Hardie Grant
BOOKS

Hardie Grant acknowledges the Traditional Owners of the Country on which we work, the Wurundjeri People of the Kulin Nation and the Gadigal People of the Eora Nation, and recognises their continuing connection to the land, waters and culture. We pay our respects to their Elders past and present.

Hardie Grant Children's Publishing
Wurundjeri Country
Ground Floor, Building 1, 658 Church Street
Richmond, Victoria 3121, Australia
Melbourne | Sydney | San Francisco
www.hardiegrantchildrens.com

ISBN: 9781761212451
First published 2024

A catalogue record for this book is available from the National Library of Australia

Publisher Marisa Pintado **Cover design** Hazel Lam
Editorial Luna Soo with Vanessa Lanaway **Production** Amanda Shaw
Typesetting Eggplant Communications

Printed in Australia by Opus Group Pty Ltd, an Accredited ISO AS/NZS 14001 Environmental Management System printer.

The paper this book is printed on is certified against the Forest Stewardship Council® Standards. Griffin Press – a member of the Opus Group – holds chain of custody certification SCS-COC-001185. FSC® promotes environmentally responsible, socially beneficial and economically viable management of the world's forests.

2 4 6 8 10 9 7 5 3 1

For my family

Prologue

Maria Petranelli had no sense of direction.

In fact, that's putting it mildly.

It would be better to say Maria was absolutely hazardous when put in charge of a map. This problem came from two sources:

1. Her tendency to assume that 'north' was whichever way she was facing at the time; and
2. Her firm belief that if she just kept moving, and quickly, she'd stumble upon the destination eventually.

This, of course, meant Maria would not only go the wrong way, she would go there with the utmost of confidence – and at lightning speed. She was continually facing the wrong direction, catching the wrong bus, ending up in the wrong suburb.

This time was no exception. And it wouldn't be long before she would be locked in the boot of someone's car, heading straight towards Florence (*completely* the opposite direction to where she was supposed to be going).

But we are getting ahead of ourselves.

CHAPTER 1

Spite

Maria Petranelli felt her height, or rather lack of it, was a curse. It gave people the impression she was cute. And cute people are never taken seriously. Maria *ached* to be taken seriously. She longed to be described as 'independent, with an air of mystery'; the type of person others suspected could be dangerous if they needed to be. But Maria was not seen as independent or mysterious, and the concept that she might be dangerous – or would want to be – was so far from the collective human consciousness that even if she donned a balaclava and held someone at knifepoint, the victim would probably hand over their wallet with a benevolent smile and a patronising 'there you go!'

Maria's cuteness was a bitter reality she fought against every day. So whenever someone declared that 'Maria would never do such a thing' or 'Maria couldn't handle something like that', it sent her over the edge. Comments like these had led Maria, out of spite, to get some Doc Martens, several karate lessons, and a belly button ring. And yet, despite these acts of defiance (which remained a secret from her family – belly button rings were next to Devil Worship in her grandmother's eyes), Maria couldn't shake the quality that made everyone around her believe she was in need of protection. But Maria did not feel in need of protection. Her mind was full of daydreams where she punched racists, tackled muggers, and broke vases over the heads of misogynists. She was small, she reasoned, but she was ready to be powerful if the situation called for it!

Though, so far, the situation had not called for it.

What the situation was calling for, right now, was surviving her family's attempts to celebrate her sixteenth birthday.

Maria knew, deep down, that her parents loved her – in their own way. It's just that Vince and Anna Petranelli did not know how to relate to her on a human level.

As soon as Maria opened her bedroom door, there they were, hovering around and trying to act natural.

'Happy birthday,' Anna said formally, handing her a card like a principal giving out certificates at assembly.

'Thank you,' Maria replied.

And they hugged with the intimacy of a handshake.

'You know,' Anna added conversationally, 'when Zia Violetta turned sixteen, she started going grey.'

'Maria! Maria!' Vince interrupted, before Maria was able to rush away and inspect her hair. 'Gotten any taller yet?'

Maria had never understood why her father felt compelled to cut her to the core. But then, Vince had never had many tools in the parenting toolbox. His main tricks, which he'd exhausted early, were:

1. Teaching Maria to swear in Italian, then telling her it meant 'hello, how are you', and sending her off to her grandparents' place;
2. Re-enacting his favourite B-grade action-comedies at the dinner table; and
3. Folding serviettes into the shape of a roast chicken.

Maria didn't realise these were Vince's clumsy attempts to connect with her. She found them perplexing, and had no idea how to respond except to stare blankly. As she was doing now.

'I'm as tall as I can be for my genetics,' she informed him.

'Ha ha ha!' bellowed Vince, who had no idea what 'genetics' were.

Maria side-stepped into the lounge room.

She didn't have a large family. Unlike most Italians, whose procreative habits may have been influenced by successive Popes' bans on contraception, Maria's family was very content with their tradition of having one child. Her grandfather was an only child, as was her father, as was she. Her grandfather would always joke, 'My parents took one look at me and thought, have another child? What for? This one's perfect,' and roll about laughing while Vince rolled his eyes – he didn't think there was room for two comedians in the family. But although the Petranellis were small in number, that did not make them easy to deal with. And despite Maria's insistence that she was not cute, nor meek, nor mild, whenever she was surrounded by the Petranellis en masse she was completely overpowered.

Her grandparents arrived in a blaze of glory.

'CHEEKY-NELLA!' Nonna Lucia cried. 'BEAUTIFUL!' She reached for the front of Maria's shirt, pulling up the neckline to what she considered a more acceptable height.

Nonno Franco brought up the rear, grabbing Maria's cheeks. 'You grow up now, eh?' he said. 'You getting old!'

It took five trips to the car to haul in the trays of lasagne, salads, meatballs, and a twenty-four pack of lemonade they'd gotten on special from Coles, and then Nonno Franco made a beeline for the couch while Nonna Lucia went straight to the laundry and started cleaning out the linen cupboard.

Maria and her mother watched helplessly. There was nothing that united them more than the overbearing presence of Nonna Lucia, who had only three purposes in life:

1. To cook better than anyone else;
2. To clean more thoroughly than anyone else; and
3. To declare that her daughter-in-law was an unsatisfactory wife and mother.

The menfolk were oblivious to the vicious undertones behind Nonna Lucia's cleaning. She would moan the whole time, and complain of arthritis, but if Anna or Maria offered to help clean out the linen cupboard (or the pantry, or the deep freeze) they'd be waved away.

Luckily, the cleaning frenzy didn't last long – Nonna Lucia had been over only a week ago, so it was more of an inspection than an intervention – and the Petranellis were soon seated and shouting at each other across the table.

'Your birthday, eh? Sixteen, eh?' Nonno Franco yelled. 'And nearly finished school.'

'I loved school,' Nonna Lucia interrupted. 'But my mother couldn't afford to send all of us.' (Nonna Lucia came from a family of twelve, which was one of the reasons she embraced the 'one Petranelli child' tradition with both arms.)

'You better get a car. I'll talk to my friend at Mister Bish.'

'It's Mitsubishi,' Anna corrected. 'But I wouldn't want a new car in this economy!'

'What does she need a car for?' Vince chimed in. 'Is she old enough to drive?'

'So when I had the opportunity to go to Australia, I thought, I will take it. I will go to Australia and I will learn. But my mother warned me, Lucia, if you go to Australia, you will cry all the time. And now I do. Now I cry all the time.' On cue, Nonna's voice started quavering. 'Oh, *Madonna mia* ...'

'You know, Zio Luigi saw you in the gelati shop last week,' Nonno Franco cut in. 'He said you were talking to a boy.'

Maria froze as every single Petranelli stopped what they were doing and turned to look at her. Even Nonna Lucia ceased her well-worn tale of misery, which usually had another two verses to go.

Maria gulped.

The Petranellis exploded with excitement.

'What's his name? Who is his mother?'

'Is he Italian?'

'I hope you have considered appropriate protection.'

'WHEN'S THE WEDDING?'

'What boy?' Maria yelled. 'Customers come in all the time! There's no boy!'

Everyone grumbled with disappointment.

'Well, what's going on? Do you have a boyfriend somewhere else?' Vince asked.

'I can't have a boyfriend right now,' she tried. 'I'm too busy with school.'

This made everyone scoff. Maria felt annoyed. She knew her grandparents didn't really 'get' education – they understood that people went to school, and then, if they were lucky, they became bank managers – but why weren't her parents more interested in her studies? Or, at the very least, *less* obsessed with Maria getting a boyfriend? They were Italians, after all – shouldn't they be panicking, eyeing every male with suspicion, and demanding life-long chastity? What was this Petranelli obsession with partnering her off?

What Maria didn't realise was that the Petranellis *were* panicking. They'd talked about it many times, and they all agreed – there was something *different* about Maria. She was too strange. Too serious. It was her sixteenth birthday, and – unlike Vince and Anna's friends, who were all hiring the Italian Club for their sixteen-year-olds' celebrations and inviting every acquaintance they'd met – Maria had vetoed any function that involved inviting friends. This might have been acceptable to the Petranellis if Maria was beyond her partying years and gearing up to get married. But at this rate, they moaned to each other, Maria was *never* going to get married. Nonno Franco's Briscola-playing friends had a lot of eligible grandsons, and Maria didn't even *flirt* with them.

But Maria didn't *want* to flirt with them! She was fine as she was, wasn't she? She looked at her mother pleadingly, desperate for an ally.

Finally, Anna seemed to get the message. 'Never mind,' she said slowly. 'Zia Pasquelina's daughter didn't get married until she was twenty-eight. Of course, no-one knows if she'll still be able to have children at that age, but at least she is happy.'

'Twenty-eight!' shouted Nonno Franco, reaching for the potatoes. 'That's too old.'

'When I was young, if a girl was twenty-eight, that was it! Finish!' Nonna Lucia declared.

Maria was affronted. 'There's nothing wrong with being single. *Or* being twenty-eight.' She glanced at her mother for back-up, and Nonna Lucia saw.

'Aha,' she said triumphantly. 'It's always the mother!'

Anna looked at Nonna Lucia as if she'd taken off a glove and slapped her across the face.

'Maria, stop joking around!' Vince said. 'What are your plans? You're sixteen now. If you don't want a boyfriend, what are you going to do?'

Maria nearly choked. 'There's lots of things I can do!'

'Like what?'

Suddenly every ambition, every goal, every life dream, went flying out of Maria's head. She racked her brains. 'Well, the other day school had a presentation about being an exchange student ...'

'Exchange student? What's an exchange student?'

'To experience what school is like ...'

'You already know what school is like.'

'In another country.'

Vince slammed his fork down. 'No daughter of *mine* is going to school in another country.'

'Who's going to another country?' Nonno Franco asked, tuning back in.

'Nobody. Maria, I forbid you to go to another country.'

'Maria? What do you want to go to another country for?' Nonno Franco shook his head. 'There are plenty of boys here.'

Maria didn't *really* want to go on exchange. When the exchange agency gave their presentation at school, Maria had briefly considered the idea; all the images of mountains higher than she'd ever seen, countrysides with completely different colours and buildings she'd only seen in movies had inspired her for a moment. But then there were the *other* photos. Photos of young people. Socialising. Laughing.

Dancing. Clinking drinks. Wearing their hair and makeup in that inexplicably correct way Maria had never mastered. It was Maria's worst nightmare, and she'd put the idea to rest immediately.

Only now, her father had forbidden it.

Maria's eye twitched.

'I'm not joking, Dad. I've spoken to the agency ...' (a complete lie) '... and I've put my name down for the group that starts in July.'

'What? Where is this group going?'

'Italy.'

A gasp of horror arose from the table, as if she'd announced she was renouncing Catholicism and joining the church of Satan. Maria was surprised; she'd expected this reaction from Vince, but she'd thought her grandparents might be more excited about her visiting The Mother Country. But Nonno Franco and Nonna Lucia's days of travelling around the world were long gone. Once the tomatoes were planted, Payneham was not only their new home, it was their entire universe. They had put down roots of concrete.

The family sat, silent and appalled, until Nonno Franco let out a chuckle. 'Oh, Maria,' he said fondly, 'you wouldn't be able to handle Italy.'

Nonna Lucia followed his lead and cackled. 'Our little Maria in Italy ... oh, Maria, I was once like you. I thought living in another country was easy. But it isn't easy! No, you'd better stay here.'

And there it was again. The incessant need everyone had to pat Maria on the head and say she couldn't cope. Maria's indignation rose all the way up her spine. 'I will be living there for three months.'

Suddenly, all traces of laughter were gone. 'Maria,' Nonno Franco warned, 'it's very dangerous over there.'

'That's right, Maria,' Nonna said. 'You are young, and you think you know everything. But you don't have any brains.'

That got a reaction from Anna. 'She *does* have brains. And if she wants to go to Italy, she will go to Italy. And she will do very well!'

Had Nonna Lucia thought an exchange in Italy was a fabulous idea, Anna would have issued warnings about harsh foreign penalties for drug smuggling and suitcases you didn't realise had been tampered with until it was too late. But with Nonna Lucia looking so distraught, she was ready to pack Maria's bags herself.

Vince looked like he was about to cry. 'But how will you get there?'

'By plane, Dad.'

'And where will you live?'

'The agency will sort that out.'

Apparently Vince had no comeback for that. He just picked up his fork and started eating sulkily, breathing out heavily through his nose.

'VINCENZO!' Nonno Franco yelled. '*MA CHE COSA HAI FATTO!*'

Maria let the ensuing avalanche of Italian pour over her as the senior Petranellis yelled at each other loudly enough to set the dog howling from the neighbour's yard. She didn't know exactly what they were saying; her family had never bothered to teach her the language. It was only ever used towards the end of family gatherings, when the inevitable fighting broke out, and Maria would excuse herself, close her bedroom door and put on her noise-cancelling headphones.

But this time, she stayed put. It was probably a bit late to try language-learning by osmosis, but she was going to Italy now, apparently.

She was going to need every advantage she could get.

CHAPTER 2

Freedom

Six months later, Maria stood at the airport terminal with a weeping Nonna Lucia, a sulking Vince and a head-shaking, lip-pursing Anna. Nonno Franco didn't come with them to see her off – he didn't deal well with goodbyes. But Maria was relishing it. As much as she loved her parents (on some level, in her own way), she couldn't wait to be independent, and she knew that crossing the ocean was the only way she could do it.

The past six months had been an emotional time for the Petranellis. Vince had attempted to forbid Maria from going, but it didn't stick, so the rest of the family didn't bother trying. Instead, they poured their energies into psychological warfare.

At first, they were worried she didn't know Italian. 'That's okay!' Maria told them. Before she started the actual exchange, she had to spend one month attending an intensive language course in Rome. That would fix it!

Next, they claimed they were concerned about her education. 'I'm not worried!' Maria said. Once she returned from Italy, she'd slot back into Year 12 and finish the year. And what could be more valuable than the hands-on learning gained from living in another country?

Then, the family announced they couldn't afford it. 'Not a problem!' Maria announced. She would just work extra shifts at the gelati shop until she could pay for her trip outright.

With Maria leaping every practical hurdle without slowing down, her family switched to fear-mongering. Anna (having long since lost the sense of victory that Maria's decision had given her over Nonna Lucia) pulled out her never-ending supply of Lifetime Channel movies about foreign trips gone wrong, and broadcast them on a loop.

'That's what happens when you go overseas,' she'd sigh, as naïve travellers were murdered, wrongly accused and thrown into prison, or sold into various slave trades. But if Anna thought the films would deter Maria, she was wrong. Maria just saw them as a learning opportunity. She scrutinised the actions of the victims, took note of their errors, and stored each scenario in her mind so she'd know what to do if it happened to her.

Maria was the *very picture* of preparedness and stoicism.

But – in the dead of night, when the dark tourism movies were silenced and her family was asleep – Maria did have the occasional whisper of doubt, a rogue inner voice asking what the hell she was doing.

Was this really something she wanted? Did she truly want to travel halfway around the world, live with a bunch of strangers, and try to fit in while speaking a language she was supposed to already know but had accidentally missed out on?

It was nearly enough to make Maria reconsider. Until she overheard Anna on the phone to one of her second cousins.

'I've decided to let her go and make her own mistakes,' Anna said. 'She won't even make it through the language course and she'll be begging to come back home. It's the only way she'll learn!'

That sealed it for Maria.

She *was* going to Italy, she *was* going to handle it, and she was going to prove her family *wrong*!

And as soon as they reached the airport, she practically ran inside.

*

Maria had invited the three Petranellis to sit with her in the airport lounge at Gate 20, but they refused: 'No, no,' Nonna Lucia said. 'We know you don't want us anymore.' Maria thought that would be that, but they didn't go home; they just shuffled forlornly to the other side of the glass, found a position where they could see Maria clearly, and stared, telepathically sending her waves and waves of guilt.

But Maria didn't let it get to her. She'd packed for every scenario up to and including an apocalypse; she'd gotten an anti-theft travel pack to carry her documents in; and the minute she boarded the plane, she started memorising the laminated safety instructions and calculating her nearest exit. Her last-minute seat at the back of the plane was a *good* thing, she decided. If the plane malfunctioned and nose-dived into the ground, the last place she'd want to be was the *front*.

She already felt like an expert in international travel.

*

Twenty-nine hours and two stops later, Maria emerged from economy class and followed the crowd of other irritable travellers with their carry-on luggage and whiny children in tow. They trudged to an enormous queue marked 'Non-European Passport Holders'. Maria looked jealously at the European passport holders, speeding through like they were on conveyor belts. She wished she were one of them. She *would* have been, but her mother had refused to take her to the embassy to apply for Italian citizenship. 'Don't you know the Australians locked up Italian citizens during World War II?' said Anna (who was born well after World War II).

But despite her exhaustion, the thrill of excitement was still alive. She had left home! She was in another country! She was free!

It wasn't until she was through customs and allowed into her adopted nation of the next three months that it hit her.

A wave of ... *something* ... swept over her – emotions she would usually have quashed without a thought, but suddenly found herself unable to.

Fear.

Panic.

Horror.

What was she doing here?

Where was she supposed to go?

What was she supposed to do?

Maria took deep breaths, trying to quell the sudden desire to turn around and get back on the plane.

Then her phone started vibrating. It took her a moment to recognise what was happening, and then the vibrations stopped … and immediately started again.

'Hello?' she picked up.

There was a long pause as her voice was transferred across the globe. The reply was panic-stricken.

'HELLO? MARIA?'

'Yes, Nonna …'

'MARIA? ARE YOU THERE? MARIA?'

'*I'm here*, Nonna!'

'HELLO! I CAN HEAR YOU! MARIA!'

Nonna Lucia burst into tears and informed the eagerly awaiting Petranelli family that Maria was alive. Maria listened to their prayers of relief and joy patiently. She was in familiar territory now.

'Maria, *why* didn't you call us before? We were so worried!'

'You can't make phone calls in the air, Nonna. It would make the plane crash.'

Nonna Lucia's scolding was immediately silenced. 'Of course, of course. You're a very brave girl.'

'MARIA?' Vince's voice echoed and distorted, and Maria realised she'd been put on speakerphone.

'I'm fine, Dad.'

'Do you know where you are staying? Are there people there to pick you up? Do you know where to go?'

'*Yes*, Dad, I've got it all sorted out.'

'Are you scared?' Nonno burst in. 'Poor Maria ...'

'*I'm not scared!*' Maria bellowed. 'I'm fine! I have to go!'

'Yes, yes, Maria, be careful, don't forget to call us when you get to the language school, and if you need anything let us know, and if you get scared you can always come home ...'

'I'll be *fine*,' Maria emphasised, and ended the call.

Fear, panic and horror were all in the past.

She clutched the straps of her backpack tightly (in case someone came up behind her, cut them with a knife and tried to take off with her belongings) and set off in search of the language school's shuttle bus.

And every time those creeper vines of doubt pricked at her consciousness, she remembered her mother on the phone to her second cousin, saying 'It's the only way she'll learn!' – and she picked up her pace and glared at anyone who looked in her direction.

CHAPTER 3

Youth

Maria tried not to show it, but the bus ride was unnerving. Everyone around her was joking around or posing for selfies, and there was far too much 'woo'-ing when the engine started. Maria had hoped, prayed even, that those terrifying exchange brochures full of fun-loving teens were just marketing. *Brochures always exaggerate,* Maria had told herself. *Hopefully I'll only have to deal with people who read a lot and want to go on quiet personal journeys.*

She cursed herself for getting her hopes up. She should have known she'd be landed with a bunch of extroverts! Even when she was on the other side of the world, it was just like being at school.

Maria had never felt equipped for relating to others. 'Mature for her age', her school reports always said, which was a very polite way of saying 'unable to relate to her peers'. Where this inability came from, it was difficult to say.

But it definitely came from Anna Petranelli.

Her mother didn't mean to be the voice of prophetic doom, but she couldn't help herself. Anna was full of warnings, especially about females, and *especially*:

1. The popular ones (in case they judge you);
2. The pretty ones (... in case they judge you); and
3. The ones who drive around on motorcycles.

Maria didn't have much experience with the motorcycle variety (which was code for something Anna refused to explain), but she was surrounded by the other types. And by the time Maria got to middle school, Anna had her so primed for confrontation that she completely missed her social cues.

Once, the most popular in girl in school told Maria she liked her T-shirt. It was a genuine compliment. But to Maria – whose mother had looked her up and down that morning and said, 'Well, that will have to do' – the compliment was so unexpected, so completely out of the blue, that she was convinced it was sarcasm and responded with an eyeroll.

But it was not sarcasm. And Elena Romanelli spent the next week telling everyone who'd listen that Maria was a snob.

Another time, Maria was forced to go on school camp. She'd tried to avoid it, but her teacher had made a personal phone call to say it would be good for Maria's social development (whatever that was supposed to mean). Just as she was about to get on the school bus, Anna called out,

'I forgot to get padlocks for your suitcase! Oh well, it's too late now. Have a good time.'

Maria did *not* have a good time. She was haunted by visions of her underwear being stolen and hoisted up flagpoles, of taking a shower only to emerge and find all her clothes were missing, of having the childish pyjamas her mother insisted she bring mocked behind her back. So Maria took her suitcase with her everywhere she went, and sat on it, while everyone else swam in lakes and climbed on obstacle courses and made videos of their synchronised dance moves. 'I just like to be prepared,' she claimed. And all her classmates called her weird.

Another time, at her first school social, a kind-hearted boy named Ahmad Almasi asked Maria to slow-dance. Maria wondered if it was a mistake, or a dare, or perhaps even an attempt to manoeuvre her so she was standing underneath a booby-trapped bucket hanging from the ceiling. She still consented, but she kept her dance style to a stiff-armed lock-kneed foot shuffle, and she glared at him the whole time. And as soon as the song ended, he beelined *straight for Elena Romanelli*, which both confirmed Maria's suspicions and put another nail in her social coffin.

These types of failed interactions were repeated again and again. Maria didn't understand her classmates, and her classmates didn't understand her. But would Maria show them she was affected? Would Maria express these bruising knocks to her self-esteem with something as human as tears?

No, she would not!

Especially not with Vince hovering in the background, ready to tease her if she showed any emotion *at all.* This habit was another of Vince's attempts at connection, after he realised his serviette roast chickens and B-grade action-film re-enactments were not getting a reaction. But Maria was a sensitive soul, and the teasing wounded her fierce pride beyond belief.

And so, Maria did what most people would do when their every vulnerable expression was met with their father cracking a joke and poking them in the ribs.

She stopped showing her emotions. To anyone.

Excellent work, Vince.

Maria didn't see emotional repression as a flaw. It felt more like a strength! And all through high school, whenever she felt a stab of self-doubt at yet another of her social failings, she coped the way she was coping with the current busload: she pulled out a book to read, and thought critical thoughts about everyone around her.

All I have to do is get to the language school, she told herself. *Then I can just focus on my studies until this whole nightmare is over.*

Maria did not allow herself to think about what would happen *after* the language school – of having to live with a family and attend a public school where she might be expected to socialise. She was going to deal with one crisis at a time.

But the young people around her were being *very* raucous. Some of them had started kissing, which Maria thought was unusually fast, even for extroverts.

It was only when someone cracked open a bottle of

champagne that she knew something was seriously wrong. Yes, they were in Europe, but surely the language school wouldn't let underage teens drink so openly?

Though, the more she scrutinised them, the more Maria realised these teens didn't exactly look underage. She looked closer. This wasn't just a case of everyone being better at fashion than her – the people around her were in their twenties, at the very least. Some of them even had grey hair.

'Happy anniversary,' one such man said.

And that's when it dawned on Maria that she was on the wrong bus.

Her stomach lurched.

Should she shout for the bus to stop? No, she couldn't do that; she didn't want to make a scene. But the crowd was getting more and more rowdy, and someone a few seats behind her was talking about 'bus karaoke'. She had to take action!

She was just about to fake motion sickness and demand an emergency stop when the vehicle slowed, then parked in front of a hotel. A hotel that was definitely not the language school, and one that seemed very popular with people going on a Contiki Tour.

The partygoers bolted off the bus and Maria waited until they'd scattered in various directions so she could sneak away.

Okay. So she'd faced her first test, and failed. But not to worry! Maria would just *walk* to the language school. Surely it couldn't be far!

It took her an hour and a half to admit she was lost.

CHAPTER 4

Inevitable

Could Maria have used her phone to get directions in real time? Yes, she could have. But she was tired, and jet-lagged, and beginning to hallucinate, and the thought didn't even occur to her until her phone had run out of battery.

It was dark before Maria gave up and got into a taxi.

It was a short trip, but a harrowing one. The driver seemed to be following only one road rule: if you see a gap in traffic, fill it before anyone else can.

He slammed his foot on the brakes and nearly threw Maria out the window. '*Sessanta euro*, *per favore*,' he said casually, as Maria peeled herself off the roof.

Maria gaped. Sixty euros! She'd only been in the country for a few hours and she'd already blown three days of her budget!

She hoisted her bags up the steps of the language school and tried the door.

It was locked.

She turned: the taxi was gone.

Maria sank onto the steps, her exhaustion making her heavier than usual.

What was she doing here? Was all this worth proving her family wrong? She didn't want to be so far from home. But what *did* she want? She had no direction, no purpose. Why was she even alive, really? She was sixteen years old, and she didn't even have a boyfriend.

Bam! That wasn't supposed to creep out of her subconscious!

As Maria set about trying to beat her brain back into submission, the door opened with a click.

'Uh, can I help you?'

Maria looked up sharply in the direction of the voice. The American voice.

Her tired eyes took her in, whoever she was: tall, jeans, zip-up jacket with the sleeves pushed up to her elbows, kind of lanky, probably about her age, black curly hair bunched into a messy bun at the base of her neck, bright blue cap with an Italian flag on it that screamed 'I'm a tourist'.

'Uh … *puoi aiutare* … I mean *vuoi* … I mean …' the girl stumbled. 'Sorry … can you speak English?'

Maria nodded, too weary to speak.

The American seemed relieved. 'Are you in this building? Like, are you here for the language school?' She was speaking slowly and loudly, even though Maria had just indicated she could understand. But Maria was too tired to feel annoyed by this, and just nodded again, sadly.

'Right! Well, this is the place!' The American laughed nervously, opening the door more widely and letting light flood the front steps. Maria could see the girl's face now: brown eyes, brown skin, smiling nervously under the god-awful tourist cap that would have filled Maria with disdain, if she had the energy.

'Uh … do you need help with your bag? Look, let me help you up,' the American offered, stretching out her hand for Maria to take.

Maria frowned. She did not take the offered hand. She did not need help with her bag, or assistance getting to her feet! Filled with sudden energy, she leapt up and nearly bowled the American over.

'Oh!' the girl said, laughing it off. 'You're good then! Okay. Uh … so I didn't get your name?'

'Maria.'

'Oh, great! Well, I'll take you to the professor. I think she was expecting everyone earlier? There was a bus? But I'm sure it'll be fine!'

The American kept talking all the way to the professor's door, clearing her throat every fifteen seconds. The throat-clearing gave Maria something to feel irritated about, rather than focusing on the unsettling feeling that she was about to be told off.

But Maria needn't have worried. 'The Professor', an older woman named Gina Giglio, was not the telling-off sort – she was all about business. Especially when *X Factor Italia* was on.

'So, uh, this is Maria, I think she's meant to be here?'

'*In Italiano, per favore,*' Professor Giglio replied.

'Oh, uh, *questo* Maria, uh ...'

The American's Italian accent was appalling. And Maria did not want to give off the impression that she needed someone to speak for her. So she racked her brains for a non-swear-word phrase that could act as an apology.

She bunched her fingers together, held them up to the sky, shook her wrist up and down a few times, and said in her most apologetic voice, '*Scusa.*'

Maria did not know she had made the hand gesture for *what do you want?* She mistakenly thought it was just how Italians talked. Her family were always throwing their hands around, so Maria tried it too, hoping it would make up for her lack of words.

It did not.

Professor Giglio sighed. 'Well, you're here to learn, I suppose,' she said in English. 'Let's sort everything out in the morning.' She turned to the American, who was standing with her hands in her pockets. 'Will you show Maria to her room?'

'Of course!'

Professor Giglio nodded and went back to her television show, and the American loped away excitedly.

'Here you are!' she announced a few minutes later, opening the door for Maria gallantly.

'Thank you,' Maria replied.

'Uh ...'

Maria watched the taller girl in front of her. She was scratching her head and smiling lopsidedly. Her hat looked forced. She looked awkward, in general. She also started all of her sentences with 'uh'. All of these things Maria observed, detached and calm. The American looked like she wanted to say something else, but settled for, 'Goodnight, then. I'm Kennedy.'

'Goodnight,' Maria repeated, and closed the door. She kicked off her shoes, crawled under the covers, and tried not to think about what the hell she was doing with her life until, finally, she managed to fall asleep.

*

It was a knock. A nervous knock. An awkward knock. Maria's eyes snapped open and, on impulse, she shot out of bed and opened the door.

'Morning,' said Kennedy.

'Oh!' said Maria.

That's right, she thought. *I'm in Italy.*

'Just letting you know classes start at nine. You missed the big orientation talk yesterday, so I thought I'd better fill you in,' Kennedy said, all breathless and arm-wavy. 'And I wanted to see how you are, actually! You looked a bit out of it last night.'

'What time is it?' Maria asked, trying to get her bearings.

'Uh … eight. There's a communal kitchen if you want breakfast. Did you … uh … want breakfast? I thought I could introduce you to the gang!'

Maria winced – both at the word 'gang', and the thought of enforced socialising, which she was not ready to do. 'All right,' she said resignedly.

Kennedy seemed to interpret Maria's long-suffering response as one of extreme enthusiasm. Hands in jeans pockets, Kennedy cheerfully led the way, occasionally turning and grinning at Maria, whose feet were dragging. She eventually found herself in a cramped, blue-and-white-tiled kitchen with several round tables.

'Hey gang! This is Maria. Maria, meet the gang,' Kennedy announced.

The 'gang' of Italian-learners, a jet-lagged bunch huddled over coffees and small tubs of yoghurt, looked up at Maria and mooed, 'Helloooo …'

'Hi,' said Maria self-consciously, scanning her new social scene. The language school was for foreigners wanting to teach English as well as high schoolers going on exchange, so, on average, the group was a lot older than she'd imagined they'd be. In fact, the only ones her age were Kennedy, a girl named Alyssa, who was taking selfies in front of the fridge and hadn't even looked up, and Chris, a guy with shoulder-length hair who was leaning back on his chair and appeared to be leering at her.

'Well,' Maria said. 'Nice to meet you.'

'Nice to meet you tooooo …' was the mournful reply,

and nobody seemed to mind, or notice, when Maria ducked into the hallway for safety.

'Actually, Kennedy, I don't feel like eating yet. I might grab something later.'

'Oh! Really? Okay,' Kennedy said, sounding disappointed but recovering quickly. 'I'll show you back to your room.' And she bounded back down the hallway.

Maria followed, perplexed. When they arrived, Maria quickly manoeuvred herself so that she was inside the room and Kennedy was outside of it.

Kennedy did not get the hint.

'So ...' she started. 'Classes start at nine. Want me to walk you? I can walk you so you know the way.'

Walk me, thought Maria, who was trying very hard to make up for the previous night's vulnerability by criticising Kennedy's every phrase. *She makes it sound like I'm a dog.*

Maria made a non-committal sound, but wasn't sure how to end the conversation that Kennedy seemed determined to have. She stoically and silently received updates about the weather and street signs and European power points, until Kennedy went too far.

'So ... how are you feeling? You sure gave me a scare last night! You looked so sad,' she said sympathetically.

That jolted Maria into action. 'Well!' Maria said in a no-nonsense voice. 'I was actually just fine. Thank you for unlocking the door.' And, with Anna Petranelli's warnings about pretty girls ringing in her head, she quickly closed the door in Kennedy's face.

CHAPTER 5

Tribulations

The next few days were a trial for Maria.

Kennedy seemed determined to help Maria 'settle in', and kept offering to walk her to their language classes. Maria found these offers very suspicious. Was this helpfulness, or some manipulative ploy to force Maria into a friendship? Did Kennedy not realise they were only at the language school for a month? A friendship for that short a time was totally unnecessary. What game was she playing? And, worse – what if Kennedy was only *pretending* to be friendly, and this was all a trap? Maria was simply not going to allow herself to be tricked into friendship, only to realise that this complete and utter stranger was just going to laugh at her behind her back, probably with the rest of the 'gang'. She would walk herself to class, thank you very much.

And so, every morning when Kennedy knocked on the door, it seemed Maria had *just* left. Usually, she had – though once, Kennedy was extra early, so Maria had stood dead still and silent, then peered out the curtains until she saw Kennedy exiting their apartment building before she made her move.

Maria was proud of nipping whatever Kennedy was up to in the bud. But it did mean she got lost every single morning. It took her four days to realise she needed to exit her apartment and turn *left* if she hoped to find the centre where her classes were held. Once again, this could have been averted if she'd used maps on her phone. But phone use was always a last resort for Maria. She abhorred social media, would rather die than take a selfie, and it's not like she had anyone to text, so she often forgot she had one at all. Besides, it was a five-minute walk from the apartments to the centre. How lost could she possibly get?

Unfortunately, the answer ranged from half an hour, to two hours and forty-seven minutes.

'Sorry, I took a wrong turn!' Maria gasped with every belated entrance, out of breath from all her power-walking.

'*In Italiano, per favore,*' Professor Giglio said on a loop, glaring a little more each time.

It was unsettling for the usually academically perfect Maria. Scorn from her peers, she was used to. Scorn from her teachers was another thing entirely, and she was determined to get back on familiar ground.

On the fifth day, Maria got the opportunity. Professor Giglio took them to a restaurant so they could practise ordering in Italian. Everyone was too intimidated to order anything but spaghetti, and Maria realised – *this was her moment to shine.*

The other foreigners poked around their plates clumsily, trying to eat without making a mess. But Maria, the only one in the group of Italian heritage, picked up a fork in her right hand, a spoon in her left, and delicately twirled the fork against the spoon until the spaghetti formed a neat mouthful. She ate with a flourish.

'Look what Maria's doing,' she heard her classmates say. 'Wow! Is that the way Italians eat spaghetti?'

Professor Giglio cleared her throat and leaned forward, and for a moment, for a blissful few seconds, Maria was *sure* she was about to be praised on her culturally authentic eating abilities. She might even be held up as an example to the group.

But perhaps Maria had underestimated how serious Professor Giglio was when she told her, every single day and with an increasingly clenched jaw, 'classes start at nine'.

The professor pulled no punches.

'No, it is not,' she said. 'In Italy, using a spoon is only for small children.'

It was then that Maria realised two things:

1. That the Petranellis had failed her, yet again; and
2. That she and Professor Giglio would never be friends.

Maria took a deep breath and steeled herself for the mocking that was sure to follow, but her classmates just ‘ohh’d’ and ‘ahh’d’ and launched into a discussion about their own cultural cutlery habits. Kennedy, who was *still* appointing herself some kind of rescuer of Maria, said magnanimously, ‘And now we know Australians eat spaghetti with a spoon!’

Maria should have been grateful, but she was appalled. She had managed to shame both her Italian *and* her Australian heritage in one fell swoop! The shame crawled up the back of her neck, and even though she was sitting straight and acting unaffected, she felt like crawling into a hole.

What am I doing here, she thought, not for the first time. She might have proved the Petranellis wrong by getting to Italy, but *succeeding* in Italy, she was not.

Thankfully, lunch finished shortly after this, in time for the Italian *riposo* – two hours when the entire country closed down so everyone could go home and take a nap. Maria was feeling more and more like a failed Italian; she’d never even heard of a *riposo*. In the Petranelli house, there *was* nap-taking after lunch, but it was gender-based. The men snored on the couch with the top button of their trousers undone, while the women participated in The Suffering: a method of doing the dishes in which you sigh a lot and say ‘*oh, Gesu mio*’ as if you are holding back tears. ‘The women do the dishes because Eve sinned first!’ Nonna Lucia would proclaim, clutching at her aching back (another direct consequence of The Fall).

But in Italy, everything and everyone slowed down in the afternoon, including the language school. This might have been a relief to Maria if she’d been able to hide in her room, but her fellow students were not finished yet.

'Who wants to sleep when there's a city to explore!' Alyssa, the most extroverted of the bunch, yelled.

Chris, the other guy their age, jumped to his feet and flung his shoulder-length hair over his shoulder. 'I'm in! Where should we go?'

Maria hoped the older, would-be English teachers would be a voice for calm, but alas, they were no better. The group was alive with ideas. The jet lag had well and truly worn off, Maria realised, and now she had to cope with everyone's enthusiasm. There was more 'woo'-ing, and then, much to Maria's horror, Alyssa shouted: 'Get in here everyone, let's take a selfie! Say "Italy!"'

'ITALEEEEE!' the group sang.

This is literally killing me, Maria thought.

*

Like many modern English speakers, Maria was using the word 'literally' inaccurately. Maria was not even close to being killed. In fact, apart from some slightly high blood pressure, she wasn't in any danger at all.

What Maria didn't realise was that her situation was going to change. And it wouldn't be long before the words 'literally' and 'killing' *would* belong in the same sentence – and they would be exactly the right ones to use.

But once again, we are getting ahead of ourselves.

CHAPTER 6

Connections

Eventually, Maria found a way to circumvent all the socialising her group insisted on during each day's *riposo*. She could have said she was going to nap, like the rest of the Italians, but napping seemed like a form of weakness and Maria couldn't bring herself to do it. Instead, she told her classmates she needed to stay behind and brush up on her verbs.

It was a reasonable excuse. Maria was behind the rest of the class, partly because she'd spent the first week turning up late to lessons, but mostly because she had so much *un*-learning to do. As it turned out, a lot of the phrases she'd thought were Italian were actually made up by her grandparents, and were an inexplicable combination of:

1. Dialect from their village;
2. English that was so heavily accented Maria hadn't even recognised it; and

3. The occasional odd noise.

So Maria diligently spent the afternoons studying, and it seemed as if she might escape socialising altogether.

But the fates were not going to let Maria off the hook.

'You will find a partner,' Professor Giglio told them in their second week of classes. 'We are going to do role plays.'

Great, Maria thought angrily. Why must everyone insist on doing role plays, all the time? She knew how this 'find a partner' thing worked, too – she'd been haunted all through primary school by being The Odd Number in an odd-numbered class. It was like her classmates intrinsically knew a dance she'd never learned the moves to; they gravitated towards each other, effortlessly finding someone to link arms with, before each couple looked at the teacher pleadingly, hoping they wouldn't be landed with The Girl Who Never Smiled as the third wheel. And now, it was going to happen to her again.

Her peers started shuffling their seats into pairs. Maria schooled her face to impassiveness and sat ramrod straight to show she didn't care that she was about to be left out.

Then she heard it.

'Uh … so, do you, uh …'

Maria turned and saw Kennedy's apologetic, lopsided grin.

And even though, up to this point, Kennedy's friendliness had been nothing but a thorn in Maria's side, something like gratitude settled low in her stomach.

‘I suppose,’ Maria replied.

Kennedy beamed. ‘Do you want to be the taxi driver, or …’

‘Whatever you want,’ Maria said dismissively. She had already decided that if the teacher made them perform in front of the class, she would ask for her money back.

To her credit, Kennedy didn’t let Maria’s impolite rendition of a taxi driver put her off. In fact, the sterner Maria was, the wider Kennedy’s smile got.

Eventually, Maria snapped. ‘What is so funny?’

‘Nothing,’ Kennedy chuckled. ‘It’s just your impression of a Roman taxi driver. It’s not just me – they’re really grumpy, right?’

Maria scoured the comment, trying to understand what she meant, trying to find the barb.

‘Maybe they just don’t like Americans,’ Maria said imperiously.

‘Ha!’ Kennedy laughed.

‘*In Italiano, per favore,*’ Professor Giglio scolded, and Kennedy and Maria both looked apologetic and lowered their voices.

‘Seriously, though,’ Kennedy whispered, rolling her eyes. ‘Role plays?’

And – even though she knew Kennedy would probably react with an over-the-top grin, which would be *very* annoying – Maria gave her a small smile.

*

As the days went on, Kennedy remained a mystery to Maria. The inevitable 'pair-up' activities continued, and they filled Maria with dread; but every time Maria steeled herself, preparing to act nonchalant at being left alone, there was Kennedy, with an open, questioning smile.

Maria kept waiting for the other shoe to drop; for Kennedy to scoff at her, judge her, or – worse – find someone else to partner with. But after a full week, Kennedy had done none of those things, and Maria was struggling to remember all the witty comebacks she'd prepared in advance of the inevitable rejection.

Plus, no matter how irritated Maria acted during the role plays, Kennedy always managed to find the funny side. Even stranger, Maria noticed, was that she was laughing *with* Maria, not *at* her, which was something Maria had never expected. She thought herself to be many things, but funny definitely wasn't one of them.

On top of this, Kennedy was effortlessly open, even when Maria remained stubbornly aloof. No matter how many times the Italian instructors looked sternly in their direction, Kennedy was recklessly chatty.

When they were asked to role play the phrase 'where are you from', Kennedy told Maria she was from Michigan, she had mixed racial heritage, and her parents were hopelessly political.

When the Italian phrase was 'what is your name', Kennedy told her that before she was born, her parents had argued about calling her 'Chisholm', but her father lost a bet to her Catholic mother, so 'Kennedy' won out.

When the Italian lesson centred around ordering food, Kennedy told her she loved peanut butter, seafood, cold weather, and hiking.

And when the phrase was 'how much does it cost', Kennedy went *completely* off script and told Maria she was bisexual, she didn't have a boyfriend, and that she'd dated a girl for a while but it didn't work out (though they'd parted on friendly terms).

Maria listened to all these facts with a practised air of disinterest, but, after multiple occasions when her only response had been 'hmm' or 'oh', she started to feel a little guilty. Kennedy had been at it for days now; perhaps she should at least try to reciprocate.

So, one day, when they were back in their communal kitchen, she took a deep breath and revealed her own personal story to Kennedy.

She told her that her parents were *not* hopelessly political, and the only Kennedy her father knew was George Harris Kennedy Jr, who Vince had watched countless times in the wacky comedies *Airport* and *Naked Gun*.

She told her that while it had never been confirmed, her mother suspected she was potentially deathly allergic to both peanut butter and seafood.

She told her she didn't mind cold weather, and that she'd only been on one hike, during which she was stung by a bee.

And then she summoned her courage, gritted her teeth and revealed that she, too, didn't have a boyfriend.

'Or girlfriend,' she blurted suddenly, and for the life of her, she couldn't understand what prompted her to say such a random, irrelevant thing. As soon as she realised what she'd said, she recoiled and stared at Kennedy in horror. What was she thinking? What madness had possessed her? Maria was appalled.

'I prefer the single life!' she exclaimed, not awkwardly at all, and then hastily excused herself, ran to her room, and locked herself in the shower.

Now who is recklessly chatty, she cursed herself, determined to zip herself back up for good.

CHAPTER 7

Action

If Maria had allowed her treacherous brain to think her moments of openness/weakness with Kennedy might lead to anything – *which she hadn't* – she would have been sorely disappointed.

Just as she thought Kennedy might possibly, potentially, be somewhat of a companion, someone who could at the very least make their non-study hours bearable, Kennedy had to leave.

'I'll be back Monday,' she assured Maria. 'It's just that we have family friends here, and I haven't seen them since I was a kid. They've got permission to pick me up for the weekend.'

Maria imagined a kindly elderly couple, probably archaic university professors or quirky archaeologists or muddled librarians. But Kennedy's 'family friends' were nothing like that. The parents were young and intimidatingly fashionable, and the two daughters – both around Maria's (and Kennedy's) age – looked like models. One in particular, when she went in for a hug, held Kennedy for a *very* long time.

Of course, Maria thought, refusing to acknowledge the pang she felt in her chest. She tried to pretend she wasn't surprised; of course Kennedy would have *real* friends. Probably ones who were fun and interesting and knew how to dance in public and drink alcohol effortlessly. Maria was just someone to study with, that was all.

'So, I'll see you,' Kennedy said awkwardly after she'd raced back inside to grab one last thing.

'Yes,' Maria replied.

'Don't do anything I wouldn't do!' Kennedy joked, and Maria attempted to smile, but it came out like a pursing of lips. And then she was alone.

And it appears that nature abhors a vacuum, because as soon as Kennedy had gone, nature sent Chris.

Chris, the other high schooler of the group (the one with the too-long hair), was one of those lucky individuals with confidence oozing from every pore – despite not having much to be traditionally confident about. His T-shirts were way too large, for one; likely because they were the 'one size fits all' variety, emblazoned with the emblems of various heavy metal bands. And he tended to be mistaken as being much younger than he was, perhaps due to his over-the-top exuberance, perhaps due to his shiny skin. But he had assets. Chris could write and read fluently in runes. He also had an unparalleled ability to spot the mistakes film editors made

– scenes where a shadow of the boom-mike could be seen on the wall, or where a main character had dirt on their face in one shot, and then a clean face in the next. Chris also had an astoundingly large bank of weaponry-related vocabulary. He was, in his mind, quite a catch.

But Maria wasn't interested in Chris. All his flirting got on her nerves. He flirted with Alyssa, he flirted with Professor Giglio, he flirted with waitresses and shop assistants and women in the street … it was disgusting to watch. Not to mention experience. And unfortunately, once he realised he would not get a response from Maria – who had long ago mastered the art of staring blank-faced into the distance as if nothing was happening – his attention to her was merciless.

At this very moment, Chris was trying to capture her interest with a prolonged and passionate description of the difference between a longsword and a broadsword. Thankfully for Maria, her phone pinged. It was an email from her mother.

She excused herself and moved into the hallway to read it.

Dear Maria, it said.

I am afraid things are not going well. Your grandfather has taken very ill and he thinks you should come home.

Maria knew it was a lie. Nonno Franco had never been ill in his life – it was something he boasted about, alongside his my-parents-saw-me-and-didn't-need-another-child claim.

It was Nonna Lucia who had been dying for the past thirty years. Only weeks before Maria's announcement regarding her future travels, Nonna Lucia had ushered her into her bedroom to show her the contents of The Drawer Without the Handle. As a child, Maria had assumed the handle had just fallen off – it wasn't until then that she realised this was her nonna's way of preventing criminals from stealing the dress she wanted to be buried in. And the shoes, and the stockings, and the undergarments. There was also a long, guilt-inducing note to her family with strict instructions on how the funeral was to be held.

'You must tell no-one,' she had whispered conspiratorially to Maria. 'But when the time comes, you will know what to do.'

The time had nearly come several times since then, but nobody had batted an eyelid; these close encounters with death had been happening since before Maria was born. Nonno Franco often referred to Nonna Lucia – out of her hearing, of course – as a vampire who would probably outlive them all.

'Chatting with your boyfriend, love?' said a cheery voice behind her. Maria looked up from her phone to see the friendly face of Milla, one of the older ladies prepping to be an English teacher.

'No, actually … just my mother.'

'Oh, that's sweet. I bet she misses you!'

'Hmm.'

'And do you have a fellow waiting for you at home?'

Suddenly Milla's face looked a lot less friendly. The smile was frozen eerily in place, waiting for Maria to answer, waiting to trap her.

'Not at the moment.'

'Ah!' She chuckled knowingly. 'In between, are we? I bet you're glad about that – now you don't have to behave yourself!'

Maria was horrified. What, forcing Maria to pair off wasn't enough – now she had to have casual sex too? Why couldn't people leave her alone!

She hastily made her escape to call her mother.

'I can't talk at the moment, Maria,' Anna rushed, Nonno's made-up illness already forgotten. 'I have to go to your second cousin's engagement party. Zia Carmelina will go on and on, of course – "why isn't Maria engaged? When is Maria going to get married?". But don't worry, I've already told her what the situation is and I'll tell her again. All right, be careful. Goodbye.'

'Wait a minute!' Maria hollered. She calmed herself and then said, carefully, 'What did you tell her the situation is?'

'Oh, you know,' Anna said airily. 'It's just that you're not as ... *confident* ... as some other girls.'

'What do you mean I –'

'Sorry Maria, I'm going to be late. Be careful, all right? Goodbye.'

And she hung up.

Maria kept the phone to her ear and listened to the dial tone in a state of shock.

And then rage.

She wanted to give her mother a piece of her mind.

Not as confident. *Not as confident!*

Whatever had given her mother such a ridiculous idea? Maria *oozed* confidence! She was in Italy on exchange! She had left her homeland, boarded a plane, travelled to the other side of the world on her own, for crying out loud! What more did she need to do?

But Maria knew that to Anna Petranelli, and Vince, and Nonna Lucia and Nonno Franco – and now Zia Carmelina, apparently – none of it counted while she was single.

But her singleness was a *choice*, wasn't it?

Quickly, she scanned through her memory, trying to find justification …

… but there wasn't a lot to work with. Maria had not dated, she had not experimented with boys, she hadn't even *kissed* anyone. The closest she'd gotten was holding hands with Toby Jordan, a fellow colleague at the gelati shop, and that had been completely by accident. They'd both reached for the pistachio flavour at the same time, and clashed knuckles, and in a moment of *extreme* weakness (Maria blamed the low temperature of the freezer room), she allowed their fingers to tangle and their eyes to lock. But then Toby Jordan had committed the cardinal sin: he rubbed her hand with his thumb.

And Maria had nearly quit the gelati shop on the spot.

Maria gasped at the memory.

Was she normal? Why had she reacted with such abhorrence because a boy rubbed her hand with his thumb?

It's true, Maria did not like public displays of affection; in fact, she didn't like *any* displays of affection. But now she realised she had made a mistake. If only she'd seized the opportunity, gone along with it for a little while, gotten it out of everyone's system. Toby wasn't so bad. He was *objectively* attractive. If only she'd persisted and put up with the hand-rubbing, she would have been able to say to Anna, 'SEE? I have plenty of confidence! I had a boyfriend, it just wasn't for me!'

And maybe she would finally be able to silence the disquieting voice at the back of her head – the one telling her she wasn't *normal* – for good.

Maria needed to take action. She was going to die alone, she already knew that. But when it happened, she didn't want anyone hovering around saying 'poor Maria'. No. She had to head off all sympathy at the pass by proudly listing all her conquests so she could proclaim that, despite all of them, she had chosen the single life.

Yes! That was the only solution.

Which meant she needed a boyfriend, and she needed one now.

And Chris was only too happy to oblige.

CHAPTER 8

Contact

They spent the rest of Saturday in the lounge room talking about medieval weaponry. Well, Chris talked, and Maria nodded. But it seemed to be working; Chris didn't show any sign of getting bored, and as the day went on, he shuffled closer and closer, until he put a romantic hand on her less-than-romantic knee.

Maria recognised the irony. There was nothing remotely sexy about medieval weaponry, at least not the way Chris was describing it. But all of a sudden, a fierce intensity invaded Chris's eyes. He was no longer talking. He was staring. He leaned forward.

He leaned forward, and Maria knew – *this was it.*

She was pretty sure she was supposed to close her eyes when it happened, but hers just wouldn't shut; instead, they stared back at him in horror. Chris didn't seem deterred. All of a sudden, his face was against hers.

His face was against hers, she realised with relief. So far, so good. True, their faces didn't appear to be moving – but, she reasoned, one step at a time. Gratefully, she closed her eyes as he breathed in heavily and progressed to the next step.

In the movies, people's lips are open. In the movies, mouths join, fit together, complete each other, slowly, seductively. But Chris's lips weren't open. They just mashed against hers fiercely, and her head moved backwards in shock. It felt … stupid.

But Maria couldn't blame him. She wasn't helping matters at all. Her lips were frozen, stiff, unhelpful, cold. He kept mashing and she knew she was meant to mash back, so she did, for a while.

This isn't working, she thought, and opened her mouth to protest.

Just as he opened his.

Their teeth connected.

Maria recoiled. *Just keep going,* she told herself. *You've already gone this far, there's no sense in turning back now.*

She was wise to push through. They finally achieved some synchronisation, though Maria's back hurt, and her arms felt like obstacles, and her eyelids kept fluttering, wanting to open against strict orders.

But despite the kissing, she felt quite good. Relief wrapped her up like a blanket.

She would not marry this boy, Maria knew. She would not walk down the street with him, her hand in the back pocket of his jeans. She would not cup his face and look deeply into his eyes, not lie in the grass with him and fit against his body, not unbutton his shirt and stroke his chest, not compliment him on his ability to write in runes.

A few more minutes, she thought. *That should be enough.*

She was smiling now. He was smiling too, which was making it all so much more awkward. But she felt complete, somehow. Confident. Taller.

And then it was over. Chris leaned his head against the couch and said, 'Wow.'

'Wow,' Maria echoed. She couldn't stop grinning. She was ecstatic.

Maria Petranelli had finally joined the human race.

CHAPTER 9

Aftermath

Now I suppose I have to break up with him, Maria thought the next day.

In a short twenty-four-hour turnaround, she had kissed Chris, proved Anna's 'lack of confidence' assessment wrong, and as an added bonus (that Maria would never admit she needed), she'd gotten some reassurance that she wasn't completely unlovable. And now everyone could move on with their lives.

But perhaps Maria should have realised that a boy obsessed with medieval weaponry would not take kindly to being rejected.

'Hey baby,' Chris schmoozed alongside her in the kitchen, 'what are you doing later?'

Maria turned sharply, took a deep breath and, exactly as she had practised all afternoon, stated, 'I'm very sorry, Chris, but I do not think it is going to work between us. I do wish you all the best.'

'What?' he exploded. 'What is that supposed to mean?'

Maria was taken aback – she thought she'd been very clear. She was not going to show weakness, however. 'Simply that I do not wish to continue our relationship.'

Chris's mouth dropped open and he stared. Maria made sure she kept looking him in the eye, but she was starting to feel uncomfortable. To make matters worse, at that exact moment, Milla appeared. She needed milk from the fridge. And then Alyssa was lurking around the doorway, phone in hand. And Maria decided that the gods must hate her – because out of nowhere, there was tall, lanky, Italian-capped Kennedy, fresh from her weekend away. She burst into the room with an overjoyed grin, oblivious as usual. 'How's it going, guys?' she said cheerfully.

Maria turned to her and stared.

Instantly, Chris's demeanour changed.

'I get it,' he said darkly, looking from Maria to Kennedy and back again.

Milla slammed the fridge door and made a hasty exit. Alyssa sniffed haughtily – and unnecessarily loudly – and went back to her bedroom.

And before Maria could implement *any* of the witty comebacks that she'd stored up for an occasion such as this, Chris inched closer, sneered nastily, and said, 'You even kiss like a dyke.'

That hit her in the stomach. Maria's heart started pounding and she couldn't think of a thing to say.

'Hey!' Kennedy growled. 'Where did that come from? Don't talk to her like that!'

'Oh, don't tell me,' Chris laughed. 'Bitches gotta stick together, I guess. What are you going to do?' he mocked, taking a step towards Kennedy. And even though she towered over him, she faltered.

'I'm going to …' Kennedy stammered. 'Uh …'

'Going to what?'

'Uh … I'm going to … uh …'

Maria appreciated Kennedy's gesture, even though it was useless. At least she'd bought her some time; Maria was ready now. She pulled herself up to her full height and declared, 'She's going to report you to the administrators of this program for sexual harassment if you don't leave both of us alone, this instant.'

Chris looked like he wanted to reply, so Maria interrupted him. 'I mean it! Right this instant!' When Chris didn't move, Maria lowered her voice threateningly and said, 'And I am *very* good at filing reports!'

Chris stared at her.

Kennedy coughed.

It was not the most imaginative threat, or the most threatening one, but Chris looked uncertain for a moment. 'Whatever, bitch,' he finally announced, and muttered insults all the way up the hallway until he was out of sight.

Both Kennedy and Maria stood in silence.

'You okay?' Kennedy eventually asked.

'Oh, yes,' Maria lied airily. 'I expected something like that might happen.'

'He's a loser,' Kennedy mustered. 'A small-minded, bigoted loser. He doesn't deserve you.'

Maria didn't reply. It was her first real attempt to prove she was normal, and *this* was how it had ended. Chris's insults had hit their mark, and Kennedy's words – though they were kind – didn't quite cut it.

'Maria?' Kennedy interrupted gently. 'Are you all right?'

Maria just frowned silently as she tried to still her racing thoughts, and Kennedy put her hand on her shoulder.

Maria blamed the shock of the situation for the fact that she didn't shake it off.

Finally, Maria spoke. 'Thanks,' she said. 'I … appreciate it.'

Kennedy exhaled, relieved, then grinned awkwardly. 'No problem-o,' she sang. It looked like she was about to say something else, so Maria edged around her, quickly walked backwards to her room, and from a safe distance called out, 'Well, good night!'

Then she closed the door behind her, locked it, got into the shower, and cried.

CHAPTER 10

Outpouring

Maria Petranelli was not usually someone who cried. She never had been. Apparently she'd come out of the womb completely silent, which of course Anna took as a bad omen. But even as a child, Maria wasn't one to let people see her emotions. It was a protective tendency she'd had to develop early – not just because of Vince's 'HO HO! IS MARIA CRYING?' style of fatherly bonding and Anna's constant refrain of 'I told you Maria couldn't handle that', but because of her grandparents' penchant for hysteria. They reacted to skinned knees with screaming, collapsing on furniture, and loud invocations to Jesus, the Madonna and all the saints. Maria learned young that she had to play it cool – otherwise, she'd get installed on the plastic-covered couch with a facecloth on her head and the TV turned off so Nonna could focus on the rosary.

So Maria resolved early in life that no matter what happened, she wouldn't let anyone know she'd been affected by anything. She was determined to be unaffectable!

But now Maria was sixteen. She was in Italy. And for the life of her, she couldn't understand why she'd been so affected by Chris.

Well after midnight, she was still tossing and turning. Her thoughts just wouldn't stop. There it was again, the despair that had been chasing her since she'd landed in this country, threatening to catch up with her and send her home. She'd been determined to prove she was independent – and look what was happening! She was falling flat on her face every time she tried to be Italian, and her first attempt to be a normal teenager led to a boy saying she kissed like a dyke. And if it hadn't been for Kennedy ...

Kennedy, who had stuck up for her countless times.

Kennedy, who had said Maria was out of Chris's league.

Kennedy, who had put her hand on her shoulder, and it *didn't feel bad at all.*

For a moment, Maria's despair was overshadowed by a confusing fluttering in her stomach. She cursed, and forbade herself from thinking along those lines any further, but the damage was done. The seed was planted.

There was something dreadfully wrong with Maria.

*

But mornings make everything better. In the daylight, Maria almost laughed at the stupidity of the night before. What an overreaction! Chris was awful, Kennedy was friendly, and Maria was *definitely not gay.*

'Morning Maria,' Kennedy, ever the optimist, sang cheerfully over breakfast.

'Morning,' she replied guardedly.

Neither of them spoke about the incident with Chris, preferring to move on as if nothing had happened. Which was good, but, Maria knew, also meant she was in for some small talk.

'So, uh, how are you finding Rome?' Kennedy said casually – *too* casually.

Maria scrutinised Kennedy's face, which gave nothing away. 'Fine,' was her cautious answer. 'You?'

'Oh yeah, I love it. It was great to get out and see a bit more of it on the weekend.'

'Did you have a good time?'

'It was fun!' Kennedy replied, trying to sound enthusiastic. 'I mean, they're good friends. We have slightly different interests, though. They're a bit wild for me. I'm … I'm glad to be back here.'

The gentle smile on Kennedy's face as she peered at Maria was far too … *something*, Maria thought suspiciously, and narrowed her eyes.

Kennedy cleared her throat awkwardly. 'But yeah, the city's pretty amazing,' she continued quickly. 'What are your favourite parts?'

Deciding that the question meant no harm, Maria replied, 'I like the cobbled streets.'

Kennedy laughed, which made Maria frown. 'Yeah, they're pretty good. It's just so amazing to be in a country where the buildings are so old, isn't it? I mean, one minute there's all this traffic, the next there's ancient ruins, you know? I feel like I want to see as much as I can before this course is over. What about you – what are you going to do next weekend?'

'I haven't really thought about it.'

'So you don't have any plans?'

Maria hesitated. 'No ...'

'Great! Neither do I. And I've always wanted to see the Spanish Steps. I mean, how hilarious, right? Why would you call them the Spanish Steps if they're in the middle of Italy?'

Maria was about to point to the section in her tourist brochure that explained the steps were built in the 18th century to lead up to the Spanish Embassy and therefore the name was logical and not hilarious at all, when Kennedy took a deep breath and blurted, 'So, what do you say? Want to check them out with me?'

I knew it! Maria cursed. *The fiend!*

Maria noticed her heart was beating faster than usual. She willed it to slow down as she thought about Kennedy's offer. Kennedy was just being friendly. They were *both* just being friendly, right?

'That would be nice,' Maria assented, and Kennedy beamed.

Maria did not recognise how much bravery was behind the invitation, nor understand that Kennedy's subsequent (and breathless) launch into possible routes, extra stops, and transport options was due to something as human as *nerves.* Maria just assumed it was typical Kennedy with her typical over-the-top cheerfulness. But she allowed the Spanish Steps invitation, and the rambling, because – not that she would ever admit it out loud – Kennedy was *not that bad*.

This was high praise indeed, for Maria, and it made her feel rattled.

But it was an unavoidable truth. Kennedy was friendly, she was kind ... she had opened the door for Maria, been her partner in their language course role plays, stood up for her when Chris was being threatening. And yes, she was pretty, and yes, she was bisexual, but that didn't have to mean anything. Though maybe ...

Suddenly, Maria realised where she had let her mind wander *again*, and snapped it shut like a suitcase. For the first time in weeks, Maria focused on conjugating her verbs.

*

It was unusually hot on the day of their outing.

The heat was different to the summers in her hometown of Adelaide, which Maria had never coped with well: months of stifling weather and nothing but an air-conditioning unit that was barely used because it was too expensive (Vince) and the unit might overheat, blow up and start a fire (Anna). But that day in Rome, even though it didn't reach the high temperatures Maria was used to, the sun seemed sharper, painfully bright, ricocheting off the cobbled streets and stabbing her skin. The streets were crowded, but rather than power-walking through them, Kennedy kept stopping to check her phone's map every hundred metres, making the sightseeing process much slower than Maria would have liked.

'Uh ... according to this we're meant to turn right ... back there, I think. I think we need to turn around.'

Maria trudged behind Kennedy, her throat dry and raspy and the top of her head feeling like it was on fire. In the heat, Maria's appreciation of Rome's beauty – its towering, ancient buildings juxtaposed with colourful bars and restaurants spilling out onto the footpaths – had long worn off. The last hour had all seemed the same to her: narrow side streets leading to a square filled with people, which you exited via another narrow side street, which led to another square filled with people.

Abruptly, Kennedy stopped. 'We're here!' she said, as cheerfully as she could under the circumstances.

Maria squinted. There was a fountain. There were some steps. This was good enough for her.

Kennedy looked deflated, but then spotted something. 'Hey, are you hungry? There's a food stand there. I'll get us something to eat!' And with this opportunity to redeem herself, Kennedy bounded over to one of the many stands selling generic food at criminal prices to similarly desperate tourists who really just wanted to be in their air-conditioned hotel rooms but were trying to make the most of their holiday.

Before she could call out 'wait', Maria was left alone in the crowd. She tried to follow Kennedy with her eyes so they didn't get separated, but Maria was very short, and it wasn't long before Kennedy was swallowed up by the sea of tourists.

So she waited.

And waited.

She's left me, she thought. *I knew it.*

And even though she told herself she'd been expecting it, this particular abandonment hurt more than usual.

So when she felt someone grab her arm, relief flooded through her. 'You're back!' she started, and then stopped. It wasn't Kennedy. It was a stranger.

'Hello, miss,' said the stranger. 'Where are you from?'

Maria was suspicious. 'Australia,' she replied cautiously.

'Wow! An Aussie. And you are here on holiday?'

'Sort of,' said Maria, noticing he had not let go of her arm. She frowned.

'I grew up here,' said the stranger. 'My name is Alessandro.' He reached into his pocket and withdrew three thick strands of thread, each a different colour – red, white and green. 'How are you enjoying Rome?' he continued, lifting her wrist and placing the bands around it.

'It's nice,' she said, while inside she screamed, *Who is this person! Why is he touching my arm!*

Alessandro started weaving the bands around each other, slowly producing a bracelet. Another man approached.

'Ah, Lorenzo, this is ... sorry, what is your name?' Alessandro asked.

'Maria?' She said it more like a question, wondering why she was standing still instead of kicking these men in the shins. She'd imagined and plotted her reactions to moments like this for years. So why was she still frozen?

'Nice to meet you,' said Lorenzo. 'You are Australian?'

The bracelet was nearly complete now, and even though the pair were acting friendly, Maria sensed danger. She looked around for Kennedy, but the men kept talking, giving a history of Rome that sounded inaccurate even to Maria. *These men are dangerous*, she thought. *This is it. Get ready. Knee them in the balls. Slap them in the face. Call for help. Do something*, she urged herself.

'There, I have finished,' said Alessandro, tying off the bracelet but still not letting go of her arm. 'That will be thirty-five euro.'

Maria nearly fainted. She was being held up by a thief! *Stab him*, she thought to herself. *Stab him in the chest!*

She felt her free arm move to her pocket.

She curled her hand around its contents and withdrew it.

And then she numbly removed thirty-five euro from her wallet and handed it to them.

'Thank you.' Alessandro grinned. 'Goodbye, miss.'

And with that, Alessandro and Lorenzo were gone, and Maria was standing in front of the Spanish Steps with a bracelet that felt evil.

She had been robbed.

She hadn't stopped it.

She hadn't done anything at all.

She wasn't powerful.

She was helpless.

She was weak.

At that moment, Kennedy arrived, practically skipping with joy. 'I have pizza! And Coke! And water, just in case!' she announced.

Maria took the pizza from her and held it in her hands.

It was cold.

CHAPTER 11

Revenge

'Hey, Alessandro. Remember me?'

Alessandro turned, surprised.

Maria was smiling, friendly, walking towards him. 'I just wanted to thank you,' she said pleasantly, and Alessandro stood there, dead still. She was close now. Close enough to smell the fear on him. He recognised her; she could see it in his eyes.

'Miss ...' he started, but his breath was cut short as Maria grabbed both his shoulders and pulled him down onto her raised knee. Winded, he gasped for Lorenzo, but she grabbed his face and pulled it close to hers, whispering, 'Like to take advantage of tourists, do you? Like to take advantage of helpless women?' She kneed him again, where it counted, then pushed the doubled-up figure to the ground, kicking him for good measure.

'Here's your bracelet,' she said, throwing what remained of it at his feet. The crowd around her were silent, and they stepped back in awe as she made her way through them.

*

Now. Lorenzo. He wouldn't be too far from here, surely.

'Hello, miss,' Maria heard someone say. 'Where are you from?'

It's him, *she realised. This was going to be easier than she thought. She moved around him slowly, assessing his position. The tourist in his grip was looking at him, too frightened to move.* Enough of this, *Maria thought.* This ends here.

'Hey Lorenzo,' she said, and Lorenzo looked up, startled.

'Yes?'

Maria moved so quickly, he didn't have time to run. The gunshot was muffled by the silencer, and Maria turned, replaced the weapon and walked casually away, not even glancing back at Lorenzo, who lay dead on the steps, blood streaming from his forehead where the bullet had gone squarely in.

*

'The pizza's cold,' said Kennedy apologetically. Her voice shook Maria out of the revenge fantasy she'd conjured to make herself feel better about her horrendous failure.

'Police,' murmured Maria.

'Ha! Good idea. We'll bust this whole operation wide open.'

'I've been robbed,' said Maria.

'Heh,' chuckled Kennedy, still trying to play along. 'Though they probably have kids to feed, so maybe we can let them off with a warning …'

'Look at my arm,' said Maria.

Kennedy obeyed, confused. 'Is something wrong with your arm?' she asked.

Maria didn't reply. Her face was blank, empty, as it always was when she was refusing to feel something, so it took Kennedy longer than usual to work out that Maria was actually in distress. 'Maria, are you okay?' she asked eventually.

The concern in Kennedy's voice kicked Maria into gear. 'Oh, it's nothing,' she said. 'I was only joking. We'd better get up those steps, don't you think? I mean, we'd really regret it if we came all the way to the Spanish Steps and didn't climb them. We can't take the food, though, we have to respect the architecture.' And she thrust her pizza back at Kennedy and set off at a fierce pace.

It took Kennedy the entire flight of steps to catch up to her. Maria was very fast for such a short person. And perhaps if Kennedy hadn't spent so long overcoming her guilt about food waste before finally putting her untouched purchases into a nearby bin, she might not have had to sprint so hard.

When they arrived at the top, Kennedy was gasping for air, but Maria stood straight and surveyed the scene.

'Hmm,' she said. 'Interesting.'

Kennedy was trying very hard not to look at Maria like she'd lost the plot, but she wasn't successful.

'I got a new bracelet while you were gone,' Maria snapped, deciding to bring it out in the open before Kennedy tried to feel sorry for her. 'And yes, it was expensive, and yes, it was unexpected, but I quite like it, really. Look! It's in Italian colours.' She scratched absent-mindedly at her wrist. *Wow*, she realised. *This bracelet is tight.*

'Oh,' said Kennedy, confused. 'It's … nice?'

'No, it's *not* nice, Kennedy!' Maria turned on her. 'Where were you? I had two strange men grabbing my arm and forcing me to buy this stupid … this stupid …' Maria was trying to wrench the thing off, but it wouldn't go past her hand.

'Here,' said Kennedy, trying unsuccessfully to help.

'No, don't …'

'If you just …'

'Ouch, that hurts …'

'Sorry, but if you just …'

'Just leave it!' she proclaimed, and Kennedy released Maria's arm immediately. 'It cost thirty-five euro. They robbed me. They robbed me!' Maria said it in a surprised voice, with emphasis on 'they' and 'me'.

'Who were they?' Kennedy asked, a bit pathetically.

'I don't know,' Maria said on impulse, but it wasn't true. She'd committed the men's names and faces to memory and had been envisioning various scenarios of revenge all the way up the Spanish Steps. She wasn't quite happy with the dialogue yet, but she would work on it later.

Kennedy looked devastated. 'I'm really sorry,' she said, sounding utterly miserable.

Finally, Maria looked up. The bloodlust ebbed as she took in Kennedy's bereft appearance. 'Oh,' she said, feeling an unfamiliar twinge of guilt. 'Well. It wasn't your fault.'

Thankfully, that was enough to make Kennedy brighten. She regained her cheerful composure and made her voice sound lower. 'If you see them, point them out, will you?'

'I will,' said Maria. 'Right before I march up and stab them in the eyes.'

Kennedy laughed, both in surprise and relief. 'Look, Maria, today wasn't great, was it? I'm sorry everything went wrong. Want to, uh … want to go somewhere, and get a drink?'

'I'd *love* to,' said Maria, the thought of stabbing Lorenzo sending a newfound rush of power through her veins.

It wasn't the most romantic of locations, in the end – they both decided they'd had enough adventures for one day, and found shelter in a nearby McDonald's. Still, as they walked back to their apartment building, Kennedy couldn't stop smiling.

And neither could Maria. When she finally got into bed she was still full of adrenaline, and she tossed and turned, excited by the fantasy (which she had extended to include fly-kicks and car chases). Eventually she floated to sleep, her mind full of images of bloody faces, broken noses, and sweet, sweet revenge.

CHAPTER 12

Repercussions

Just as Maria started getting used to life at the language school, her month in Rome was nearly over. *This is it,* Maria thought. *I'll actually have to go on exchange.* She had a twinge of something that an emotionally healthy person would call 'sadness', but which Maria described as 'slight annoyance'.

She wasn't nervous about the exchange; she would be going to school, after all, and she knew how to survive school. She just had to focus on her studies and she would get through. But she found she didn't want to leave Rome. She was finally getting the hang of it. The roads looked familiar. The language was becoming less of a mystery. She was getting yelled at by passing motorists less and less. The fact that she would be leaving Kennedy had *nothing* to do with it, of course. Maria was adamant about that, and every time a stray thought tried to suggest otherwise, she banished it immediately. Despite the theft incident at the Spanish Steps, she was back to her fierce self. In fact, she felt more powerful than ever. Yes, yes, she'd had her first test of street bravery and had failed miserably; but, she told herself, it was just because it was unexpected. She had never encountered anything like that before, except in her imagination. Now that she knew what danger felt like, she was never going to be paralysed by fear again. She was almost itching for a chance to prove herself.

'I think,' Kennedy said on their second-to-last morning in Rome, 'that we should celebrate.'

'Celebrate what?' asked Maria.

'Surviving a month in a foreign country; staying awake during all those classes; the fact that we're about to head off into the wider Italian landscape … take your pick.'

'All right … how should we celebrate?' Maria asked.

Kennedy paused, took a deep breath, and then said it. 'The Spanish Steps.'

Maria opened her mouth involuntarily.

Kennedy hurriedly continued. 'It was such a terrible day last time … we didn't get to see it properly. And you know what they say about getting back on the horse …'

Maria had no idea what they said about getting back on the horse. Her exposure to common sayings was limited to Vince Petranelli's usage. He used them often, but incorrectly:

1. Don't throw the baby in the bathwater.
2. That has just broken the camel's straw!
3. You can take a duck to hot water, but you can't make it drink.

'Yes, I suppose so,' said Maria, catching Kennedy's meaning despite the horse analogy. *Besides*, she thought, *maybe we'll see Alessandro and Lorenzo.* She fingered the bracelet thoughtfully. She had decided not to take it off: it was a symbol, a reminder that she would never be helpless again.

And Kennedy, unaware of Maria's violent thoughts, beamed.

This time, the weather was much nicer. The sun was warm, and there was a cool breeze: it was the perfect weather to explore Rome on foot.

Everything was beautiful that day. The scooters zipping in and out of traffic; the old men sitting on benches and laughing together; the buskers with piano accordions who all seemed to be playing a rendition of Frank Sinatra's 'My Way'; it felt like a film.

Maria and Kennedy wandered slowly, taking their time at landmarks that appeared to be significant. They admired the ancient ruins and elaborate churches and, on Maria's insistence, walked quickly past the naked statues. Sometimes they accidentally bumped into each other, and their hands brushed, which meant Maria had to leap away as if she had been burned, and Kennedy had to cough and say 'uh' and make a terrible joke. But overall, and despite these awkward encounters, neither wanted the day to end. Maria was daydreaming the whole time, of course; she kept imagining catching a glimpse of Alessandro and Lorenzo, and how the scene would play out. After the twentieth iteration, she started to imagine it was Kennedy in their grip, and that she, Maria, would leap in, beat them up, and rescue her. *Just to show Kennedy I can stand up for myself, that's all,* Maria was rationalising, when Kennedy's voice cut into her thoughts.

'This doesn't look right,' Kennedy said. She checked her phone map again. 'I thought we were only a few side streets away.'

'Hmm,' said Maria, only just tuning into her surroundings and realising they looked a lot less … safe. The beautiful cobbled streets and restaurants with chequered tablecloths were gone; all that was around them was bitumen, broken glass, and graffiti. And these streets seemed deserted, though – twice – Kennedy and Maria passed an old woman sitting on the pavement, her back against the wall, crying, '*Un euro, solo un euro …*'

'Do you think we should turn around?' Kennedy asked uncertainly, after giving the old woman ten euro for the second time.

'Absolutely not,' Maria replied confidently.

It was time for her to take charge.

It was time to start power-walking.

It was time to head north.

Before Kennedy had a chance to protest, Maria took off at a furious pace, determined to reach a more familiar, and safer, part of town.

And, against all odds, she did – she emerged from the confusing twist of bitumen streets and into a square. It was a small square, but it was a square nonetheless.

'Okay,' she said to Kennedy. 'Where are we now? Let's check the phone again.'

Kennedy was silent for a few minutes as she assessed their whereabouts and tried to compare them to the map. 'Wow!' she exclaimed. 'The Spanish Steps are literally around the corner! How did you do that?' She looked admiringly at Maria, who shrugged off the praise as if this was a regular occurrence – which, of course, it wasn't.

'All right then,' said Maria in a no-nonsense voice, already marching towards a narrow laneway. But then she stopped dead.

Which, when you think about it, probably isn't the best choice of words.

Because there, in front of her, was the thief Lorenzo, on his back, his eyes open.

Dead.

CHAPTER 13

Consequences

Lorenzo was someone who many people would describe as 'fit'.

Not in the 'could probably run a marathon' way – in fact, Lorenzo did not care for sports – but in the 'I am God's gift to women and I know it' way.

He had an *excellent* metabolism. And to celebrate his excellent metabolism, Lorenzo liked to eat. And eat. And eat. 'You just need to exercise more,' he would say, with his mouth full of food, to his scowling sisters.

When Lorenzo moved into the side street that day, his left arm felt heavier than usual. It sent sharp ... no, dull ... pains through him, and he was short of breath. And suddenly his chest folded into itself, crushing everything inside.

Lorenzo collapsed.

Some would say it was because his sisters had put the evil eye on him.

Some would say it was because his cholesterol level was through the roof.

But Lorenzo might have recovered – if he hadn't hit his head on a windowsill as he went down.

His death was, you could say, an accident.

CHAPTER 14

Guilt

'Oh no,' Maria gasped. 'Oh no. Oh no!'

'What ...' Kennedy stopped as she caught up with her and saw Lorenzo's body gruesomely splayed on the pavement.

'Oh my god,' Kennedy gasped. 'Oh ... my ... god. Is he dead?'

'Did you kill him?' Maria asked. Then, before Kennedy could reply with a resounding 'What Are You Talking About?', she answered her own question. 'No, of course you didn't. You couldn't have! You were with me. Did I kill him? Oh God ... it's my fault. It's all my fault!'

Kennedy's eyes were nearly popping out of her head. 'Maria, what are you talking about?' she yelled.

'I didn't really want him to die! I mean, I know I imagined it ... but I never meant it ... Oh God, it's all my fault ...'

'Who? Maria, what are you talking about?'

Suddenly, Maria realised she was showing way too much emotion. She reined it in, scratched at the bracelet and took a deep breath. 'Lorenzo,' she said.

'Who?'

'The bracelet guy!'

'The bracelet guy was called Lorenzo?'

'Yes. Yes! And that's him!'

Kennedy looked at her in horror, then realisation, then determination. This was it; this was her time. Filled with heroic energy, Kennedy took a deep breath, puffed out her chest and announced, 'I'll get help!'

And then she turned and ran.

Maria frowned, but Kennedy was not there to see it.

I knew she would leave me, Maria told herself grimly, trying to stop her head from spinning.

Maria had not killed Lorenzo. Revenge fantasies aside, she hadn't even wanted him dead. Just maimed. Not dead!

But now Kennedy was gone, and Maria was standing in the middle of an empty square in the backstreets, completely alone – unless she counted Lorenzo's dead body, which made her feel even less safe. What if Lorenzo's murderers were still nearby? What if they heard her, and saw her, standing alone? She looked for somewhere to sit, somewhere less obvious, where she could wait for Kennedy. *If she bothers to come back,* she thought bitterly. There, across the square, beside the entrance to another long, narrow laneway, was a bench. *As good a place as any for my last moments,* she thought fatalistically, and moved towards it.

She imagined what Kennedy would say when she came back and found her lifeless corpse. She hoped she would feel guilty; she hoped she would regret having left her to face Lorenzo's murderers, alone.

Then Maria forgot about Kennedy, and started worrying about what she'd say to Lorenzo's murderers when they arrived to kill her. Would she try to fight them? No – she had no chance of winning, and losing the fight would only make her look weak. She wouldn't say anything, she decided. Or ... she would say 'just get it over with'. Would she raise her eyebrows when she said it? She played around with the words, suddenly so weary she wanted to lie down. She reached the bench and was just about to collapse on it when she saw a shape in the shadows.

*

They say lightning doesn't strike the same place twice. This is a proverb. It means it is extremely unlikely that an extremely unlikely event will happen to the same person, a second time. For instance, a tourist seeing a dead body in a side street in Rome.

But Maria was staring at another dead body, in a side street, in Rome.

And this dead body also had a bracelet on his wrist: one made of three bands, red, white and green.

And this was not at all like Lorenzo's death. This was not an accident.

CHAPTER 15

Beginning

All of a sudden, Maria didn't want to die. She didn't care if she had witty last words, or if her death would teach Kennedy a lesson. She wanted to *live*.

She clawed at her wrist, wrenching the symbolic bracelet from her arm and hurling it to the ground. Then she realised it had her DNA all over it, and, worrying that the murderers might use it to track her, she picked it up again and stuffed it into her pocket.

Was Maria completely misunderstanding forensic science?

Yes.

Was she overreacting?

No!

First, they had killed Lorenzo. Then they had killed the man with the bracelet. She knew she would be next.

She heard footsteps. Her heart lurched and she froze, wide-eyed with fear.

This wasn't a side street at all, she realised. This was an alley. There was no more stereotypical location for an untimely death than an alley, she knew – she had to get out of there!

But they had seen her.

*

Kennedy came running back through the square, having failed to find a single reinforcement (and having completely forgotten there was such a thing as a police force), just in time to see Maria being ushered away by two suspicious-looking figures. Kennedy broke into a sprint. 'Maria!' she called dramatically, but they had already disappeared into the labyrinth of Rome.

And that is how Maria found herself locked in the boot of a car.

CHAPTER 16

Rescue

Great. I've been kidnapped by the mafia, Maria thought. *I knew this would happen!*

Maria put up only a minimal struggle. She knew a direct confrontation was not wise. She had to bide her time. She was careful not to look into their faces; there was much less reason to kill her if they believed she couldn't identify them. But she used her peripheral vision as best she could, taking in hair colour, eye colour, nose sizes, facial hair, build, scars – anything that might help. *The smaller one looks a bit like a skinny Robert Downey Jr.*, she decided just as the boot lid closed, leaving her in darkness.

Fortunately, Maria adjusted quite quickly. It only took a few moments to realise the boot was not as terrifying as she thought it would be. It was actually quite spacious. The two men hadn't spoken to her, but then, they hadn't shot her in the head either. And the car had *not* started straight away and driven off at lightning speed – in fact, it seemed she had been left alone in the vehicle until the men finished whatever business they needed to finish. So, in theory, there was plenty of time to escape. Maria was feeling quite optimistic, considering the circumstances.

Then her phone vibrated.

Oh no, Maria thought, imagining the Petranelli family huddled around the speakerphone, ready to call her a 'poor girl'. How on earth was she going to explain this turn of events?

But it was a mobile number, one she didn't recognise. She answered it cautiously.

'Hello …?'

'Maria!' It was Kennedy, so relieved she sounded close to tears.

Maria frowned. 'How did you get this number?' she demanded, forgetting, in the drama, that *she* was the one who'd insisted they exchange them 'in case our luggage gets mixed up'. (Though, Maria had greatly regretted her moment of weakness and deleted Kennedy's shortly after.)

But Kennedy didn't have time to remind her of any of this. 'Where are you? Are you all right?'

'I'm fine … I'm in the boot of a car.'

Kennedy gasped. 'Where are they taking you?'

'We're not moving – it's still parked.'

'Okay,' Kennedy said, relieved. 'Where is it? I'll come get you.'

'I don't know, but I think we went north!'

'What type of car am I looking for?'

Maria cursed herself. She'd paid so much attention to the men that she'd forgotten to pay attention to the car! She racked her brains. 'It's black, I think.'

'Okay. I'll be right there.' And she hung up.

Kennedy spent the next twenty minutes running up and down side streets and knocking on the boot of every black vehicle she came across, which caused at least two alarms to go off and several passers-by to swear at her. Just when she was about to give up, she heard it: banging, coming from a car behind her.

Maria had been kicking as hard as she could, trying to smash through the tail-lights so she could stick her face in the opening and yell for help. She had seen someone do this in one of Vince's B-grade action-comedies. But then she heard voices, and stopped kicking. The boot opened and light flooded in. Kennedy's face appeared, and nothing Anna Petranelli could ever say would make Maria believe this was anything short of a miracle.

'Kennedy!' she exclaimed happily.

'In you go,' said the two men, tipping Kennedy over and landing her on top of Maria.

Now they had two witnesses in the boot that they didn't know what to do with.

*

Just as Maria manoeuvred herself out from beneath Kennedy, the car came to life and started driving serenely and smoothly through the streets of Rome (as serenely and smoothly as one can drive through the streets of Rome).

Maria and Kennedy travelled in silence for a very long time. The scenery changed from apartment buildings and street signs to open countryside and sweeping plains. Not that they could see the scenery, of course.

They were both embarrassed, but for different reasons. Kennedy was embarrassed that she had failed so dismally to save the day. Maria was embarrassed that she was in such close proximity to Kennedy. To combat the awkwardness of the situation, she listened intently to the two men in the passenger section of the car, but their voices were muffled.

It's time to take action, Maria finally decided. Despite not wanting the men to hear them talking, she chose not to whisper; whispering seemed too intimate at a time like this.

'We need to kick the tail-lights out,' she said, in a voice slightly above a whisper.

'What?'

'We need to kick the tail-lights out!'

Kennedy, who had not been forced to watch as many B-grade movies as Maria, was taking far too long to catch on. Maria rolled her eyes and realised she would have to take matters into her own hands – but Kennedy was in the way.

'We need to swap places,' she said.

'What?'

'We need to swap places!' She was getting sick of this pattern of dialogue, so just started shimmying. Kennedy, still being slow to get with the program, unexpectedly found

Maria completely on top of her. Now their bodies were pressed together. Again. And the road was far too bumpy.

'Uh ... Maria ...'

'Oh, for goodness' sake, Kennedy! Will you just move over?' she hissed, exasperated.

'Right ... sorry ...'

After much fumbling, the two managed to swap places, and Maria was once again kicking with all her might at the area where she imagined the tail-lights would be.

The movie Maria had been basing her escape plan on was hopeless. The dialogue was clichéd, the characters stereotypical, and it featured more than one scene where the hero's well-timed punch caused an explosion. But the 'kicking the tail-lights out' plot point wasn't actually implausible, in theory; it's just that the film was made in the 1980s, and apparently, twenty-first-century cars are much harder to kick through.

The car stopped abruptly. Maria and Kennedy heard a car door open, and shoes crunch on gravel.

They froze.

The boot opened.

'Stop it,' commanded one of the men, in English.

'Okay,' said Maria meekly.

The boot slammed shut again, and the journey continued.

CHAPTER 17

Physical

It was meant to be a simple job.

The instructions had been straightforward – get in, make the hit look like a mugging, get out.

But Giovanni and Felice did not get out fast enough.

They'd been stealthily walking towards the getaway car when they heard two foreign girls gasping like industrial vacuums, and Felice insisted they stop.

Giovanni said the girls hadn't seen them. Felice said they'd better stop and make sure.

Giovanni repeated they were in the clear. Felice wanted to wait and watch, just in case.

Giovanni said Felice was being ridiculous. Felice countered that if he was being so ridiculous, why was one of the girls sitting on a bench and loudly reciting a death monologue?

The boot was a snap decision, one Felice made when

he heard pounding footsteps approaching, and Giovanni – the one who looked like a skinny Robert Downey Jr. (a comparison he would not have liked, as he could not abide Marvel films) – had spent the entire drive since then cursing him. Especially when the girls started kicking his car.

*

'Where do you think they're taking us?' Kennedy asked.

Maria was quiet, trying to think it through. 'Wherever we're going,' she said finally, 'when the boot opens again, we should kick them in the face and then run.'

'Maria,' Kennedy replied, a natural diplomat, 'I don't think kicking is always the answer …'

Kennedy didn't have a chance to make a better suggestion. The car screeched to a stop, and Maria tensed, preparing herself for confrontation.

But it was very anti-climactic.

The boot opened, Maria and Kennedy were ushered out, the two men gave them stern words in Italian … and then they closed the boot and drove away.

Kennedy watched the car leave, her mouth open.

Maria watched it leave and memorised the numberplate.

'Well,' Kennedy said, when the car was no longer in sight. 'I really didn't expect any of that!'

'I did,' Maria muttered.

'What?'

'Oh … never mind,' Maria sighed. Kennedy was innocent,

she knew. Kennedy didn't understand how cruel and terrible the world was.

'Did you catch what they said to us?'

'It was "Something something see you in Rome",' Maria said helpfully.

Giovanni and Felice had *not* said 'something something see you in Rome'. What they had said, after much deliberation in the car, was 'you saw nothing in Rome', combined with threatening hand gestures that Kennedy and Maria had no trouble translating.

'We should call the police,' Kennedy said.

'*What?*' Maria nearly shrieked. 'We can't do that!'

'Why not?'

'We don't know the number,' she said.

This, of course, was not the real reason. The real reason was she was scared the police wouldn't believe her and would say 'now get off the line in case somebody is trying to report a *real* crime' before hanging up on her.

This fear was not unfounded; Maria had actually heard a police officer yelling this exact line to her mother. To be fair, it was not just any police officer – it was Anna Petranelli's cousin's son, Matteo, who, upon graduating, made the mistake of gallantly announcing to Anna that 'any time she had a problem, she could call him personally'. And so, Matteo listened patiently when Anna called to tell him that:

1. The neighbours' son kept parking his car in front of their house, and it was leaking oil;

2. She saw someone back into a pole and then drive off without leaving a note; and
3. She had been watching Adelaide Crime Stoppers, and even though she did not recognise any of the criminals, she wanted Matteo to know she would be keeping a special eye out.

Matteo, a good Italian boy, tried to be respectful, and at the end of each phone call he politely thanked her. But he had made the 'any time you need anything' promise to a *lot* of female Italian relatives. So when Anna called to say she was having an argument with Vince and needed someone to back her up, Matteo was no longer able to contain himself.

Unfortunately, Anna had him on speakerphone. So when he shouted, 'NOW GET OFF THE LINE … (et cetera),' Maria heard it all.

And so did Vince.

Not willing to let Vince gloat, even for a second, Anna had grabbed nine-year-old Maria by the shoulders and said, 'Let that be a lesson to you. *These* are the types of people we have running our country!'

And when Matteo and his fiancé of six years finally tied the knot, Anna refused to attend the wedding.

Kennedy, of course, did not know any of this, so she did not recognise Maria's flimsy 'we don't know the phone number' excuse for what it was. 'Hang on, I'll look it up,' she said, pulling her phone out. '… Damn it. My battery's dead!'

'Oh no!' Maria said, managing not to sound too relieved.

'What about yours?'

That's right. She'd forgotten about her phone.

Maria took it out of her pocket. The battery bar was glowing red – her phone would be useless soon. 'I have a tiny bit left,' she admitted, 'but it doesn't look like I have a signal.'

Kennedy looked concerned.

'Don't worry!' she reassured her, feeling much more positive now that she didn't have to call any authorities. 'Let's just walk north. We'll reach help eventually!'

Maria set a gruelling pace, but it was only a short while before they both slowed to a walk, and then a shuffle. They were too tired to appreciate the rolling green hills dotted with olive trees, the vineyards bursting with colour, or the tall, thin cypress trees lining the Tuscan countryside. Actually, they didn't even realise they were in Tuscany. Kennedy might have worked it out if her phone wasn't dead, but even if Maria did have a signal, it wouldn't have occurred to her to check a map. What they did know, however, was that they were walking up a slope that never seemed to end, and there were no buildings to be seen.

'So those men, they killed that Lorenzo guy?' Kennedy eventually asked.

'Yes, they must have – and the other man. But I didn't recognise him. It wasn't Alessandro.'

'*The other man?* What other man?' Kennedy cried.

'When you left … I walked over to the other side of the square … and there was another body.'

'Are you serious?'

'Yes,' Maria said. 'Then those two men showed up and started pulling me away.'

'I can't believe this,' Kennedy murmured. 'I honestly can't believe this.'

'I know,' Maria said.

Neither could think of anything to say for a good few seconds.

'Apparently the gods are determined not to let us see the Spanish Steps,' Kennedy sighed.

Maria looked at Kennedy in surprise, and saw her give a small smile. She considered several responses before replying, 'Well, you must have done something to offend them.'

'Me?' Kennedy snorted. 'Why do you assume it was me?'

Maria just shrugged haughtily, which made Kennedy laugh, and Maria felt something fluttery in her chest (which she hastily repressed).

They walked until sunset, when they finally saw a couple of old stone farm buildings in a field ahead. But when they reached them, they discovered the buildings didn't have lights, and there were no people nearby. Animals, yes; old farm machinery, yes; but that was it.

It was getting dark quickly, and it was difficult to see.

Kennedy walked over to one of the sheds. 'This one seems okay. Should we try to sleep here, and find help in the morning?'

Maria didn't like to give up, but she recognised it was foolish to keep roaming the roads at night, so she agreed. She wandered away from Kennedy, looking around the dark interior to pick an appropriate space for herself.

'Over here,' Kennedy called. 'This corner looks good!'

It was an innocuous phrase, intended to be helpful. But Maria's brain did not know what to do with it.

What did she mean, *this corner looks good*? Was Kennedy bragging? Wanting her to know she'd found her own suitable sleeping space so Maria didn't need to worry about her? Or was she implying they sleep *together*? What was happening!

Underneath all the social confusion was something else, something Maria was working in overdrive not to allow into her conscious thought.

It was the thought of lying next to Kennedy. Yes, they'd already been together in a closed car boot, but that had been under duress, so it didn't count. But now the thought of them sleeping close together was … it was making her body feel … there was no other way to put it … *pleasantly electric.*

Maria was horrified.

'Uh, I mean, if you want,' Kennedy amended, in response to Maria's alarmed expression. 'It's okay if you, uh, want to sleep somewhere else.'

Maria pulled herself together and marched over to Kennedy's corner. 'Here will be fine,' she said properly.

They lay down next to each other without a word. Maria stayed a good foot away from Kennedy, and tried to make herself comfortable. It didn't really work. The ground wasn't too hard, and they were shielded from any wind, but now that she'd stopped moving, the cold seeped into her bones. Try as she might, she couldn't stop herself physically shivering.

'Maria?'

'Yes?'

'Are you … cold?'

Maria cursed herself inwardly. There was no denying it. She realised she had only two options: admit it, and risk Kennedy thinking she was a 'poor girl'; or deny it, and have Kennedy think she was shivering from fear.

She made her choice.

'I *am* cold,' Maria said, but she said it with surprise in her voice, as if it had only just occurred to her.

She heard Kennedy muffle a laugh, which she felt mildly indignant about. Then Kennedy shuffled closer to Maria's back and – so slowly that Maria had ample time to shout 'NO' if she wanted to – gently wrapped her arm around her waist.

Damn it.

'Is that better?' Kennedy asked hesitantly.

Maria's body was stiff as a board. But she couldn't deny it was warmer this way. (Though she could, and would, deny absolutely everything else she was feeling.)

'Yes, that's better,' Maria conceded, and she felt Kennedy relax and hold her a little tighter. It filled her body with a fire that had nothing to do with sharing their body heat.

Maria was incredibly relieved Kennedy would not be able to see her cheeks burning.

In survival situations like this, physical contact is a must, Maria reasoned to herself, over and over again, but it wasn't until she heard Kennedy snoring quietly that she was able to fall asleep.

CHAPTER 18

Sanctuary

Maria woke up when an egg smashed against the side of her head.

She opened her eyes. Had an egg just smashed against the side of her head? Surely she was dreaming. She lay still for a moment, trying to wake up properly.

Where was she? She was warm, and comfortable, and there was a pleasant weight across her chest. What was that? Slowly, and with a growing sense of alarm, Maria realised it was Kennedy's arm. Which was attached to Kennedy. Who was snuggled against her back. Which felt …

No! Maria told herself firmly. *Kennedy is not 'snuggled' anywhere. We are surviving in the wild. That is all.*

Though, now Maria was taking in her surroundings, calling it 'the wild' was a bit of an exaggeration. It was actually a very respectable barn. There was hay. A pile of sacks stacked against a wall. A few rogue feathers. A cow.

And now, yolk sliding down her neck.

That's right, Maria remembered. *I'm in Italy*.

Another egg landed, hitting her squarely on the shoulder. She sat up. 'Hey!'

Maria glared at a little boy, who glared right back at her.

For a moment, neither made a move. Then he turned and ran, yelling in Italian, 'Nonna! There are thieves in the shed!'

Maria elbowed Kennedy, who had managed to avoid the artillery fire.

'Maria?' she said, confused. 'What's that on your face?'

'Shh!' she hissed. They listened to the sound of distant voices coming rapidly closer.

'*Two* thieves,' the boy confirmed.

'Of course there are, Gabriele,' said a patronising voice. 'Of course. I believe you. Two thieves in the shed.'

The boy and an older woman appeared in the doorway. Maria and her nemesis glared at each other. Kennedy and the older woman widened their eyes in shock.

The older woman let out a wail. 'There are thieves in the shed!' she shrieked. 'Rocco! Thieves! They are going to kill us all! They have come to murder us in our beds!'

'Shut up, old woman,' a man's voice hollered. 'Thieves. Murderers. Always the same. Can't a man get some peace and quiet?' He joined the glaring child and the wailing woman.

Kennedy and Maria sat among the hay, waiting.

'Hmm,' he said. 'Thieves in the shed.'

And with that, he turned and left.

'I threw eggs at them,' Gabriele told his nonna proudly.

‘What are they saying?’ Kennedy asked.

‘I’m not sure …’ Maria replied. She recognised the melodrama, but, thanks to the very wholesome curriculum of the language school, she didn’t recognise the words. ‘I think they’re calling us thieves?’

Rocco reappeared a moment later, carrying a rifle.

Everyone went hysterical.

‘I’ll show you freeloaders how we deal with thieves here!’ roared Rocco.

‘No! Rocco! Don’t! You’re out of control!’ the woman shrieked.

‘I’ll show you!’ Gabriele echoed Rocco, picking up more ammunition – fistfuls of hay, clumps of dirt, and occasional clods of manure.

‘Wait!’ yelled Kennedy in English. ‘Wait! Don’t shoot! We’re sorry!’

‘Lost! We’re lost! Lost!’ yelled Maria in Italian.

Something soft hit her in the mouth.

I’m going to kill that kid, she thought.

*

Everyone calmed down once they realised it was just two lost foreign girls taking shelter in their barn. The gun was put away and Maria and Kennedy – dirty, bedraggled and more than a little overwhelmed – were ushered into the kitchen and seated at the table. Rocco, an older man with sharp tufts of white hair, eyed them curiously while his wife, Nicolina, transformed from wrathful to magnanimous and put plate after plate of food in front of them.

'You poor things,' Nicolina said periodically, which drew no reaction from Maria – but only because she didn't recognise that phrase in Italian yet. 'Look at the poor children, Rocco. They are starving! We'd better get the good wine. Poor things. I wonder where they came from?' Nicolina hovered and fussed and stroked their hair and pinched their cheeks, to which they had no defence except to smile politely.

Rocco put on his foreigner voice and tried to communicate. 'I am Rocco. ROCCO. And this … this is my wife. WIFE. NI–CO–LI–NA,' he yelled in Italian, gesturing wildly.

'Rocco, you stupid man, they are English, not deaf.'

'Hey! Nicolina! This is none of your business!' he hollered back.

Nicolina shook her head and sat at the table next to Maria, grabbing her hand and stroking it. 'YOU POOR GIRL,' she yelled (somewhat hypocritically) in Italian. 'You are lost?'

'Yes,' Maria replied, trying to put sentences together. 'We … I am from Australia …'

'Australia! That's the other side of the world,' said Nicolina.

'We were in a car … and we walked here.'

'Poor girl,' Nicolina said to Rocco. 'She's lost her mind.'

'Maria,' Kennedy whispered. 'Tell them about the murder.'

'I don't know the word for murder,' she replied.

'What about dead?'

'No.'

'Killed?'

'No!'

'Phone?'

'Do you have a phone?' Maria asked in Italian.

The old couple stared at her for a moment, then exploded into rapid-fire Italian.

'You see, Rocco! They need a phone.'

'All right, all right! They need a phone! What do you want me to do about it?'

'I told you, you need to pay the bill, but what do you say? You say, we don't need a phone.'

'We *don't* need a phone!'

'Of course we do! How are we supposed to help the lost children without a phone?'

'Maybe they aren't lost children. Maybe they're thieves!'

'Oh, you'd like that, wouldn't you! Then they could murder us in our beds, and we couldn't call the police for help, and do you know why? Because you didn't pay the phone bill!'

Maria and Kennedy sat quietly, waiting, until Nicolina noticed they'd stopped eating. 'Look what you've done, Rocco! You've scared the poor children.'

Rocco huffed, crossed his arms and glared at the floor.

'Don't worry, young people,' Nicolina crooned. 'You can stay here as long as you need.'

'They need to go home, Nicolina!'

'All right, all right!' she snapped. She took a deep breath and tried again. 'Did you come from the city? Did you come from Firenze? FIRENZE?'

'She asked if we came from Florence!' Kennedy said victoriously, glad she could participate.

'No, we came from Rome,' said Maria.

'They came from Rome, Rocco. What are we going to do?'

'Well, I can't drive that far. We'll ask the kids. They'll be here tomorrow to pick up Gabriele.'

Nicolina nodded. 'Good,' she said, and then looked at the guests. 'Paola and Alberto will come tomorrow. They will fix everything. You will stay here tonight.'

'What are they saying?' Kennedy asked.

Maria didn't answer. Gabriele had entered the room. Maria was still upset about all the egg throwing, and her eyes narrowed.

What she didn't expect was for the kid to narrow his eyes right back.

CHAPTER 19

Violation

Maria didn't say it out loud, but she was very eager for nightfall. The sooner it was night, the sooner they could sleep.

Maria's motivation for this was, of course, completely pure. It had nothing to do with the possibility of being close to Kennedy again, which could potentially lead to more 'spooning'. Maria loathed that term, anyway, and didn't know why she'd thought of it. Surely they should call it something less stupid? Though, as much as she hated the word, the activity itself – even though it had been strictly for survival purposes – had been …

What is wrong with me, Maria thought, forcing her mind to stop wandering.

The *main* reason Maria wanted nightfall was because nightfall meant sleep, and sleep meant morning, and morning meant that Paola and Alberto, whoever they were, would arrive and fix things. And then Kennedy and Maria would be able to escape participating in farm life.

Participation had been mandatory so far. Nicolina had looked at the two girls and decided that Maria, being short and therefore more in need of mothering, was the perfect person to share her culinary expertise with. Neither Nicolina nor Rocco had encountered many foreigners before, and tended to view anyone who couldn't speak fluent Italian as simple-minded. Unfortunately, Maria was playing right into the stereotype, dropping ingredients left, right and centre, and holding knives as delicately as if they were firearms.

Maria's culinary inadequacies were not entirely her fault. Anna Petranelli always cooked with the aggression of one whose every move was being passive-aggressively criticised by their mother-in-law (which, to be fair, happened quite often), and she snapped at anyone who set foot in her cooking space. Maria never learned from her grandmother, either. For some reason, Nonna Lucia saw every attempt at Maria contributing to a meal as a personal rejection. One time, just so she could prove she could do it, Maria made pumpkin soup and served it to the family, and Nonna Lucia cried the whole time.

In the end, Maria decided it was better for everyone if she avoided the kitchen.

And her inexperience was definitely showing now.

While Nicolina would have found it a disgrace in an Italian girl, foreign Maria's clumsiness only made her more endearing. Every time Maria sneezed because she'd got flour up her nose, or cracked an egg only to have half the shell end up in the yolk and some of it in her eye, Nicolina would clasp her hands together, shout '*CARINA!*' and grab the utensils from her. 'Now let me show you!'

Meanwhile, Rocco had grabbed Kennedy by the arm and was giving her a tour of the farm, making many sweeping arm gestures and using the phrase 'all this is mine' often and proudly. Rocco and Nicolina appeared to be the only ones in the area, and their modest farm had remnants of much grander days. The stone buildings and sheds had mostly fallen down, except for the house, and the barn where Maria and Kennedy had spent the night.

'All this ...' shouted Rocco in Italian, gesturing to the vibrant, hilly landscape. 'All this is mine.'

'IT'S BEAUTIFUL,' Kennedy shouted back in English.

Shouting slowly and gesturing wildly – that was how everyone was going to play it, apparently. (Except for Maria, because she was too dignified, and Gabriele, who was watching Maria warily from a kitchen chair.)

'Come this way,' said Rocco, grabbing Kennedy's arm. 'Come this way. I will show you.'

Kennedy was led to a small wooden shed, which was old and dusty. It took some effort to open the thick door as the doorframe had long since swelled from moisture. 'Come in here,' said Rocco.

Kennedy followed, trying not to cough. The air had become thick and musty, and the smell of hay – and something else that Kennedy couldn't put her finger on – immediately overwhelmed her.

'Rabbits,' said Rocco. 'Do you like rabbits?'

'Oh! Rabbits!' Kennedy said, once again sheltering behind her English. 'I had a pet rabbit when I was a kid!'

'We'll have these for dinner soon,' said Rocco, not the least bit worried that he had no idea what Kennedy had just said. 'And these,' he pointed. 'Quail.'

They were not quail. They were pigeons. Rocco knew this, but hoped Kennedy didn't. Quail were a lot more expensive, after all. Rocco opened a cage, grabbed a pigeon expertly and, pinning its wings to its body, placed it in Kennedy's hands.

'Oh, right,' Kennedy stammered, trying to grip the bird for dear life without crushing it to death. 'Right. It's, uh … it's beautiful,' Kennedy said in English, and then, knowing she was being ridiculous for refusing to at least *attempt* her language skills, finally tried out her Italian. '*Bello*,' she managed to choke out.

Rocco raised his eyebrows at the adjective and took the pigeon back.

'Hmph,' he said, his fingers curling around the pigeon's neck.

*

What happened next was extremely unpleasant.

But it was more unpleasant for Maria.

'*CARINA*,' yelled Nicolina. 'Now let me show you.' She grabbed a fistful of feathers and yanked hard.

Maria tried not to scream.

*

It had only been a day since Maria and Kennedy had stumbled upon a dead human body (two, in Maria's case). But neither of these experiences had as much effect on them as did the dead birds, which now appeared before them on a platter in the centre of the table.

Rocco was not helping matters. He grabbed a bird with both hands, plopped it on his plate, and started hacking at it with a knife, oblivious to the foreigners' discomfort.

Instinctively, Kennedy reached for Maria's hand, and instinctively, Maria let her.

'They're holding hands,' Gabriele hollered.

Maria released her grip immediately.

'It's bedtime soon,' said Nicolina to Gabriele.

Rocco dropped a wing and part of a breast in front of Maria, who paled.

'Thank you,' she bleated.

Kennedy wasn't even able to say that. She had held the thing while it was alive, and now most of its neck was on her plate.

They choked their way through dinner, gulping as much homemade wine as they could. Maria tried to cut the bird into tiny pieces and spread them around the plate so her hosts would not realise she hadn't eaten it, but Gabriele noticed.

'She's not eating the quail!' he sang.

'It's bedtime soon,' repeated Nicolina. She was also eagerly awaiting nightfall so she could put her hellion grandson to bed.

He wasn't usually this difficult, but ever since the foreigners had arrived, he hadn't stopped hollering accusations against them in her ear. 'Now,' said Nicolina to Maria. 'Tonight, you and your friend will sleep in Alberto's old room …'

'That's not her friend,' Gabriele interrupted. 'I saw them kissing in the shed.'

If only Maria or Kennedy had learned the Italian word for 'kiss', they would have understood why Nicolina froze, stared, moved her mouth a few times, and then became hysterical. Unfortunately, romantic interludes did not feature in the Italian language school's role plays, and so her behaviour was a complete mystery.

Rocco appeared to understand what was going on, though; he closed his eyes slowly and took a deep breath.

'Gabriele!' Nicolina yelled. 'Go to your room right now!'

'Why do *I* have to go to my room? It's not my fault they were kissing!'

'*Now,* Gabriele!' Nicolina repeated. She was pacing back and forth, wringing her hands. 'Go, go, *go!*'

'Homosexuals, Rocco,' Nicolina said once Gabriele had finally exited. 'Homosexuals snuck into our barn, and now they are in our kitchen! What do we do?'

'I don't know, Nicolina,' Rocco sighed.

'Is this a sign? Is this a test? Oh *Madonna mia*, what would you have us do?' She stormed out of the room. And then she stormed back in. 'HOMOSEXUALS!' she yelled.

Unfortunately, the Italian school's role plays hadn't featured the word 'homosexual', either.

Nicolina's angst on the topic was recent. For most of her life growing up in the village, she had never even heard of a homosexual. But over the past few years, it seemed like everyone was talking about them. Even the Pope. And so Nicolina had to get up to speed, and fast. The subject was one of great speculation among her similarly aged friends, who had heard lots of rumours and even claimed to know a few, but, as far as she knew, Nicolina had never come across a homosexual in her life. It didn't take her long to catch up with the centuries-old fears and prejudices, especially with some of her friends' wild descriptions. But then, the next thing she knew, there was a new Pope who turned everything on its head. All of a sudden, Pope Francis said good Catholics had to be *kind* to homosexuals.

Fear them, be kind to them … Nicolina couldn't keep up. But the Pope had declared it! Yes, the Pope! So what was she supposed to do, with two of them sitting in her very kitchen?

Finally, Nicolina made her mind up. 'This is a test from God,' she told Rocco. 'If the Pope says we have to be kind to homosexuals, we are going to be kind to homosexuals.'

Rocco breathed a sigh of relief.

'But, by Jesus, Mary, and all the saints,' she amended, '*I will not have them fornicating in this house!*'

In an instant, Nicolina transformed back from friendly to fierce. 'You!' she pointed to Maria. 'You will sleep with me. Rocco, you will sleep in Gabriele's room.'

'All right, all right!' muttered Rocco, who knew better than to argue when Nicolina was in one of these moods.

'Caterina!' she addressed Kennedy, having made up her own version of her guest's name. 'I will show you Alberto's old room. And the door will remain closed, all night!'

*

That night, Kennedy lay staring at the ceiling, contemplating the events of the past few days. She was miles from home, in a foreign country, and she had seen a dead body, been locked in the boot of a car, and been forced to eat a pigeon. But ... she and Maria were together. They would get through this. She finally drifted to sleep with the knowledge that no matter how lost she felt right now, Maria would be there in the morning.

*

If she survived the night, that is. Maria began to doubt her safety (and made sure she assessed how far a drop it would be from the window if she had to make a hasty escape) when Nicolina closed the bedroom door behind them and locked it meaningfully. The key, one of those old brass ones Maria had only seen in horror films, was then attached to Nicolina's very low-hanging crucifix necklace, which she slipped underneath her billowing nightie. Maria was worried that she would be forced to wear something similar, but instead, she was presented with a pair of Rocco's pyjamas; pyjamas with drawstring pants, which Nicolina personally did up for her, then tightened, and then knotted.

'Goodnight,' she snapped, turning her back to Maria and yanking the covers around herself.

'Goodnight,' said Maria, lying deathly still. She didn't know what she'd done wrong, but wondered if it had something to do with Gabriele dobbing her in for not eating the pigeon.

I'm going to kill that kid, she thought, not for the first time that day, and scarcely dared to breathe for the rest of the night.

CHAPTER 20

Translators

It was late afternoon when Paola and Alberto arrived. When they saw Rocco and Nicolina standing in the driveway waiting for them, each with grim looks on their faces, they immediately thought the worst. *Our son has really done it this time,* they thought. *He's set fire to the house. He's stolen Rocco's wallet. He's poisoned the horse.* Paola and Alberto were not jumping to unreasonable conclusions – Gabriele had done worse, each time claiming amnesty by saying it was an accident. So they were relieved when they realised that Rocco was only grim because Nicolina had been nagging him all morning, and Nicolina was only grim because there were foreign homosexuals in her house.

Interestingly to both Alberto and Paola, it was not the girls' sexual orientation that was making Nicolina wring her hands; rather, it was the enormous burden she'd put upon herself to keep them apart and/or supervised, at least until they were wed.

'Mama, you need to stop being so old-fashioned!' laughed Alberto. 'You think we were angels before we got married?'

Nicolina's eyes widened, her mouth opened, and she started to hiccup.

'He's kidding, Mama,' Paola, her daughter-in-law, cut in hastily.

(He wasn't.)

'Good,' said Nicolina, recovering slowly. 'Now you'd better come inside.' She turned brusquely and marched towards the house.

Rocco waited until she was out of earshot before slapping Alberto on the side of the head. 'Idiot boy! Are you trying to get yourself killed?'

'I'm sorry, I'm sorry!' Alberto laughed.

(He wasn't.)

Paola and Alberto entered the kitchen to see Kennedy and Maria sitting at the table, looking desperate and miserable.

'What on earth,' said Paola, taken aback by the pitiful sight. 'Where did they come from?'

'God only knows,' Nicolina sighed.

'Well, what are we supposed to do?'

'God only knows.' Nicolina had become a lot more religious overnight.

'I'll fix it,' said Alberto. 'I speak English.'

This was an exaggeration. Alberto might have sat through years of classes when he was at school, but the only English he used regularly was 'hello, my name is Alberto, I am very good-looking'. He had looked it up on the internet.

'Hello!' he announced. 'My name is Alberto, I am very good-looking.'

Maria and Kennedy looked at each other, alarmed.

'Alberto … so help me …' warned Paola. She sat down at the kitchen table and looked at the pair of bedraggled strangers. 'Hello,' she said clearly, in English. 'My name is Paola … excuse my husband, he thinks he is a funny man.'

'You speak English!' Maria and Kennedy both cried, overjoyed.

'Yes.' Paola smiled.

'Find out where they're from so we can send them back there,' Nicolina snapped. Paola paused, as if wondering how to phrase it.

Kennedy noticed. 'She's been really angry since last night. We don't know what we did.'

'My mother-in-law,' Paola tried, 'is upset because you were … kissing?'

Kennedy was about to set the record straight, but was beaten to it.

'NO!' protested Maria, hoping her face wasn't turning red. 'We're not even dating!'

'Oh,' was Paola's non-committal reply.

But Maria was not satisfied with Paola's answer. 'I don't even like her like that!' she yelled.

Why Maria felt the need to announce this, she did not know. It certainly had nothing to do with the way her body, the traitor, had reacted when Kennedy had tried to protect her from the cold. And absolutely *nothing* to do with the unbidden, unhelpful dream she'd had overnight, which she could barely remember because her brain was working overtime to repress it, in which Kennedy had gently cupped her face and …

'Kennedy!' hissed Maria desperately. 'Did you tell them we kissed?'

'Of course not!' she stammered.

'Because we didn't, you know!' Maria repeated, addressing the whole assembly now. 'We did not kiss! We have *never kissed!*'

'What's she saying?' asked Alberto.

'She says they never kissed,' said Paola.

'There now, you see?' Rocco bellowed, relieved. 'You stupid woman! Always yelling about something!'

'Well,' said Nicolina slowly. 'Maybe I was wrong.'

Maria huffed in relief.

She noticed too late that Kennedy was frowning, staring directly ahead, and sitting very, very straight.

CHAPTER 21

Dinner

Back in Payneham, Adelaide, the phone was ringing.

'Anna!' Vince Petranelli yelled. 'Anna!'

Vince waited for a few moments, then tried again. He took a deep breath, and used his diaphragm to project.

'AN-NA!'

'WHAT?'

'THE PHONE'S RINGING!'

'I CAN HEAR THAT, WHY DON'T YOU ANSWER IT?'

Vince had no comeback for this. He sank deeper into the couch in disgust. 'That woman expects me to do everything,' he grumbled.

'Eh?' said Nonno Franco, snorting awake. He sat up and looked around, confused. Had he fallen asleep? *Oh look,* he thought. *Channel Nine News is on.*

The phone continued to ring. Nobody made a move to answer it.

'ANNA!' Vince tried again, but Anna appeared to have selective hearing.

'Let the machine get it,' said Nonno Franco.

'We don't have a machine,' sulked Vince.

'She's very lazy, your wife,' Nonna Lucia commented, shaking her head. 'She does not know how lucky she is to have such a good husband. When I was young, if I dared say no to my husband, he would ...' Her hand chopped the air in a hitting motion.

'Ha!' bellowed Nonno Franco. 'I wouldn't dare! If I had even tried it, she would ...' Nonno Franco pretended to slit his own throat.

Vince was ignoring their hand gestures. The phone was still ringing.

'AN-NAAAA!'

'What! What is the matter!' An exasperated Anna emerged from the hallway just as the phone stopped ringing. 'There now, you see? We've missed it! Why couldn't you have just answered it?'

'I didn't know who it was,' Vince complained.

Anna sighed loudly and rolled her eyes. 'I've got to go and do the shopping. Do you think you'll be able to manage by yourself?' Without waiting for an answer, she left the house, closing the front door a little louder than necessary.

'In my day women didn't leave the house to go shopping, shopping, shopping,' claimed Nonna Lucia. 'We stayed home to take care of the family.' She waited for a response from the menfolk, but got none, so she continued. 'And now Anna is gone, I suppose *I'll* have to do the dinner … oh, *Madonna mia* … my back … oh, my knees …' She managed to inch herself up from the sofa and limp into the kitchen, gasping in pain every now and then.

'Change the channel, will you?' said Nonno Franco. 'I want to watch my show.'

The phone started ringing again.

'ANNA!'

'She's gone *shopping*,' Nonna Lucia spat.

Vince looked alarmed. 'Can you answer it?'

'Me? It's not my house! Why is my son not acting like a man? I know why it is. It is because your wife does everything for you, isn't it! She doesn't let you act like a man. I'm ashamed of you!'

'What's wrong with the TV?' Nonno Franco asked. 'Where is *Deala Deala*?'

'*Deal a No Deal*,' Nonna Lucia corrected.

'What happened, did I miss it?'

'Yes,' Vince replied, which wasn't true, but he hated *Deal or No Deal* and refused to change the channel.

The phone continued to ring.

Finally Vince got up from the couch. He approached the phone nervously, slowly, hoping whoever it was would hang up before he got there. But the caller was persistent.

'Hello …?' he finally said into the mouthpiece.

'Hello, my name is Professor Giglio from the School of –'

Vince, recognising a foreign accent when he heard one, immediately slammed the phone down.

'Who was it?' asked Nonna Lucia, plunging her hands into a sink of tomatoes.

'Telstra. Trying to sell me a phone, I bet.' He picked up the receiver again. 'You hear me? I've already got a phone!' As he slammed it down, it started to ring. Filled with sudden confidence, Vince picked up the receiver again and barked into it. 'Yes?'

'Professor Giglio calling from the –'

'No thank you!' Slam. 'Bloody Telstra. Why can't they leave a man in peace!'

The phone rang again. And again. And again.

Vince ignored it until Anna got home, but by then it was too late. Professor Giglio had long since given up.

At any rate, the phone calls were forgotten, because just as Anna entered the kitchen with bags full of ingredients for beef stroganoff, Nonna Lucia turned off the oven in triumph.

'Oh, were you planning on cooking dinner?' she said innocently to Anna. 'Sorry, I didn't know.'

Vince and Nonno Franco looked at each other and, without a word, moved to another room in the house, far away from the kitchen, where they could watch *A Current Affair* in peace.

There was a lot of yelling in the house that night. But it was not because the Petranellis had discovered Maria had gone missing, was in violation of her visa, and was now considered an illegal immigrant: it was because the Petranellis had cannelloni for tea.

CHAPTER 22

Accommodation

Nicolina wiped the tears from her eyes and sighed. 'Such nice young people, those homosexuals,' she sniffed, waving at her family and her charges as they drove away.

Rocco shook his head. 'Three months ago you were calling homosexuals the children of the devil.'

'Hush! Be quiet!' snapped Nicolina, then sighed. 'Poor children.'

Rocco shook his head again and followed her inside.

*

It was dark when they finally left the farm. Nicolina had insisted they stay for dinner (thankfully, there were no pigeons this time), and now Maria, Gabriele and Kennedy were squashed into the back seat.

'It will be late when we get to Florence. We are staying in a hotel. You can stay with us, and tomorrow you can catch a train back to Rome,' said Alberto.

'Speak slowly, will you? They can't understand you when you speak that fast,' Paola admonished.

Yes I can, Maria frowned, but was quickly disarmed by Paola asking kindly, 'Are you all right back there?'

'Yes, thank you,' both Kennedy and Maria replied. Neither had spoken until then – not to their hosts, and not to each other. And Maria, who had finally had time to reflect on the kissing accusation and her poor response to it, knew it was her fault.

'So, uh, do you live near here?' Kennedy asked politely.

'Yes, our house is not far from where we picked you up. We will be staying in Florence for a few days to do some shopping and visit my family,' Paola replied. And the car settled into silence.

'They're very quiet,' Alberto whispered.

Paola looked at him wryly. 'They've been through a lot! They had to stay with your mother for a whole night.'

Alberto chuckled.

The kids were a mystery. Neither Paola nor Alberto had been able to get the whole story. Back at Rocco and Nicolina's, Alberto had given them his mobile phone to use, but, as it was already after hours, the language school hadn't picked up. And even though Paola had tried her best, it hadn't exactly been a calm atmosphere for conversation, what with Rocco still shouting everything, Nicolina interrupting every few sentences with a dramatic prayer to the heavens, and Alberto attempting to crack jokes until he realised Gabriele had disappeared again and was probably up to no good.

Maria was not bothered by the lack of opportunity to tell their implausible story to strangers who might not believe them. But, though she would never admit it, she *was* sorry about the lack of opportunity to talk to Kennedy alone.

She shuffled in her seat and looked out the window. Even if she *did* know what to say, she couldn't say it in front of Alberto and Paola, who had been so kind, and certainly not in front of the devil child, who would probably ruin everything. But the guilt sat heavy on her chest. Ever since they'd met, Kennedy had done nothing but try (albeit unsuccessfully) to stand up for her; had done nothing but try to be her friend. So what if people mistakenly thought they were together? And a rogue, scary thought kept ringing in Maria's brain – so what if Kennedy *did* kiss her one day? Would that be so bad?

But when she tried to catch her eye, she saw Kennedy was studiously avoiding looking at her.

They drove on, and tiredness settled over them all. Maria had just closed her eyes when a voice rang out.

'Maria's kicking me!'

'Good for you, Maria!' laughed Alberto. 'If I were you, I'd kick him harder!'

Gabriele opened his mouth to protest as he turned and glared at Maria. She smiled sweetly in reply, then put her head back and fell asleep.

*

Alberto slowed to a stop and let the car run for a few seconds before turning off the engine. He stretched and looked at his sleeping passengers. Paola was sitting upright, her eyes closed, looking very dignified. Kennedy, on the other hand, had her head bent back and her mouth open. Maria was curled against the side of the car, and Gabriele, unbeknownst to him, was leaning on her arm.

'Wake up, everyone …' Alberto said gently.

'Hmm?' Paola yawned. 'We're here already?'

Gabriele opened his eyes and shot upright.

'Wait here a moment,' Alberto said, opening the door. Maria offered to come with him and pay for the hotel rooms, but he wouldn't hear of it. So they just sat, sleepy and silent, squinting slightly from the car's interior light. A few minutes later, Alberto returned. 'We're ready,' he said, opening the boot and getting out the suitcases.

As Kennedy and Maria emerged from the car, he grinned at them. 'Have you ever been to Florence before?' he asked in Italian.

They shook their heads.

'No,' replied Kennedy.

'Hey, you understand me now! I knew you were faking it,' he laughed, clapping her on the shoulder. He led the way up some outdoor cement stairs to a balcony. At room 206, he stopped. 'Here,' he said, passing them a key. 'This is your room.'

Maria and Kennedy suddenly felt very awkward.

'Oh,' said Maria.

'Oh, uh …' started Kennedy.

Alberto smiled cheekily, pretending not to notice their hesitation. 'We will see you in the morning.'

Before they had a chance to reply or protest, Alberto opened the door of room 207 and disappeared inside.

Maria and Kennedy stood on the balcony for a moment.

'Hmm,' said Maria.

'Should we …'

'Um …'

The tension was palpable. Maria wanted to apologise, but how could she without bringing up the uncomfortable topic in the first place? And now Kennedy was standing very straight again, and looking very nervous. It made Maria's heart beat even faster. She was not good at vulnerable conversations, and she was scared she was about to have one, and she wished she could run away and hide. But apparently that wasn't a choice. So she opened the door, and they stepped inside.

The room was small. The mauve carpet was not quite fitted to the floor and rose in ripples near the far wall. There was a tiny bathroom, two bedside tables with lamps, and a moderately sized television mounted on the wall facing the bed.

The double bed.

Maria was unaware that this was all a calculated ploy from Alberto. She had no idea that Alberto:

1. Was a hopeless romantic;
2. Genuinely believed that 'forcing two people to share a bed' was a legitimate way to progress love stories; and
3. Was, at this very moment, being told off by Paola, who knew exactly what he was attempting to do.

But if Alberto was imagining the two girls would look into each other's eyes, seize the moment and fall into a passionate embrace, he would be sadly disappointed.

'Uh ...' started Kennedy, staring at the bed.

'Hmm,' Maria replied. She tried to think of a solution. The room was too small to insist someone sleep on the floor. Finally, she uttered the most neutral words she could think of: 'I'll just take my shoes off.'

'Me too,' said Kennedy.

Shoeless, they sat on the bed.

Kennedy opened her mouth to speak, and Maria prepared herself.

'It's been a wild couple of days, hasn't it?'

Okay. She's starting neutral, Maria thought. *I'll play along*. 'Yes,' she replied.

'Still, I guess it's been an adventure ...' Kennedy halted as Maria looked incredulously at her. 'I mean ...' she stammered. 'I mean, it hasn't ended badly or anything, has it? And we got to see a lot more of Italy!'

'I suppose so,' said Maria, realising vaguely that, despite being stranded in various parts of Italy on more than one occasion, she hadn't taken much in at all. 'It doesn't seem real.'

'No!' Kennedy agreed, giving a short laugh and rubbing the back of her neck. 'So …'

Maria felt herself tense up again. *Here it comes* … she thought.

'… when we get back to Rome … I guess we'll have to go on exchange.'

It took a moment for Maria to realise what Kennedy had said. She'd been expecting criticism, a demand for an explanation and an examination of each others' true feelings, and she wasn't ready for any of that. But once again, Kennedy was being kind – this time, by keeping their conversation on safe ground.

Maria was so relieved she almost felt light-headed. 'I don't really want to go on exchange,' she admitted, feeling her shoulders relax.

'Me neither,' said Kennedy.

Maria looked at her in shock. 'Really?'

'Really.'

'Then why did you come to Italy?'

'I don't know … it seemed like a good idea at the time. I love my parents so much, but they can be a lot, you know? And I guess it seemed pretty neat to travel …'

'That's exactly the same as me!' Maria exclaimed. 'And ever since I got here, I just keep thinking, have I made the biggest mistake of my life?'

'I know!' Kennedy laughed. 'I mean, it must be a sign, right? Getting robbed? And eating pigeons? And getting kidnapped?'

They both stopped laughing as they remembered the reality of their situation.

'I feel lost,' said Maria suddenly.

Kennedy looked at her, surprised.

Maria was frowning at the floor. 'I just don't know ...' she started, and then cleared her throat. 'I just don't know where I'm supposed to be.'

As soon as the words escaped her mouth, she knew she'd gone too far. This wasn't just vulnerable conversational territory, this was *dangerous.* She had to snap out of it, and she had to snap out of it *now*. She sat a little straighter, blinked a few times, and was about to say something frivolous when Kennedy put her hand on her knee, sending a rush of heat through her whole body.

Kennedy swallowed hard, cleared her throat, and then said boldly: 'Maybe *this* is where you're supposed to be.'

Maria frowned at the line, and Kennedy shook her head and laughed self-consciously. 'Sorry, that didn't make sense. Stuck in this hotel is definitely not where either of us are supposed to be! But since I *am* here, I'm glad I'm here with you,' she recovered. 'Because I think you're ... pretty great.'

Maria felt like she was about to faint. Kennedy's eyes were so soft, and the hand on her knee was sending shivers through her, and this was not like Toby Jordan rubbing her hand with his thumb *at all.* This was something else entirely, something she wanted fiercely, and it was terrifying.

'I think you're pretty great too,' she whispered, her heart racing as she looked into Kennedy's eyes. And Kennedy was staring back, wistfully, longingly, and then she was leaning forward …

All of a sudden, Maria felt like she was underwater. Everything was slow and fluid; the sound was muffled, the air was thick and her arms were leaden.

But it was all broken the second a sharp yell rang through the air.

Maria's hands flew to her mouth and her eyes widened in shock.

She had just pushed Kennedy off the bed!

'Ow,' Kennedy said, startled.

'Kennedy! I'm so sorry!' she gasped.

The silence was prolonged. For a few moments there was a standoff, in which both girls stared at each other in horror and confusion.

'Ow!' Kennedy said again, louder this time.

'Kennedy, I'm really, really sorry! It was just a reflex!'

'A *reflex?*' she shouted.

'Yes! I thought you were trying to kiss me!'

'I wasn't trying to *kiss* you!' Kennedy yelled.

Now Maria felt stupid. 'I know, it's just that …'

'Is this how you treat everyone who's *nice* to you? You push them off the bed in case they *kiss* you? God, Maria!' Kennedy snapped. 'Now I understand why you're single!'

The words stung.

And no matter how much time Maria had spent preparing herself for rejection, no matter how many comebacks she'd practised in case she ever found herself in a situation like this, there was nothing at all she could say or do to prevent the pain rising from her stomach into her chest, then into her throat. And it stayed there. Had she been any other girl, she might have cried. But she didn't. She said nothing.

And this failure wasn't like the one when she kissed a boy only to be called a 'dyke' a day later, or when she let herself get robbed at the Spanish Steps, or when she managed to get kidnapped and put in the boot of a car. This failure was far, *far* worse.

'Sorry,' Kennedy mumbled eventually.

'Oh, me too,' Maria replied, sounding as if she were shooing away a fly. 'But it's late, so ...'

'Yeah, we probably should ...'

Kennedy didn't finish that sentence. They both shuffled around until Maria coughed, then made her way to the left side of the bed. 'I'll take this side, should I? I'll try not to hog the blankets,' she joked.

'All right,' Kennedy chuckled. 'I'll try not to kick you in the middle of the night.'

What a hilarious conversation *this* was turning out to be.

'Goodnight, Kennedy,' said Maria.

'Goodnight, Maria,' said Kennedy.

They lay still for a while. Eventually, Maria rolled over just as Kennedy pulled the blankets her way.

'Sorry,' Kennedy said, realising Maria was still awake.

'Sorry,' Maria replied.

And they lay awake, as close to the edges of the bed as humanly possible, for a very long time.

CHAPTER 23

Truth

'Kennedy, I'm really, really sorry! It was just a reflex!'

'A *reflex?*' she shouted.

'Yes! I thought you were trying to kiss me!'

'I wasn't trying to *kiss* you!' Kennedy yelled.

(Yes, she was.)

CHAPTER 24

Hangover

She was running. She didn't know what she was running from, she just knew something was after her. But there was no noise outside herself; all she could hear was her ragged breathing and the sound of her footsteps pounding the cement. The Roman streets all looked the same, no matter how many times she turned a corner. She fell, and threw her hands out to lessen the impact. The bracelet was on her wrist. She gasped and clawed at it, but it wouldn't budge.

'I need scissors!' she yelled. 'Somebody give me some scissors!'

'If I cut the bracelet, your arm will come off,' said Kennedy, appearing out of nowhere, a pair of scissors in her hand. 'It's not a good idea.' And then she ran away and left her.

'No!' Maria screamed. Whatever it was, whoever it was, was catching up to her. She pulled at the bracelet and tried to scramble to her feet. A door slammed.

*

A door slammed.

'Sorry,' whispered Kennedy, emerging from the bathroom.

Maria's eyes flew open and she sat up, breathless, her heart pounding in her chest. She checked her wrists – they were free of bracelets.

'I just wanted to have a shower,' Kennedy whispered again, grabbing a towel.

Maria, still recovering from her dream, glared at her. 'Well, have a shower, then!'

'Sorry.'

Maria ground her teeth in frustration and collapsed back onto the pillow, trying to slow her heartbeat.

Stupid Kennedy! Why was she always apologising? Why hadn't she given her any scissors? She was so infuriating! And, with this new sense of rage coupled with the vivid memory of her nightmare, Maria's shame over the Not-Trying-To-Kiss-You incident was well and truly repressed.

*

Alberto made a lot of noise as he came out of his room. 'Are you ready, Paola?' he yelled.

'I'm right here, Alberto, will you be quiet?'

'Okay,' he yelled. 'Gabriele!'

'Alberto!' Paola hissed, embarrassed. 'What are you doing?'

'I'm giving them plenty of warning.'

Alberto continued to stamp and cough and yell his way next door, but before he got there, Maria and Kennedy emerged, fully clothed and smiling as if everything was completely normal.

'Oh, did you … did you sleep well?' asked Alberto.

'Yes, thank you,' they replied, giving nothing away.

The mid- to low-range-priced hotel offered a self-serve 'continental breakfast' buffet in the cramped dining room. Anxious for some semblance of home, Maria reached for the cornflakes just as Kennedy reached for the jug of orange juice. Their hands collided.

'Sorry!' Kennedy said, flinging her hand back as if she'd been electrocuted.

'*Will you stop apologising!*' Maria hissed with such force that Kennedy took a step back.

'Sorry,' she said again, and Maria rolled her eyes and ignored her until they were back at the safety of the breakfast table, buffered by Paola and Alberto.

Maria looked at everyone's food choices and realised she was the only one eating cereal. Everyone else had fancy pastries on their plates and tiny cups of black coffee, including Kennedy. *That is so like her*, Maria thought, criticising Kennedy's every move. *Always giving in to peer pressure.*

Gabriele was also criticising every move. 'Why is she eating *that?*' he asked, pointing accusingly at Maria's cornflakes.

'Okay,' Alberto interrupted. 'I will speak slowly so you can understand me. All right?'

Kennedy and Maria both nodded.

'Good. Now, we need to get you two back home. But I want to understand – how did you end up at my parents' place?'

Kennedy and Maria looked at each other. This had been the topic of conversation all morning: what were they going to tell Paola and Alberto? Kennedy was all for telling them the truth, but Maria knew that if they did, Paola and Alberto would take them to the authorities, and the police wouldn't believe her and would tell her off, and she could only take so much rejection in such a short time. Not that she admitted this to Kennedy, of course. Instead, she took a very firm stance that it was better to just get back to Rome and not burden the family. Maria was very convincing, and Kennedy was very persuadable – especially when she had a giant crush on the persuader – and so Maria's plan won out.

'I don't know the words in Italian …' Maria started. 'Is it all right if I speak in English?'

Alberto nodded, and Maria took a deep breath and launched in. 'It's a funny story, actually! We got lost. We're both studying in Rome, and we decided to go on a tour on our day off, but we caught the wrong bus, and ended up completely stranded in the countryside!'

'And you couldn't call anyone?' Paola asked.

'Our phones went flat,' Maria said.

Paola translated unquestioningly for Alberto, who nodded, and asked, 'Who was it you were trying to reach yesterday when I lent you my phone?'

'Our school,' Maria continued, looking at Kennedy for backup.

'Yeah, uh, the school,' said Kennedy, and Maria was annoyed that even when she was telling the *truth*, Kennedy managed to look guilty.

'Well, make the phone call after breakfast, and then we'll organise the train tickets,' Paola suggested.

As soon as Maria finished thanking her, Paola turned to Gabriele and rattled something off in Italian.

'But …' Gabriele started. Paola raised her eyebrows warningly, so Gabriele got up and dragged his feet over to the game consoles in the kids' entertainment area.

'I think I left something in my room,' Paola said, rising from the table. 'Alberto?'

'Well, go get it, we'll meet you back here,' said Alberto. But Paola fired out her rapid Italian again, and Alberto, much like Gabriele, got up and dragged his feet after her.

As soon as they had left, both Kennedy and Maria sighed.

'They don't believe us, do they?'

'No.'

'You know, I had the strangest dream last night,' said Kennedy.

Maria couldn't stop herself from shouting, 'Really? Me too,' with way more enthusiasm and solidarity than she'd intended.

'Yeah?' Kennedy said excitedly. 'Mine had that guy from *Jurassic Park* in it …'

'Oh,' said Maria, disappointed, cutting Kennedy off.

'Why? What was yours about?'

'Well … it was about the bracelet.'

'The …' Kennedy lowered her voice. 'The Spanish Steps bracelet?'

'Yes. What do you think it means?'

'What, the dream?'

'No, the bracelet!'

Kennedy looked sceptical. 'I don't know, wasn't it just something to scam tourists?'

'That doesn't make sense!' Maria said sharply, then looked around the room to make sure no-one was listening. 'If it was just a tourist scam, then why did someone kill Lorenzo? And why was the other dead guy wearing one? I've been thinking about it a lot. Maybe it's gang colours.'

But Kennedy hadn't seen 'the other dead guy'. And unbeknownst to Maria, Kennedy was still a bit wounded from last night's Pouring-Your-Heart-Out-Only-To-Get-Pushed-Off-The-Bed incident, which had happened while she was still recovering from the unprompted I-Don't-Even-Like-Her-Like-That declaration. So she gave a disbelieving laugh that came out a bit too bitter.

'Really?' Kennedy said doubtfully. 'Italian-flag-themed gang colours on a bracelet?'

Maria was affronted. 'Just because you're from America,' she snapped.

'What's that supposed to mean? Are you saying that just because I'm from America I'm in some kind of a gang?'

'Hardly,' Maria scoffed, looking pointedly at Kennedy's button-up collared shirt.

'What's that supposed to mean, that I *couldn't* be in a gang? Because neither could you, you know!'

And then they entered into a fierce argument, each girl overcome with a ferocious desire to prove they could handle being in a gang, while simultaneously pointing out each other's ineligibility.

Just as Kennedy was about to claim that her *cousin* was in a gang, and had asked her to join thousands of times (which was, of course, not true), Paola and Alberto re-entered the dining room.

'Have you seen Florence before?' Paola asked, ignoring the tension at the table and smiling in a way-too-friendly fashion.

Somewhat surprised by the question, the pair shook their heads.

'We will go sightseeing before we take you to the station. It would be terrible to come all the way to Florence and leave without seeing it. Have you finished eating? Let's go. Maria, you come with me, Kennedy will go with Alberto.'

Paola broke into Italian and gave Alberto instructions to meet them at 'the usual place'.

Maria watched Alberto nod solemnly, and had a terrible feeling they were about to be divided and conquered.

*

Even though Maria was determined not to give in without a fight, Paola's strategy was effective. She dragged Maria up and down the streets, pointing out the sights – old churches with frescoed walls, cobblestoned piazzas with sculpted fountains, artisan workshops and market stalls bursting with shoppers, the glittering Arno River flowing steadily under the breathtaking arched bridges. But there was little time to concentrate on the scenery: Paola was ruthless. In between every 'here is the Ponte Vecchio' and 'over there is the Fountain of Neptune', Paola rattled out questions like a machine gun and narrowed her eyes suspiciously at every answer.

'So you were on a tour, and you got lost?'

'What was the name of the tour?'

'What did you see?'

'What was the bus doing so far outside of Rome?'

'How did you manage to get separated from the group?'

Luckily, Maria was quick on her feet. She answered all of Paola's questions with flying colours. She invented bus companies, she created tourist destinations, she gave a very convincing description of Michelangelo's *David*, and she even invented a bus driver with a receding hairline and a monobrow. She was beginning to believe her story herself at this point. But Paola, even though she had been nodding along, didn't buy a word of it.

'Maria,' she said eventually, grabbing Maria gently by the shoulders and turning her so she was looking her in the eye, 'I know this is not true. Michelangelo's *David* is not in Rome. It is here, in Florence.'

'Oh,' said Maria, sheepishly. The jig was up.

'Why don't you tell me what really happened?' Paola guided Maria to a bench and adopted a sympathetic and understanding pose. It made Maria uncomfortable. She sat up straight and frowned, but knew there was nothing else to do but tell her the whole story. The bracelet, Lorenzo, the second body, the boot of the car ... Paola's sympathetic and understanding pose became more shocked and horrified as the story went on.

'Maria, is this a true story?'

'Yes,' Maria sighed.

'You need to go to the police! Why didn't you go to the police?'

'I was afraid,' she admitted.

'This bracelet ... do you still have it?'

Maria nodded and fished it out of her pocket.

Paola shook her head in wonder. 'What could this mean?'

*

Not long after this, Kennedy, Gabriele and an obscenely grinning Alberto loped up to them – apparently, this bench was 'the usual place'.

'So! How was the sightseeing?' Alberto asked.

'Can I speak to you for a minute?' Paola said, leaping up, grabbing his arm and dragging him away.

'What did you find out?' she asked as soon as they were out of earshot.

'Everything,' Alberto said confidently. 'She does like her.

She likes her a lot. She tried to kiss her, but Maria pushed her off the bed.'

'What? Didn't she tell you about the murder?'

'What murder?'

Paola sighed in exasperation.

*

While Paola was filling Alberto in on the details, Kennedy sat next to Maria on the bench, looking sheepish.

'So,' she said. 'Uh … Florence is nice …'

'I told her, Kennedy. I told her about the murders.'

'Oh.'

'I think they're going to take us to the police.'

'Okay,' Kennedy said, looking relieved.

But there was some unfinished business that Maria had not been able to get out of her head.

'I'm sorry for saying you couldn't be in a gang,' she admitted, and she looked apologetically into Kennedy's eyes.

Kennedy softened immediately. 'Me too.' She smiled.

And so, Kennedy forgave Maria for pushing her off the bed.

And Maria forgave Kennedy for voicing her greatest fears.

And nobody ever needed to talk about it, ever again.

CHAPTER 25

Justice

The five of them sat in the police station, waiting. They had already spoken to a senior officer, whose English was impeccable. Maria had shown them the bracelet. And – much to Maria's surprise – nobody had scoffed, yelled at her for making up stories, or called her a 'poor girl'. In fact, everyone took her very seriously. All in all, it was a success. Maria berated herself for not having done it sooner.

'Excuse me.' Another English-speaking officer approached them. 'I need to speak to Maria once more. There are a few questions I need to ask her.'

'What about Kennedy?' Maria asked.

'I need to ask you specifically about the second body. Kennedy was not present during this ...?'

'No,' Kennedy replied.

Maria hesitated, unsure.

'It's okay, I'll come with you,' Paola said encouragingly, so Maria got up and followed the officer.

'My name is Roberto Spinelli,' he said with a smile, and showed them each to a chair on the opposite side of his desk. He smelled like cigarettes and aftershave, and he had serious dark eyebrows and a five o'clock shadow, which Maria felt made him more impressive.

'Now, I am not asking about' – Roberto looked at his notes – 'Lorenzo, but the second body. The man with the bracelet. Can you remember what he looked like?'

'No ...' Maria said, disappointed with herself. 'Not really. I just saw the bracelet and that's all I focused on.'

'And the men who grabbed you ... did you get a chance to see what they looked like?'

'Yes!' she said excitedly. 'I did! There were two of them ...'

'Can you describe them to me?'

Maria had already described them in her initial interview, but she did so again. She even threw in the Robert Downey Jr. reference, to which Roberto Spinelli, a connoisseur of American films, nodded knowingly.

'Now, you need to be certain of your description, miss. Would you be able to identify these two men? If you saw photographs?'

'I think so,' Maria said, uncertainty briefly sapping her confidence.

Roberto Spinelli pulled a folder from the filing cabinet behind him. 'I have several of these for you to look through.

Would you mind spending a few minutes …?'

Maria opened the folder and tried not to feel a thrill of excitement. She knew it was probably immoral, but she was enjoying this moment. She felt like the heroine in an action movie. There she was, Maria Petranelli, looking at portraits of the criminal underworld, potentially bringing them to justice. She imagined casually dropping it into the conversation the next time Zia Carmelina decided to bring up Maria's unmarried status. 'Not as confident' indeed!

She stopped abruptly.

'There,' she said.

'What is it?' Paola and Spinelli both said at once.

'That one. I recognise that one.' It was the man who had opened the boot and told her to stop kicking the tail-lights out. In the photo, his chin was raised defiantly, and he looked fairly young.

'This is the man? You are sure?'

'Yes.'

'Miss, I need you to be absolutely certain that this is the man who kidnapped you. One hundred per cent sure.'

'I am, it's definitely him,' Maria said. 'I'm one hundred per cent sure.'

Maria was feeling so victorious that she didn't notice the change in Officer Spinelli. She didn't notice he was clenching his teeth and shaking his head and looking annoyed about something. She didn't think it was suspicious that he took his phone out of his pocket and began typing a message. And she certainly couldn't read his mind, so she had no idea that he was cursing to himself and thinking, *Felice Bitte, you idiot.*

Unfortunately, Paola, who was usually more observant, was too distracted to notice either. 'I'm sorry,' she said, sounding exasperated. 'My husband is messaging me. My son has snuck away from him.' Paola got to her feet. 'I'm so sorry, are we finished? I need to …'

'Of course, of course,' Roberto Spinelli said, pressing 'send' on his phone and putting it back in his pocket. 'You retrieve your son, I'll escort Maria back to the front desk.'

'What we saw in Rome …' Maria asked, while she had the chance, 'has it got something to do with the bracelet?'

'Yes,' said Roberto Spinelli, opening his office door so Paola could start searching for Gabriele. 'It has definitely got something to do with the bracelet.' And he grabbed Maria's arm and led her the opposite way.

If Maria had any sense of direction at all, she would have immediately realised they were not heading back to the front desk. But she did not. In fact, she wasn't even paying attention to which way they were going. She was feeling too smug about the bracelet. *I knew it*, she thought. *Just wait until I tell Kennedy.*

Roberto Spinelli was walking faster now, and his grip had tightened. They power-walked through corridors, and Roberto Spinelli didn't make eye contact with anyone. It wasn't until Maria tried to shake his arm from hers, and his grip became painfully tight, that she realised something was wrong. Something was very, very wrong.

Should I do something? she wondered. *Should I shout for help? Should I struggle?* But Maria didn't want to make a scene. What if she was just imagining things? What if Roberto Spinelli was holding her arm so tightly because he was making sure she didn't get lost in the crowded police station? What if he was pushing her so quickly because he was in a hurry to see justice done? She would look absolutely ridiculous if she elbowed a police officer in the stomach in the middle of the station when all he was doing was trying to uphold the law. Then the police might *really* yell at her. But, despite all of her justifications, deep down, she suspected something sinister was afoot. And when he opened a door, and they stepped outside, and she saw the car waiting, she *knew*. It was a black car. And a waiting black car could only mean one thing …

Roberto Spinelli opened the back door, put his hand on Maria's head, and was about to push her inside when he gasped in surprise and pain. Maria had kicked him squarely in the shin.

'What the –' he started, but Maria wasn't finished. She raised her knee and plunged it into Roberto Spinelli as hard as she could, and then, as he was gasping for breath and clutching at his groin, she pushed him into the car door.

'Don't even think about it!' she shrieked. 'Not this time, you don't!'

And with that, she began sprinting victoriously. Enough was enough – this time she was ready, and she was fighting back. She had no idea where she was going, but she was going to get away!

But Maria was not a fast runner. Or a particularly coordinated one. And it wasn't long before she was in a sprawling heap on the ground, her jeans torn, her knees bleeding, and bitumen embedded into the palms of her hands.

Before Maria even had a chance to curse Anna Petranelli for her fear of organised team sports, a shadow came over her. Maria looked up. It was not Roberto Spinelli. It was someone tall, heavy, and intimidating. He had greying hair, an old face, and an expression of steel.

'Maria Petranelli,' he said in Italian. 'You will come with me, please. You will not argue, you will not fight. You will come with me, and you will get in the car. And if you do all of these things, I will not kill your friend.'

Maria froze. Her friend?

'Let go of me!' someone yelled. It was a high-pitched, annoying, childish voice.

Maria recognised it at once.

It was Gabriele.

Roberto Spinelli didn't have a gun pointed at Gabriele's head, or a knife poised at his throat – but he had his hand on Gabriele's shoulder, and he pulled him roughly back inside the police station before Maria had a chance to stand.

I'm going to kill that kid, Maria thought. But she knew it wasn't true. She liked Paola and Alberto too much. She stood up slowly, and the man nodded approvingly and walked over to the car. Maria limped behind him, her knees stinging furiously.

This will backfire, she thought. *We're outside a police station. There's no way I could go missing without anyone noticing.*

But Gabriele hadn't seen her, and he'd already been taken inside. How was anyone in the station supposed to know what was happening to her? She hesitated, and the tall man noticed.

'*Signorina*, this is not a time to disobey.' His face was serious and, Maria admitted, a little terrifying. She weighed her options. There weren't really many to choose from: Roberto Spinelli had Gabriele, and she was still too out of breath to try attacking the tall man.

This will backfire on them, she thought again, getting into the back seat of the car. *It has to.*

The tall man opened the driver's door and sat behind the wheel. He adjusted the rear-vision mirror so he could look directly at Maria (she frowned in return), and started the car.

At least she wasn't in the boot this time, she reasoned. But why was this happening? What did they want? *And all because of that stupid bracelet,* she thought. She couldn't believe this was happening to her again. She thought back to that blissful time ten minutes ago, when she was safely inside the police station, casually flicking through photos of criminals. When would this all end?

'It is good that you are cooperating,' the tall man said. 'We are in the process of contacting your father. If you behave, and if he does what is right, you will be back home soon.'

Now Maria baulked. Her father? What on earth did Vince Petranelli have to do with all of this? She sat back in her seat, exhausted and completely confused.

There was nothing else to do but put her seatbelt on.

CHAPTER 26

Obedience

It was a long drive. They left the city and drove through the countryside for a good hour at least; Maria just put her head back and watched the scenery pass. She knew she should be worried, but it was hard to feel that way when the drive was so calm, so peaceful. Every time the car slowed, her heart would jolt and nausea would hit her like a wave, but as soon as the tall man resumed driving at normal speed, she found herself relaxing again.

She spent the first part of the drive contemplating her situation. If she had been forced to wear a blindfold or had a canvas bag thrown over her head, it would have made more sense; instead, she'd seen faces and the route they were taking (which, when asked, Maria would describe as 'north, on the open road, past a lot of trees and fields'). This apparent lack of interest in what Maria saw was unsettling.

Did it mean they were going to kill her so she wouldn't be a witness? But then, the tall man *had* said something about her father …

Her father. Vince Petranelli. She searched her memory for clues. Had she missed something? Was the man who invited his mother over when his wife was sick because he didn't know how to boil water, the man who thought it was funny to teach five-year-olds Italian swear words and tell them it meant 'how are you', the man who didn't like going out at night because he didn't want to miss *A Current Affair* … was this man capable of manipulating the criminal underworld? If it was true – if the tall man had kidnapped her purely with the intention of returning her to her father – then she had *seriously* underestimated Vince Petranelli.

Also, the tall man seemed like an extortionist. There had to be money involved, surely. Was Vince Petranelli rich? He certainly didn't act like it. Every time the collection plate came their way at Mass, he grew uptight and restless until he grudgingly put in a five-dollar note, and then spent the rest of the service and the drive home calling the priest a thieving con artist. Vince had been taken to a Pentecostal church once and was so thrilled that the collection was taken up in bags, not plates (meaning he could pretend to put something in and nobody would be any the wiser) that, for a brief period, he had considered becoming a Protestant. *Was this the behaviour of a rich man?* Maria pondered. Maybe. Maybe he was one of those eccentric rich men – the ones who acted poor but were actually sitting on millions. Was her father sitting on millions?

Maybe everything about her father was an act.

For about three minutes, she managed to convince herself that it was true: that Vince Petranelli was going to storm the castle with machine guns and save her. But then reality got the better of her. Even if Vince *was* a criminal extortionist underworld figure, he wouldn't be able to pull this off. He had failed her a million times in the past, and he would probably fail her now.

No: once again, it was up to Maria to save herself.

Though, she admitted, the last time she had saved herself, Kennedy had been involved.

Awkward, kind Kennedy.

Maria spent the rest of the drive contemplating this.

She was sorry she had pushed her off the bed.

She was sorry she had thought bad thoughts about her tourist hat with the Italian flag.

She was sorry she had yelled at her for saying 'sorry' all the time.

Not that she wanted to *marry* her or anything, she clarified to herself. But, as the car turned off the main road, and her heart jolted and her stomach became sick with fear about what would happen next, she wished, more than anything, that Kennedy was with her now.

*

They pulled into an estate with an obscenely long driveway, luscious, sculpted gardens and an oversized house. Two men were there to open the door and guide her inside as soon as the car slowed to a stop.

'Take her to the kitchen and give her something to drink,' the tall man ordered, and everyone complied, even Maria, who accepted the glass of water and glared at everyone with every mouthful.

She drank slowly, studying their faces, trying to make sense of it all. The tall man – who was clearly the boss – had grey hair, a lined face and permanently raised eyebrows. His two henchmen kept their faces completely neutral as Maria memorised them. One was fair-haired, stocky and mean-looking, while the other was more Southern in appearance, with darker hair and skin, an athletic build and an air of impressive aloofness.

As Maria swallowed her last mouthful, the tall man spoke. 'Very good, Maria. Now you should rest. I am sure it has been a big day for you. Luca, Dominic, show Signorina Petranelli to her room. Maria, I will see you later.'

Luca and Dominic gently held Maria's elbows as they guided her to a bedroom, deposited her inside it and left. As soon as the door was closed, she tried to open it again – but it was locked.

*

Vince Petranelli did, in fact, have connections in Italy. His uncle and cousins owned a flour mill. But this was not likely to inspire fear and terror into the hearts of man.

Angelo Petranelli, however – who was no relation – had just had a CEO murdered, and had paid enough money to ensure that it looked like a drug overdose.

And his daughter was missing.

'Where is she, Bertoluccio?' Angelo Petranelli yelled into the phone. He stood up with rage.

'She is fine, she is safe,' the tall man assured him calmly. 'She is resting. But, you understand, it is very lucky that we found her. If we had not come by when we did, who knows what could have happened?'

Angelo recognised the edge in Bertoluccio's voice. 'What do you want?'

'Something for our troubles. You see, we have done you a very big favour, keeping her safe from those who might use her for their own ends ...'

'How much?'

Bertoluccio paused. 'Two million.'

'Two million!'

'I'm going to lose two of my men over this. That can't be for nothing.'

Angelo Petranelli clenched his teeth. *That girl* ... he thought to himself, shaking his head. His daughter had been missing for over a month now and this was the first time he had heard anything about her whereabouts. He was going to have a serious talk with her when she got home.

Bertoluccio interrupted the silence. 'I trust you understand this is a sign of friendship, Petranelli. I am on your side – I am only trying to protect the girl.'

Angelo was having none of it. 'When? Where?'

Bertoluccio rattled off some directions. 'Eleven o'clock, tomorrow morning.'

'Fine,' said Angelo, slamming the phone down. 'Bastard!' He pulled a handkerchief from his pocket and wiped the sweat from his forehead. *Daughters*, he thought to himself, shaking his head. This was the last time he would come to her rescue with two million euro and a semi-automatic, that was for sure!

But Maria Petranelli – daughter of Angelo the crime boss, not daughter of Vince the roof tiler – did not need rescuing. What she needed was better taste in men, but she would figure that out for herself in a few years. For now, she and her husband of two days were crossing the border to Spain, ready to set themselves up in defiance of their old-fashioned parents. This Maria had also grown up in Australia; she'd been taken there as a child by her mother, who wasn't keen on Angelo Petranelli's career choices. But she had been seduced back to Italy by a tourist who wouldn't stop complimenting her eyes. And now they were about to start a new life together; change their names, change their identities, and live as they pleased. So Maria Petranelli – daughter of Angelo and new wife of Marco the perpetual uni-student and part-time anarchist – might have been missing, but she did not need rescuing: she had never been more content.

And our Maria Petranelli didn't need rescuing either. She had already surveyed her room critically for possible escape scenarios. A heavy vase next to her bed ... a window ... hedges and a stack of garden chairs directly outside ...

She was ready.

But she was also, she admitted to herself, a bit weary.

She waited over an hour for her oppressors to appear so she could make her move, but they were taking so long; so long that she didn't see the harm in lying down, just for a moment.

*

Maria had no idea that as she was 'resting her eyes', Bertoluccio had pulled Giovanni and Felice into his office and quizzed them on the existence of witnesses. She did not know that they lied, poorly, until Giovanni couldn't help himself and blamed Felice for everything. She didn't hear Bertoluccio's silenced weapon go off twice, a harsh penalty for their mistake but one Bertoluccio didn't hesitate to dish out, because he – unlike the two idiots he had just dispatched – was much better at getting rid of bodies. And she didn't know that Bertoluccio was feeling confident because, in his mind, the other foreign student hadn't seen anything, and even if she had, there were no longer any (living) links back to him. Plus, now he was getting two million euro, as well as getting up the nose of his rival Petranelli, which was one of his favourite power plays.

No, Maria was completely oblivious to all of this. The only thing she was aware of was her escape plan. And every time an unbidden thought pushed its way in – a memory of Kennedy's soft smiles, of a gentle arm around her waist or a hand on her knee – she pushed it away by replaying that victorious moment when she had kicked Roberto Spinelli in the shin.

CHAPTER 27

Attack

'But that doesn't make sense. Why would she run?' Kennedy demanded.

Roberto Spinelli shrugged apologetically. 'I began to notice inconsistencies in her story. Obviously there was a dead body, and obviously the two girls were kidnapped, but a second body ... *signora*, I showed Maria those photos deliberately. The men in those pictures are not criminals. It is a tactic we use sometimes, to determine what is fact, what is fiction.'

Paola frowned. 'That seems dishonest. Why didn't you just ask her outright?'

'In my experience, some people do not tell the truth.'

'Hang on,' Kennedy interrupted. 'Are you saying Maria has been lying this whole time?'

'Not at all,' Spinelli said. 'It may be she was suffering from shock. She has been through a lot in the past few days, perhaps it was too much for her.'

Alberto shook his head in disbelief. 'But how did she get away from you? Why didn't you stop her?'

'She claimed she needed to use the bathroom. I was trying to be polite. Luckily, I was able to spot this fellow before it was too late,' he said, clapping his hand on a sulking Gabriele's shoulder.

Paola switched her attention to her returned son. 'And you … what were you thinking? Why did you run?'

Gabriele shrugged. 'I was bored.'

'What about Maria? What's going to happen to her?' Kennedy pressed.

'We are doing everything we can. As soon as she shows her passport or tries to travel by train, she will be found.'

'But anything could happen to her. Can't you just track her phone?'

Alberto cleared his throat and held up his hand apologetically. In it was Maria's phone. 'She didn't take it with her to the interview. She left it on the chair,' Alberto said, handing it to the officer.

Kennedy wanted to argue, but she was speechless. How had everything gone so wrong?

Roberto turned to Alberto and Paola. 'Look, you have both been very kind to these young people. You have done more than most people would. Now, do not fear, Maria will be found.' He turned to Kennedy and switched to English. 'As for you, *signorina*, we have contacted the language school and they've been informed of your situation. Do you have a way back to Rome?'

'We can take her to the station,' Paola said.

'Good,' Spinelli said. '*Signorina*, it is very important you get on the train, and do not get off until you reach Rome. I will contact the local authorities so someone can meet you there and take a statement.'

There was nothing else to say.

Roberto Spinelli made his goodbyes and playfully pinched Gabriele's cheek, telling him not to run away from his parents again. And then the group was alone.

'This doesn't make sense,' Kennedy said. 'Maria is … determined, but she wouldn't just make up stories and run off.'

'That policeman is a weirdo!' said Gabriele, way too loudly.

'Gabriele! Shh!' Paola hissed, and Alberto yelled, 'Hey! Woah! Ha ha, easy there!'

But Kennedy felt the same. This all felt off. Roberto Spinelli was right about one thing, though: for now, there was nothing else they could do.

*

There was a knock on the door. Maria's eyes flew open and slowly adjusted to the dark. How long had she been asleep? The room was strange, and she couldn't figure out which way she was facing. She sat up and saw the vase next to her bed.

That's right, she remembered. *I'm in Italy.*

With a surge of energy and determination she leapt out of bed, grabbed the vase with both hands, and launched herself behind the door. *This is it,* she thought to herself. *Get ready …*

The door opened an inch, and then further, and Maria held the vase high above her head …

… and swung it straight into the hands of a very alert Dominic.

'*Signorina*, no,' he said politely, putting the vase back where it belonged.

Maria stood, vaseless and incredulous, and allowed him to lead her back to the bed.

'I have brought you some dinner,' Dominic said in Italian. He stepped outside her door and retrieved a tray laden with a plate of risotto and thick slices of bread.

'Oh,' Maria replied. 'Thank you.'

Dominic nodded and left, and Maria didn't look at the tray for a good few minutes. *How on earth did he catch that vase …?* she wondered. But eventually, hunger got the better of her. It was dark outside, after all, and she hadn't eaten anything since breakfast.

When Dominic entered twenty minutes later to retrieve the tray, the window was open, and Maria was gone.

'What the hell …' Dominic cursed, running to the window … and Maria emerged from underneath the bed and ran out the door.

Dominic sighed, and caught up to her in four or five strides. '*Signorina*, no,' he said.

Maria was surprised by how polite he was, considering he was a criminal. She hadn't had much to do with criminals – at least, not that she was aware of – but she had seen a lot of Vince's films. In Vince's films, the criminals were always old men who:

1. Wore long black coats and turtlenecks;
2. Spoke exclusively in either British or Russian accents; and
3. Ended up being blown up by their own bombs.

But Dominic looked nothing like them. He was young, for one thing. He wore a fitted white button-up shirt, rolled up at the sleeves; and, rather than hiding his chest with a turtleneck, the top few buttons of his shirt were undone, revealing smooth, brown skin. He seemed too good at anticipating things to ever get blown up by anything, Maria thought, and his wavy hair and handsome eyes and polite Italian made her *very* annoyed.

She didn't have time for this. She'd been kidnapped, she was being held by criminals, and God only knew what was happening to Kennedy!

She needed to get out of this mess and get back to Florence, fast.

It was time for new tactics.

'Excuse me,' Maria said later, 'could I use the shower?' She held up her hands to show him the dirt and dried blood.

'Of course,' Dominic said politely, and led her to a

bathroom – an ornate, marble-tiled room with gold faucets and a water feature.

Maria washed the dirt from her face, cleaned the dried blood from her hands and knees, and surveyed the room, plotting.

It was quiet in there for a very long time.

Eventually, Dominic knocked on the door. '*Signorina*?' he called. '*Signorina*, are you all right?'

Maria flung the door open and threw a handful of hot water in his face. It was meant to blind him; she imagined it would have the same effect as flour, or soup, or acid. But it didn't. He was meant to hop around, screaming in pain, leaving room for her to duck around him and escape. But he didn't.

He just wiped the water from his eyes, said, '*Signorina*, no,' and led her once more to her room.

This is getting ridiculous, Maria thought as Dominic closed the door and locked it behind him. *I'll just have to go for it.* So, as soon as everything outside her door was still, she rushed over to the window, opened it and, as quietly as she could, backed out, her feet scrambling for a foothold.

It was an awkward experience. Maria was not what you would call 'graceful', or 'coordinated', or 'good at quietly sneaking out of windows and dropping from significant heights'.

A few moments later, she opened her eyes to find herself sprawled in the garden, once again covered in dirt, with Dominic standing above her, shaking his head.

'Come on, *signorina*,' he said, reaching towards her. Maria sighed, and let him pull her to her feet. But standing up made her cry out in pain.

'Are you all right?'

'My ankle ...' she gasped.

'Can you walk?'

Maria tried and cried out again, then quickly pulled herself together. It was bad enough that this way-too-attractive man was foiling her escape attempts; she was *not* about to let him *Bodyguard* her back to the bedroom as well!

'It is a bit painful,' she said in as proper Italian as she could muster. 'I will have to walk very slowly.'

Dominic nodded and helped her back to her room. As soon as Maria was seated on the bed, he examined her ankle. 'There's no obvious bruising,' he said. 'But do you want some ice?'

'Yes,' Maria said, and Dominic left to retrieve some.

Maria leant back on the bed, cursing her failed escape plans. At least now she knew for sure: her father, Vince Petranelli, must be intimidating. Why else was Dominic still being so patient after she had tried to hit him with a vase, thrown water in his face, and orchestrated two window incidents?

Indeed, like a complete gentleman, Dominic had just returned with an ice-filled plastic bag wrapped in a towel, pulled a chair over so she could elevate her leg, and placed a pillow under her foot. Maria let him do these things, though she made sure she narrowed her eyes.

'What is this place?' she asked eventually.

'It is a villa, belonging to my boss,' said Dominic.

'Is your boss the tall one?'

'Yes.'

'Do you work here all the time?'

'Sometimes I work here,' Dominic replied non-committally.

'What do you do?'

'I do not wish to bore you, *signorina*,' Dominic said smoothly.

Maria sighed. This was going nowhere. She appraised the man kneeling in front of her. 'How old are you?'

'Twenty-five,' he replied.

Still eligible, said the voices of the Petranellis in Maria's head. She took in the twenty-five-year-old holding a plastic bag of ice to her foot. He *was* attractive, she could admit. Tall, patient, nice eyes, seemed kind, though she'd describe him as more well-built than lanky …

Stop it! she commanded herself. *Stop comparing everyone to Kennedy.*

She was so exhausted she was hallucinating, she realised. She needed sleep. It was the only solution.

*

She was back home. In her bedroom, in her bed.

'Anna!' she heard her father call. 'Anna!'

Maria got out of bed and opened the door. Vince was there, dressed in a long black coat and a turtleneck, a new scar over one eye, stroking a cat that was nestled in his arms.

'Maria's awake!' he yelled. 'Did you sleep, Maria? Did you have any nightmares?'

'You'd better not go in the shed,' Anna interrupted, popping up from behind Vince. 'You wouldn't handle being in the shed!'

Maria felt her body glide into the yard, across the garden, and through the shed door.

The salamis that usually hung from the ceiling were missing; instead, there were guns. Hundreds and hundreds of guns. Vince walked in, selected one, and exited without saying a word. He slammed the door behind him.

Maria heard a noise, and looked around her.

There, on the floor, was Lorenzo.

Still. Dead. His wrists tied together with half-woven bracelets.

Then his eyes flew open.

'I TOLD YOU NOT TO GO IN THE SHED!' Anna shrieked from the doorway. 'YOU'VE REALLY DONE IT NOW!'

Maria's hair stood on end as Lorenzo got up slowly. 'I'm tired,' he said. 'I'm tired, Maria.' He made his way towards her, saying it again and again. 'I'm tired. I'm tired, Maria.'

Maria's heart was in her throat. She backed away, trying to find the door, but it had disappeared. She looked around to find a weapon, but the shed was suddenly empty – no guns on the ceiling, no strings of salami to strangle Lorenzo with, no bottles of tomatoes to smash. Just empty walls, as far as the eye could see.

Lorenzo was so close now. 'I'm tired, Maria ...'

'Kennedy!' Maria screamed. 'Help me! Kennedy! KENNEDY!'

*

And she woke up.

She scrambled out of bed, turned on the light, and took in her surroundings.

There were no guns. No corpses.

Lorenzo was not back from the dead and lurching towards her.

She was okay.

She was fine.

She would figure out how to escape.

Then she would find Kennedy, somehow, and casually tell her what had happened.

She wouldn't admit how scared she was, and she would definitely, *definitely* not tell her that, at the moment she had felt most terrified, she had called out for her in her dreams.

CHAPTER 28

Rejected

Early the next morning, Paola, Alberto and Gabriele stood with Kennedy as she prepared to board a train.

Paola scrawled their email address and home number on a piece of paper. 'Mobile coverage is not good in our village – I'm giving you our landline. I hope you'll keep in touch!'

'I don't know how I can thank you enough,' Kennedy said.

'Don't worry about it. It's been a pleasure,' said Paola, drawing her into a hug. 'We're glad we could help. Aren't we, Alberto?'

Alberto nodded and pulled Kennedy aside. 'She's a funny girl, that Maria,' he said. 'But she likes you. I can tell. Kiss her again – and if she pushes you off the bed, get back up and kiss her anyway. What have you got to lose?'

'Uh, thanks,' Kennedy replied. She wasn't quite so brave,

and she certainly wasn't keen on kissing anyone without their consent, but it was nice that someone had confidence in her. She looked at the large clock above the train platform. It was time to go.

'Goodbye, Kennedy,' Alberto said. 'We will see each other again, I think ... our paths have crossed for a reason!'

'Yes,' Paola agreed. 'And let us know when you find Maria!'

And then, one by one, everyone leaned towards her so they could say their traditional Italian goodbyes. Kennedy didn't mind the kissing-on-both-cheeks thing, but she could never work out which direction her face was supposed to go first. As Alberto leaned towards her and Kennedy narrowly avoided kissing him full on the lips, she couldn't help but wonder what Maria would do in this situation. *She'd probably push him off the platform,* she thought longingly, a stab of sorrow hurting her insides.

She got onto the train, smiling and waving, and the family smiled and waved back.

*

While Kennedy was settling into her seat on the train, Maria was at the villa, sitting on the bed as the door opened.

'It's time, *signorina*,' Dominic said.

Maria stood up and followed him out of the room. The fear from her nightmare had not left her, and all she wanted was to feel safe. For some reason, her dream had revealed, this was very much linked to seeing Kennedy again. But Maria did *not* have time to be delving into her subconscious or analysing her rogue dreams, so she was stubbornly refusing to think about it. She just needed to get through the day.

Maria walked quickly behind Dominic and was soon met by Luca, who was much less friendly than his counterpart. He grabbed her arm roughly and escorted her to the car, not noticing or caring that she was still limping from the night before.

Bertoluccio climbed into the driver's seat, and Maria's heart beat faster and faster with anticipation. *This will all be over soon,* she promised herself, urging the car to start. She couldn't believe how eager she was to see her family.

The car reversed out of the driveway and turned onto a main road, where it was met by a convoy of another three vehicles. The convoy was not a surprise to Maria; by now, she earnestly believed her father would be at the drop point with a posse of thirty people, a gold tooth and a machine gun. For the first ten minutes of the drive all Maria could do was wish the car would go faster, so it would all be over.

But, as with all long drives, the motion of the vehicle and the peaceful, monotonous scenery made her mind wander. She started to imagine the reconciliation with her father. Would it just be Vince there? He might have flown Anna in as well. But what about Nonna and Nonno? Would they all be standing there in a tight little group, surrounded by people with machine guns? All huddled together like they had been at the airport? Maria swallowed. She could picture it vividly: their stern, disapproving, knowing faces; her mother raising her eyebrows, her nonna shaking her head; the whole lot of them ready to say 'I told you so …'

Maria felt herself becoming annoyed. Honestly. That would be so like them!

We told you that you wouldn't be able to handle Italy, Maria.

You think you know everything, but you have no brains.

Why don't you have a boyfriend, Maria? You should have a boyfriend by now.

Were you scared, Maria? Look at Maria! Maria's scared!

Now Maria's heart was beating even faster. Was she ready for this? The cars slowed in unison and took a right turn onto a dirt road. Her stomach turned queasy. She tried to feel excited to see her family, but she knew the reunion was going to be unbearable.

And then she saw them – another group of cars, already parked, waiting. She looked with a mixture of eagerness and dread for the familiar figures of the Petranellis, but nobody had emerged from the cars.

'Luca, Dominic,' Bertoluccio ordered. 'Stay in the car until my signal. Then bring the girl out.'

The two men nodded. As if on cue, a lot of car doors opened and a lot of intimidating people, from both teams, got out at once.

But Vince was not present.

Is he still in the car? Maria wondered. *Is he loading ammo into his weapons? Cracking his knuckles so he can take on Bertoluccio with his bare hands?* She tried to picture it, but she couldn't shake the much more realistic image of her father twisting the corners of a serviette, holding it up and saying, 'Look, Maria! A roast chicken! Look! Look!'

'Angelo!' Bertoluccio called.

Maria didn't recognise the name. Was this one of Vince's contacts?

'Where is she, Bertoluccio?' Angelo Petranelli called.

Bertoluccio smiled and walked right over to Angelo Petranelli, kissing him on both cheeks. Then he nodded to one of his associates, who took a step forward, and Angelo nodded to one of *his* associates, who handed a suitcase over. Maria watched from her car. It was like some strange kind of dance. And it seemed to be going just fine, even though Vince still hadn't appeared. But it didn't quell the disquieting feeling gathering in the pit of her stomach.

Bertoluccio's man, now armed with the suitcase, got into one of the vehicles and headed back the way they'd come. Once the car had reached the main road, Bertoluccio looked over at Maria and flicked his fingers. Dominic and Luca snapped to attention and escorted her from the car, giving the appearance of gentleness and respect despite the painfully tight grip they had on her arms.

Maria saw Angelo look at her and breathe in heavily through his nose.

'Is this some kind of a joke, Bertoluccio?' he asked. 'Where is my daughter?'

The smug look on Bertoluccio's face froze. 'What do you mean?'

'You lying son of a bitch, that's not my daughter!' Angelo roared.

Dominic crossed himself. Luca froze. And Maria realised there had been a colossal mistake. As likely as it had seemed a few minutes ago, Vince Petranelli was *not* going to emerge out of an armoured car with a gold medallion around his neck and several guns blazing. Instead, every single person in the area had pulled out some kind of weapon and aimed it at someone else's head. Maria was the only person left unarmed and, she had to admit, she felt quite vulnerable.

'Where's my daughter?' Angelo said again, his voice dangerously low.

Maria, her arms freed so Dominic and Luca could handle their weapons, took two steps back.

'Wait, wait,' Bertoluccio said, arms out. 'This girl witnessed a job, spoke to *Spinelli*, has an Australian passport –'

'Either you're an idiot or you've betrayed me,' Angelo cut him off. 'You have my money and you have my daughter!'

'No! There has been a mistake!' Bertoluccio protested. 'I thought this *was* your daughter!'

And then there was chaos.

Some people jumped straight back into a car and tore towards the main road in hot pursuit of the sorry soul with the two million euro. Some dove behind vehicles and opened fire on those who were also ducking behind vehicles. A brave minority ran towards each other and tried to wrestle their foes to the ground. But nobody paid any attention to Maria.

Without giving it a second thought, she edged to safety, taking cover behind a car. She ignored the shouting, yelling, gunfire and cursing, even the errant body flying through the air, and sidled around until she reached the front of the car and slipped inside.

She was in the driver's seat.

And the key had been left in the ignition.

She turned the key and the engine roared to life. She slammed her foot on the accelerator. She was going to get away!

But Maria did not know how to drive. She had not taken the car out of 'park', and so all she did was rev the engine dramatically.

Everyone turned and stared at Maria as she panicked and fumbled around for the gear stick. Everyone except for Dominic, who sprinted, faster than anyone Maria had ever seen, until he was level with the vehicle. The car jolted forward just as Dominic wrenched the door open and threw himself into the back seat. Maria slammed her foot on the accelerator, and, with the back door still swinging wildly, she drove as fast as she could, swearing loudly as bullets rang past and occasionally collided with the chassis.

'Be careful!' shouted Dominic.

'I DON'T HAVE TIME!' Maria shrieked.

Come on, she urged. *Faster! Go faster!*

She tore onto the main road and kept driving with

absolutely no regard for the speed limit. She knew they would be chasing her soon, and this was no time for obeying the law!

Maria was following this philosophy in more ways than she realised. It didn't occur to her that Italians drive on the right side of the road, even when an oncoming Vespa swerved around her, tyres screeching.

'Idiot!' Maria screamed, ignoring Dominic, who had buckled himself in and was yelling both obscenities and prayers in the same breath.

But then another car came, and then a truck, and Maria finally realised that *she* was the one in the wrong. She wrenched the steering wheel to the right, hard … too hard.

Everything was happening too fast for her to process. She didn't notice the car was no longer swerving along the gravel and was now bumping over the edge of the road until it was too late. All she could do was brace herself as it went jolting down a hill, rose up onto two wheels and then banged down and bounced to a stop in the middle of a field, completely invisible from the road.

The car was silent now. So was Dominic. And, somewhere along the line, Maria had hit her head quite hard. Everything was hazy, and then everything was black.

*

Gentle arms lifted her out of the car … and everything was black again.

Someone was wiping blood off her face … and everything was black again.

'Are you all right, *signorina*?' someone said. 'I think she's waking up.'

And she *was* waking up, but only for long enough to vaguely think of Kennedy, and wonder where she was.

And then everything was black again.

CHAPTER 29

Sense

When Maria did wake up, her first thought was that she had stumbled into a different century. She was in a wooden bed covered by a handmade quilt and a crocheted blanket, the room smelled like pine, and the walls, floor and sloping roof were made of raw, dark timber. Her second thought was that she was going to throw up. But, she realised after a few moments, her stomach was not upset, just empty. She sat up, but regretted it when a sharp stabbing pain struck behind her eyes, making it difficult to see.

'Careful,' said an old voice, though it was hard to understand – it sounded Italian, but with an accent she'd never heard before. Maria held a hand to her head and squinted, trying to make out where the voice had come from.

If only people had subtitles, Maria would have understood what the old woman leaning against the doorway was saying.

As it was, all she heard were words – very friendly, very cheerful, but nothing Maria could make out.

'Where am I?' Maria asked – in English and then in Italian – but she couldn't understand the response. The woman smiled and tutted and checked Maria's temperature with the back of her hand, then made her way out of the room.

'Wait!' called Maria.

The woman turned, held up one finger, said, 'One minute, one minute,' in that heavy accent, and left.

She returned with a bowl of soup. 'Eat,' she said, picking up a spoon and holding it to Maria's mouth. Maria, not accustomed to being fed, opened her mouth to explain that she was perfectly capable, thank you very much, and the spoon was shoved in.

'Good,' said the woman. 'Good. Good.' She was slightly hunched over, her wiry grey hair tied under a headscarf, and she was dressed completely in black except for a pair of electric blue Crocs. When the soup was gone, the woman put the bowl aside and started speaking again. 'Rovena … Rovena …' she kept saying, waving her hands at herself.

'Is that your name? Your name is Rovena?' Maria guessed.

'Yes! My name is Rovena! Good!'

'I'm Maria,' she replied, relieved they had gotten this far. 'Where am I?'

Rovena's mouth set into a determined line, and she pointed at Maria.

'Yes? Me?'

Rovena nodded, and then, in a sudden, wild gesture, slammed her hands together, making the sound of an explosion with her mouth.

Maria remembered. 'I was in a car crash?'

Rovena pointed to herself and mimed walking, then threw her hands up into the air, let out a cry, and put her hands to the sides of her shocked and horrified face.

'You saw the crash?' Maria asked.

Rovena's face grew stern, and her posture straightened. She mimed scooping something up and carrying it.

Maria shook her head, confused. 'Sorry? I don't get that last bit ...'

Rovena frowned and tried again, holding up one of her arms and flexing a bicep.

'You have muscles ...?'

Rovena grew frustrated, and said something insistent in a deep, guttural voice.

'Are you pretending to be a man?' Maria guessed.

'She's pretending to be me.' There was Dominic, standing in the doorway. 'You're awake. I thought I heard talking.'

'You're speaking English!' Maria gasped.

'Yes,' Dominic admitted. He, it seemed, had escaped the accident unscathed. 'How are you feeling?'

Suddenly Maria was full of energy, and she felt like yelling. She was sick and tired of all these ridiculous things that kept happening to her, *that's* how she was feeling! She was sick of finding dead bodies! Sick of being thrown into car boots! Sick of being caught up in conflicts between criminal outfits with only one month at a language school to help her understand what they were saying! Sick of waking up in European versions of *Little House on the Prairie*! And now, she was sick of discovering that one of the members of the aforementioned criminal outfits had actually been able to speak English all along! All she had wanted was to go on exchange in Italy. Was that really too much to ask?

But she didn't say any of this.

'Fine,' Maria replied. And for the first time in a long time, she didn't bother looking for possible weapons or escape routes. What was the point, really? It didn't seem worth the effort when, no matter what she did, things just kept getting worse.

Dominic took a deep breath and came closer, and Rovena dragged a chair over to the bed. Dominic said something to her in a language Maria couldn't understand – though she guessed it was 'thank you' – and then sat.

'I should tell you the truth,' Dominic said, sighing, and Maria raised her eyebrows expectantly. 'I'm not who you think I am. I am actually a member of the Raggruppamento Operativo Speciale.'

Maria wondered why, whenever anyone said anything in Italian, they felt it necessary to speak at three times the regular speed.

'We are an arm of the Carabinieri, the police, specifically targeting organised crime.'

'So …' Maria asked, trying to make sense of this. 'What were you, undercover or something?'

'Yes.'

'Hmm,' said Maria.

'Bertoluccio is a very bad man. But I promise you are safe here.'

Maria waited for him to continue to explain himself, but he didn't. It was his solemn silence that convinced her to hear him out.

'What was going on back there? At the handover?' she asked.

'Bertoluccio mistook you for the daughter of Angelo Petranelli. He is another dangerous person who is under investigation. He was going to exchange you for two million euro.'

Maria frowned. 'How could they mistake me for ...'

'You both have the same name. Maria Petranelli.'

'Oh.'

'And his daughter has been living in Australia for many years.'

'Oh.'

'So the name, the passport, that is why the confusion happened.'

'So, my dad ... my real dad, Vince Petranelli ... is he a part of this?'

Dominic shook his head. 'I am unaware of anyone called Vince Petranelli. It was all a big mistake.'

Maria nodded. Deep down she had known this was the case, but she couldn't help but be disappointed, and sank back into the pillows.

'You should rest,' Dominic said. 'I can explain everything to you later ...'

'No!' Maria said quickly. 'I mean ... please, I'm fine, really. I just want to know what's going on. I have so many questions.'

'All right,' said Dominic. 'Where should we start?'

'With the bracelet. That's where this whole thing began.'

Now it was Dominic's turn to look confused. 'I'm sorry, *signorina*, which bracelet?'

'I've got it here ...' She reached into her jeans pocket and pulled out the now faded band. 'Here it is,' she said, passing it to Dominic. 'What does it mean?'

Dominic frowned, looking it over. 'I do not know. It has the colours of the Italian flag ... it looks like a tourist item ...?'

'I know that,' said Maria impatiently. 'But what does it *mean?*'

'Perhaps it means, "I have visited Italy". A keepsake, a souvenir to remember your trip?' Dominic's voice was too gentle, too sympathetic, too much like he was humouring her. It made Maria clench her fists and bang them on the bed.

'But what does it have to do with the *murders?*'

Dominic blinked. 'I'm afraid it doesn't have anything to do with organised crime, miss.' Maria huffed in exasperation, and Dominic looked confused. 'I'm sorry, do you *want* it to have something to do with organised crime?'

'No! It's just that, the guy who scammed me with this bracelet ended up dead, and then the second dead guy had one around his wrist as well ...'

'Oh,' said Dominic. 'Well, I know it sounds unlikely, but perhaps it is just a coincidence.'

'But the police officer said it was likely the bracelet had something to do with it,' she persisted.

'The police officer at the station who took you out to Bertoluccio?' Dominic asked.

'Yes!'

'Maria, you have become involved in something very dangerous. It has nothing to do with this bracelet. I don't know why he told you it did. He was handing you over to be killed.'

Maria gaped. 'What do you mean ...?'

'The police officer you spoke to was corrupt. He has deals with both Petranelli and Bertoluccio. And sometimes, they have deals with each other. You are part of a deal that went wrong.'

'But ...' Maria shook her head, trying to understand, but failing.

'Let me explain,' Dominic continued. 'Bertoluccio discovered you had witnessed a murder *he* arranged. You saw that body just before you were put in the car by two men, right?'

'In the *boot* of the car,' Maria clarified.

'Okay,' Dominic said. 'But those men who kidnapped you are dead now.'

'Dead?'

'Yes. Bertoluccio is a very tough man. He does not tolerate mistakes.'

That made Maria pause.

Dominic nodded. 'To him, it was a mistake you had seen the body. Then it was a mistake you were allowed to live, because you could become a witness. You could identify the ones who committed the murder, and that could lead back to him. Usually he would have killed you for that.'

Maria tried to reconcile this with the way Bertoluccio had treated her. Driving her without a bag over her head. Sending Dominic in with food. Promising her that if she behaved, everything would be fine. It didn't make sense.

Dominic noticed her confusion, and continued. 'When you went to the police station, the corrupt officer ... do you remember his name?'

'Roberto someone?' Maria tried.

'Roberto Spinelli,' Dominic confirmed. 'Spinelli recognised that you were the witness who'd seen Bertoluccio's job. He knew Bertoluccio would pay him if he handed you over. So he did.'

'Even though I might have been *executed?*'

'Yes, *signorina*. I am sorry. But Bertoluccio wasn't going to kill you, because when he heard your name and that you were from Australia, he thought you were the missing Petranelli daughter. So he decided to hold you ransom. Only a small ransom, because he and Petranelli sometimes work together, but still, it was a ransom.'

Maria tried to let it all sink in, but her head was spinning.

'The problem now is that you are *not* the missing Petranelli daughter. So, you are still a witness. To the murder, and also to Bertoluccio's and Petranelli's connection to corrupt police.'

'Oh my god,' Maria said, sinking back into the bed.

'I am sorry, *signorina*.'

Maria was quiet, struggling to process how much danger she was in. One thought wouldn't leave her mind. 'What about Kennedy? Will she be okay?'

Dominic frowned. 'I am not sure who Kennedy is ...?'

'She's my ...' Maria paused. Acquaintance? Fellow traveller? Bane of my life? 'Friend,' she landed on. 'She's my friend. She was kidnapped with me. But Spinelli didn't hand her over. I think ... maybe because she didn't see the body. The man Bertoluccio killed, I mean. She just got put in the boot because she was trying to save me.' The memory made Maria's chest ache. She frowned.

'You are safe here,' Dominic reassured her, mistaking her silence for something else. 'This is a safe house, and I am here to protect you.'

Maria exhaled. She had a million questions, but she settled on an easy one to take her mind off the things that were really worrying her. 'What do you have to do with all this?'

'I was undercover.'

Maria waited for more, but that was all Dominic would offer.

'Did you do what you needed to do?'

'Partly,' he replied.

'Did you blow your cover because of me?'

'Yes.'

'I'm sorry.'

'It is all right.'

Maria sighed. It was a heavy sigh. 'I guess it all makes sense,' she said eventually. 'Except for one thing.'

'What is it?' asked Dominic.

'Who killed Lorenzo?'

Dominic lifted his arms apologetically. 'I am sorry, Maria. I do not know who Lorenzo is. But I believe that his death is unrelated.'

'Do you think you could find out?' Maria asked. 'Could you find out how he died?'

Dominic raised his eyebrows. 'It is possible, I suppose ...?' There was a question in his voice.

'It's just that ...' Maria hesitated. 'I feel a bit guilty. I know it sounds stupid, but ... I imagined killing him.'

'Hmm,' said Dominic.

'I mean, because he robbed me. Because of the bracelet.'

Dominic nodded slowly, as one nods to someone who has both suffered a blow to the head and tried to inflict blows to *their* head, and still seems very capable of having violent thoughts.

But Maria was leaning back against the pillows now, and her eyes were heavy. 'To be clear, I don't actually want to kill anyone,' she said, and yawned.

'You should rest,' he said.

'Yes,' she agreed. 'I am very tired.' She sighed and closed her eyes.

Dominic said something to Rovena, who nodded.

Maria's eyes opened again. 'What language are you speaking?' she said sleepily.

'We are speaking Albanian,' he said.

'Are you Albanian?'

'No, but I have picked up a bit here and there.'

Undercover, multi-lingual, strong enough to pick her up and carry her out of a dramatic car-crash … this was getting ridiculous.

'Rest now,' said Dominic as he left the room, and Maria was so tired she obeyed him.

Rovena, who'd been watching silently this whole time, picked up Maria's hand and held it until she fell asleep.

CHAPTER 30

Meanwhile

Paola and Alberto sighed as they watched the train leave. They couldn't help but feel sad as they said their goodbyes. They were such interesting girls. They both hoped Maria would be all right.

'Well, we should get going,' said Paola as Kennedy's train disappeared from sight. Alberto agreed, and they started to walk away.

A moment later, they stopped.

Paola said it first. 'Where's Gabriele?'

CHAPTER 31

Appendage

While Maria was recovering with an Albanian woman and an undercover cop, trying not to think about being hunted by the many enemies she'd accidentally made, Kennedy was having her own difficulties. Obviously, going on a sort-of date with Maria that had ended with a dead body was not ideal. Nor was getting put in a boot and ending up in Florence. But Kennedy had always been a forgiving sort of person. She was safe now, on a train heading back to Rome, and she would have chalked it all up to a (briefly terrifying) travel adventure if it weren't for Maria.

Oh god, Maria. Kennedy couldn't stop thinking about her. She hadn't been able to, ever since they'd met. The intensity of Kennedy's feelings had taken her by surprise. Maria wasn't the type Kennedy was usually drawn to; not least because she carried herself as if there was a forcefield around her, one that might electrocute you if you got too close. But that moment when Kennedy first saw her was etched in her memory. There she was, this lonely, strange Australian girl hunched on the steps of the language school, looking up at her with the saddest eyes she'd ever seen – until Kennedy offered to help her up, of course, at which point Maria turned into a determined, self-reliant machine with an energy that made her seem a lot taller that she actually was. But Kennedy knew there was much more to Maria than she let people see. She acted so tough, so disinterested, so determined to kick everyone in the face … but then she'd slip up and accidentally smile. And every time it happened, Kennedy immediately wanted to make it happen again.

Kennedy was a goner, there was no question of that. But she didn't know if Maria felt the same way. There were times she was *sure* something was there; casual comments, side glances, accidental touches, a sense of humour Maria didn't seem to show to anyone else. But then, she could be snappy, and grumpy, and there were some very excessive reactions when anyone even *suggested* they were attracted to each other.

Kennedy didn't know what to make of it. But at that moment, it didn't really matter; all she wanted was for Maria to be safe.

She wished she'd gone with her to that second interview in the police station. Something had to have happened to make Maria run like that. Kennedy was no hero, she knew that, but she wondered if maybe she could have done something. Convinced Maria it was all right, that she would stand by her no matter what, that she didn't have to run …

The dialogue Kennedy was creating for this scene was compelling. There was practically an orchestra. The train was moving now, and Kennedy closed her eyes, letting her mind wander. It wasn't easy; the train's movements kept jolting her head, passengers kept getting up to wander around, and a nearby English couple were having a very heated argument about whose job it was to look after the passports. But Kennedy kept her eyes closed. She wanted to concentrate. She wanted to play the conversation out just right.

*

'Kennedy?' Maria would say, shocked, but full of hope. She would squint, frown, then shake her head, as if she couldn't believe what she was seeing.

'Hi.' Kennedy would smile.

'Is it really you?' Maria would say, taking a step forward, her eyes opening wide with wonder.

'Yeah, it's really me,' Kennedy would reply casually, with a small laugh, not moving as Maria came closer and reached up to touch her face.

'You're here … I can't believe it … you came back for me …'

'Of course I did,' she would say, and Maria would fling her arms around Kennedy's neck, and Kennedy would lift her and swing her around, laughing, and they would kiss …

*

'Hi.'

Kennedy opened her eyes.

Someone was staring right into her face.

Gabriele.

Gabriele was staring right into her face.

Kennedy scrambled backwards in shock. Gabriele was sitting opposite her, his legs too short for his feet to touch the floor, his arms casually resting on the armrests. 'I'm hungry,' he sniffed.

'Tickets!' said a man in a uniform, and everyone in the carriage came to life, reaching into bags and pockets and waving blue passes at the man as he passed.

'Oh my god,' Kennedy gasped, though Gabriele seemed unmoved.

'Tickets!' the man in the uniform bellowed, towering over her.

Kennedy let out a nervous laugh and said, 'Hello,' as she handed up her ticket. She swallowed hard as the man frowned at Gabriele.

'Ticket,' he said again.

'I'm with her,' Gabriele said, pointing at Kennedy.

The ticket inspector looked at Kennedy and held out his hand expectantly.

'Uh … well … I … uh … I don't …'

'TICKET!' boomed the man, turning to Gabriele.

And Gabriele jumped off his seat and hurtled down the aisle.

'WAIT!' shouted the ticket inspector. 'You stay there!' he ordered Kennedy, and turned to chase after the kid.

Kennedy's heart was beating fast, her breathing had become very shallow, and her forehead glistened with sweat. 'It's really hot in here,' she said to the lady sitting across the aisle. 'Is there a window we can open?'

Kennedy wasn't asking simply because she was desperate for fresh air. There was a small part of her that wondered if it would be possible to avoid the ticket inspector by leaping from the train.

Kennedy's overblown fear of the ticket inspector, and in fact all public transport workers, had developed when she and her family were on holiday in the UK, and she witnessed a man being arrested for drug smuggling at the airport. The incident was particularly scarring for Kennedy because:

1. She was very young at the time;
2. It involved high-speed chases, batons, dogs, and a fist fight; and
3. Her uncle, not wanting Kennedy to be upset, tried to lighten the mood by saying, 'See, this is what happens when people try to board a plane without a ticket, ha ha ha!' Thus traumatising her for life.

Kennedy eventually found out the truth, but still, the damage had been done. It really was lucky for her that the train windows were not of the opening variety.

She looked around nervously, half expecting to see Gabriele being dragged back by the scruff of his neck, but Gabriele was not stupid. He was also small for his age, and very fast. He had ducked through the doors at the end of the carriage, darted into a baggage compartment, and rolled underneath a bag rack on the floor before the inspector was even halfway down the aisle.

Gabriele stayed put as the inspector's shoes went past him and into the next carriage, returned through the baggage compartment, and then went back the way they had originally come. When there had been no sign of the inspector's shoes for a good few minutes, Gabriele emerged and walked calmly back to his seat.

'Hi,' he said casually, and Kennedy jumped.

'Gabriele!' Kennedy yelled. 'What are you doing on the train?'

'I don't understand what you're saying,' said Gabriele, though he could probably guess.

Kennedy repeated it in Italian, but Gabriele just shrugged.

The truth was, he didn't know what he was doing on the train. Gabriele was one of those kids who did things because:

1. It seemed like a good idea at the time

... actually, that is the only reason Gabriele made any of his decisions.

A muffled voice rang over the loudspeaker. 'Next stop, Arezzo. Next stop, Arezzo ...'

Kennedy stood up and grabbed Gabriele by the arm. They had to get off the train before the ticket inspector came back. A few other passengers shuffled to the exits. Kennedy followed them, doing her best to look inconspicuous while hopping nervously from foot to foot and praying under her breath that the slowing train would just stop already so she and Gabriele could get off.

Finally, the doors hissed open, and Kennedy pushed Gabriele off the train and along the platform until they were well and truly blended in with the crowd. Kennedy breathed a sigh of relief.

'I'm hungry,' Gabriele said, and Kennedy looked down at him incredulously.

'What are you doing here?' she exploded in English. 'What were you doing on the train? Your parents will be panicking! I wasn't supposed to get off until I got to Rome! And now we're in the middle of nowhere and I'm stuck with an eight-year-old!'

'I don't understand what you're saying,' Gabriele said again (though, again, he could probably guess).

Kennedy was at her wit's end. She turned on the spot, looking around desperately as if hoping some kind of answer would appear. Paola and Alberto would be so worried … they would blame her forever … she had no idea where she was …

'I'm hungry!' Gabriele was now pulling on her pants leg, trying to get her attention.

Kennedy huffed in exasperation. *All right*, she told herself, *first things first. Just take it one step at a time.* Her mobile phone was dead; she needed a pay phone. And she needed the kid to be quiet, which meant she had to buy him some food. She reached into her back pocket.

Her wallet was gone.

Kennedy started to panic. Was this really happening? How long had her wallet been missing? Was it still on the train? Was it back somewhere in Florence? What was she going to do?

'*Huuun-gry,*' Gabriele sang, and Kennedy couldn't take it any more.

'*I don't have any money!*' Kennedy shouted in Italian, and Gabriele, who hated being yelled at, bared his teeth at her and took off.

'Gabriele!' she yelled after him. 'Wait!'

Thankfully, he did not go far. He waited at a distance, watching Kennedy from behind the legs of a regal-looking woman, until Kennedy had stopped chasing him, put her hands on her head, and looked as if she might cry. Only then did Gabriele emerge, strolling back to Kennedy as if nothing had happened.

When Kennedy saw him, she gasped and hugged him – partly out of relief, partly to stop him from disappearing again. He wriggled out of her grasp.

'Gabriele,' she said in her best Italian, 'don't run. I need to call your parents to tell them you're all right.'

'Okay,' he shrugged.

'It's just,' Kennedy continued, holding up the black screen of her phone and then pointing to a phone booth, '... I don't have any money.'

Gabriele seemed to understand. He nodded way too confidently. 'How much do you need?'

'Oh, uh …'

'There's probably some in here,' he said, holding up the regal woman's purse.

Kennedy gasped. 'Where did you get that from?'

Gabriele shrugged and pointed vaguely behind him.

'Did you steal it?'

Gabriele shrugged again.

I am dealing with the spawn of Satan, Kennedy thought, ready to give Gabriele a lecture about how it was wrong to steal. But as soon as she opened the purse and found that all it contained was some ID, she couldn't help wishing Gabriele had picked a wealthier mark.

'That's her,' Gabriele said, pointing as his victim walked past.

Kennedy leapt into life. 'Excuse me, ma'am!' she called gallantly, thinking this would be a good opportunity to show Gabriele some basic morality. 'You may have lost this?'

The woman looked at the purse, looked at Kennedy, snatched the purse away, opened it, snapped it shut, and glared.

'We thought you'd need it back,' Kennedy said heroically, putting her arm proudly around Gabriele.

The woman narrowed her eyes and opened her mouth. 'Police!' she yelled.

'No … wait … I …'

'POLICE!' she hollered again, and this time Kennedy didn't wait around to explain. Instead, she followed Gabriele, who was already flying through the crowd.

When they were at a safe enough distance, they stopped abruptly, and Kennedy put both hands on her knees and tried to get her breath back. Gabriele grabbed the side of Kennedy's jeans and pulled.

'What?' Kennedy asked.

'Here,' Gabriele said, holding up a few one- and two-euro coins. 'I took these.'

Kennedy decided now was not the time for moral lectures after all.

*

It took three phone booths before Kennedy found a telephone that was still in working order. She dialled the number nervously and waited as she heard ringing, but it went straight to voicemail.

'Hi, it's uh, Kennedy here,' she faltered. 'Gabriele's with me, he's safe … we're in Arezzo, but I'm going to try to catch a train back to Florence. Maybe you could meet us at the station, but if you're not there I'll keep calling until I get through. But don't worry, he's okay. Uh … bye.'

Kennedy hung up and looked down at the kid, who seemed completely oblivious to the trouble he had caused. 'Gabriele, your parents aren't answering … do you know their mobile numbers?'

Gabriele shook his head and looked away. Kennedy sighed. This was useless.

'I'm still hungry,' Gabriele said, and this time Kennedy didn't yell or panic or hyperventilate; she just nodded. 'Me too.'

But her wallet was missing. And she was no good at singing, or dancing, or magic tricks, so she couldn't exactly put a handkerchief on the ground and expect people to fling coins at them. What was she going to do?

'Gabriele,' she said, kneeling down so she could look him in the eye. 'You're hungry, and we need train tickets to get back to your parents. But I don't have any money. Do you think ...' Kennedy swallowed, feeling immoral as the words slid out. 'Do you think you could ...'

'Sure,' said Gabriele.

'I'll wait here,' said Kennedy. 'Be careful.'

Gabriele nodded, and Kennedy wondered what she had become.

CHAPTER 32

Mortality

Maria recovered quickly.

In truth, there was very little to recover from – just minor bruises and a cut above her right eye – but Rovena insisted Maria remain in bed and do as little as humanly possible. Every half hour, Rovena would come in, fluff the pillow and re-adjust the bed covers until Maria was practically strapped down by the sheer tightness of the tucked-in sheets. Rovena would talk the whole time, and sometimes sing, and sometimes pray, and Maria wished she could speak Albanian so she could understand or have a conversation or explain that the sheets were making her claustrophobic. But she couldn't, and now she didn't even have Dominic to translate for her.

He had not reappeared since the conversation when he'd revealed everything to her. Maria tried finding out where he'd gone, but Rovena just shook her head and said

'Dominic will be back soon' (which Maria could understand, even without the hand gestures).

At least I'm safe here, she tried to reassure herself, but she felt so unmoored. If Kennedy had been there, it would have been different; no matter what mess Maria had gotten herself into, there would have been something, some*body* that was familiar.

And maybe the outcome would have been different, too. Maybe, if they'd been together, they would have actually been successful in stunning Dominic and escaping before the handover – and then Maria wouldn't have Angelo Petranelli blaming her for losing two million euro, as *well* as Bertoluccio wanting to kill her for being a witness. And, okay, maybe Dominic would be a bit annoyed at getting knocked out, but if she and Kennedy had escaped by themselves, he could have stayed undercover.

Maria didn't realise it, but she was resorting to her most common coping mechanism for failure and feelings of vulnerability; replaying the events, but giving herself the strength and skill of the characters in Vince's B-grade films. She imagined kneeling down to check that Dominic was still breathing, then stepping over his prone body and vaulting effortlessly out the window. She imagined stealing a getaway car, Kennedy in tow, and actually knowing how to drive it. She imagined speeding in reverse down that long driveway, then spinning around dramatically at the last minute and launching like a rocket onto the correct side of the road. She imagined deftly manoeuvring the steering wheel with one hand as Kennedy held on for dear life, and envisioned herself using her free arm to shoot holes through the cars that were chasing them.

Maria's fantasies were making her feel better, and were all fairly par for the course. But then, out of nowhere, her mind decided to ditch the action-movie driving scenes and replay the car crash as it had happened in real life – only now, it was *Kennedy* lifting her from the vehicle, *Kennedy* sitting by the bed, reaching out, intertwining fingers, squeezing gently, slowly rubbing her hand with her thumb …

Maria felt her temperature go from boiling to ice cold in a second.

Right! she thought. *Time to get out of bed.*

*

Rovena's home was very small. It didn't take Maria long to find her way to the old-fashioned kitchen, complete with an open fire and a woodheap.

'Ah! You look much better,' said Rovena. She put a steaming bowl of white bean soup on the table. 'Sit! Eat!'

Maria accepted the soup gratefully and tried to think of something to say. She saw a few photos on the wall and pointed to them. 'Your family?' she asked.

Rovena smiled, and fetched a photo album that was falling apart at the seams. She pointed out sons and a daughter, and her late husband, and a sister she had lost. Maria couldn't understand all the words, but she understood that this was a painful topic. She sat quietly while Rovena went through the pages, saying names, sometimes laughing, but mostly silent.

When Rovena closed the book with a sigh, Maria looked at her, and gave a small, sad smile. 'I'm sorry,' she said, feeling extremely inadequate.

They were interrupted by a knock on the front door.

Rovena patted her hand and stood up to answer it.

Dominic must be back, Maria thought.

But it wasn't Dominic. The man at the door was shorter, stocky, and had northern features, and it took a moment for Maria to place him.

He was at Bertoluccio's mansion, Maria remembered. He was Dominic's partner. Luca.

For a brief, wishful moment, she wondered if Luca was undercover too, and if he was here to help.

But the look of absolute menace on his face made her heart leap into her throat.

'Rovena!' Maria called, jumping up. 'Run!'

But there wasn't time. Luca pushed Rovena aside roughly and bounded towards Maria.

She couldn't let this happen. She had to fight back.

'Get away!' she shouted, and looked around wildly for a weapon. Completely overlooking the knife-block, cast-iron saucepan and iron poker, she reached down, grabbed her bowl of soup, and flung it at him like a frisbee.

And – against all odds – it hit his forehead! Maria would have been drunk with the victory of throwing something that actually made contact with its intended target (it really was a first for her), but Luca wasn't thwarted for long. He growled, one hand on his forehead, and kept walking towards her.

Maria picked up a chair, holding it in front of her like a lion tamer. 'Stay back,' she warned, but he grabbed the chair's legs and pulled. Maria struggled, but Luca wrenched it away from her with so much force she toppled forwards. He flung the chair to the side and grabbed her roughly. Maria could hear Rovena shouting for help, but it sounded like she was far away. All the sound was muffled and she realised she couldn't breathe. She couldn't *breathe*. Her head and heartbeat pounded as Luca's hands tightened around her throat. Was she dying? She couldn't be. She wasn't ready to die. This was all happening way too fast ...

But then Luca's grip loosened, and Maria was on the floor. She gasped for air, nearly choking on it, but gradually the pounding in her head ceased and her throat stopped aching. She could hear shouting in the background and briefly wondered where Dominic had come from. She heard scuffling. Swearing. Rovena crying out. The sound of fists against flesh. The crack of furniture breaking.

And then everything was silent. Maria coughed and hiccupped and leaned back against the kitchen bench.

'Are you all right?' Dominic asked, gasping.

'Yes,' she said, ignoring his outstretched hand and standing up, extremely slowly, by herself.

He nodded and moved towards Rovena, helping her to her feet and reassuring her as she muttered and shook her head and threw her hands to the heavens.

'Where's …' Maria coughed. 'Where's Luca?'

'He's gone. And we need to go too. It is not safe here any longer.'

He turned to Rovena and started speaking rapidly in Albanian. When she nodded and left the room, he turned back to Maria. 'I will take you to Rome. The embassy will arrange for you to be taken home. Until then, you will be safe with me. Do you understand?'

'Yes,' said Maria, without argument.

'Good. I have got a car. I am sorry I left you, but I had to get transport. We'll drop Rovena off in Florence. She has children there. She will stay with them.'

'Okay,' Maria said.

Dominic peered closely at her.

'Are you all right, *signorina?*' he asked cautiously.

'I'm fine,' Maria replied, as if this sort of thing happened all the time. Because, she was rapidly realising, this sort of thing *was* happening all the time.

As they left Rovena's house, Maria, unlike the Maria of Yesterday, did not look at Dominic and hope he wasn't judging her for not being able to defend herself. She did not replay the fight, giving herself much more raw strength, or come up with impressive scenarios she would use next time.

No. Maria was not thinking courageous thoughts of power and bravado. Maria was trying not to think about anything at all.

Because she had nearly been killed. And for the first time she realised, *really* realised, that this might not end well.

CHAPTER 33

Batteries

The car trip was silent. Well, Maria and Dominic were silent. Rovena, who had relinquished her right to the front seat to give 'the young people' a chance to talk to each other, was chatting happily from the back. Maria was grateful; the steady stream of commentary was helping to keep her mind off things.

'What's she talking about?' she asked Dominic eventually.

'She is excited to see her children,' Dominic replied.

But Maria saw the twitch of a smile. 'Is that all?'

Dominic paused, as if deciding whether to tell her. 'She says a few of them are single.'

Maria peered in the rear-view mirror and saw Rovena waggling her eyebrows. Usually, Maria would have been appalled, but nearly being strangled to death made this potential matchmaking seem like less of a threat than usual.

'I don't understand,' Maria said after a few moments.

Dominic looked at her questioningly.

'I mean, it's just … how can she be so happy after what just happened?'

Dominic nodded. 'That was not the worst thing Rovena has seen or experienced, not by far. Rovena is a refugee. She has had a hard life.'

The Maria of Yesterday would have been affronted by this comment. The Maria of Yesterday would have questioned the criteria by which Dominic judged 'a hard life', reasoning that having to live with Vince and Anna Petranelli wasn't exactly a walk in the park either. But Maria had changed a lot in the past few days. She had begun to realise that the world was a lot bigger, and more dangerous, than she'd ever thought. And – despite all her planning for worst-case scenarios – she was slowly starting to understand that she might not be able to take the whole world head on, all by herself. And maybe she needed to stop trying to. Maybe she needed to stop viewing everyone around her as A Potential Enemy who she needed to prove wrong. Now that she'd encountered A Real Enemy – or enemies, plural – the rest of the human race didn't look so bad. Even her family; sure, they were overbearing, frustrating, occasionally self-esteem shattering, but right now, Maria would give anything to see them. And the people she'd met in Italy – Nicolina and Rocco had taken them in, even though she and Kennedy had appeared in their barn without warning. Alberto and Paola had driven them all the way to Florence, put them up in a hotel, and tried to get them help, even though she'd lied to them. Rovena had taken her in unquestioningly, cooked her soup, stayed with her until she'd fallen asleep. Dominic had blown his cover to save her life. And before she'd met any of them, tall, awkward, Italian-capped, always-attempting-to-be-gallant Kennedy had shown up at her door and wanted to be her friend …

*

Though currently, Kennedy was not behaving very gallantly. She was still standing by the telephone booth, waiting for the child that *she had sent off pick-pocketing* to return. She felt incredibly guilty, but kept telling herself, over and over again: *I wouldn't be doing this if it wasn't absolutely necessary, I wouldn't be doing this if it wasn't absolutely necessary.*

Gabriele returned ten minutes later.

'How did you go?' she asked.

Gabriele handed her two wallets, a purse and a duffle bag. Kennedy's eyes widened and she tried to act natural, looking around warily at a patrolling security guard.

'Good job,' Kennedy affirmed, her voice higher than usual. 'Let's go sit down.' Kennedy led them to the outskirts of the train station, where trees and lawn were plentiful and roaming police officers were few. They sat on a bench and looked through Gabriele's collection. There was an awful lot of money when she added it all up. She decided she would take twenty euro from each; hopefully, no-one would notice the loss.

'Gabriele,' Kennedy said, 'can you take these over there' – she pointed to an information booth – 'and say someone lost them?'

‘Okay,’ said Gabriele, skipping away.

Now I’ve asked him to lie, Kennedy thought as she watched Gabriele throw everything onto the information booth’s counter, yell ‘LOST!’ and start running back towards her.

But Gabriele didn’t have a trace of guilt on his face. ‘Now can we eat?’ was all he said as soon as he reached her.

I wouldn’t be doing this if it wasn’t absolutely necessary, Kennedy reminded herself, again.

*

One shared pizza, two lemonades and an awkward interaction with the ticket seller later, and they were on a train back to Florence. The train lights flickered on, and Kennedy and Gabriele leaned back against their seats. A woman sitting opposite looked from one to the other, and smiled at Kennedy. ‘Is this your brother?’ she asked.

‘Uh …’

‘Yes,’ Gabriele replied.

‘How sweet.’

Kennedy marvelled at Gabriele’s quick response. A stowaway, a thief, a liar … this child was something. And he sure was useful to have around.

The lady opposite Kennedy reached down into her bag, pulled out her mobile phone, flipped back a panel in the train wall, and plugged her charger into a power socket.

Kennedy’s gasp was theatric.

Gabriele looked at her disapprovingly. ‘What are you doing?’

'Power sockets,' she said in English, not knowing the Italian term. 'Power sockets!' She pointed, then reached into her own pocket and pulled out her phone. 'I can call your parents again!' she tried in Italian. And in her head, she thought, *I can call Maria!* She knew Maria's phone was at the police station, but maybe, just maybe, she had returned, and picked up her phone, and would be on the other end of the line ...

Gabriele took Kennedy's phone. 'Excuse me, *signora*,' he said. 'My sister would like to use your phone charger. We need to call our parents ...'

'Of course, dear! Of course! Here you are!' She unplugged her phone and passed the connection point to Kennedy. 'Mine has plenty of battery. I was just charging it out of habit.'

'Thank you,' Kennedy said enthusiastically. 'Thank you!' She brought her phone to life and could barely contain her joy.

Maria Maria Maria ... she thought, her finger poised over the number pad. But then she looked over at Gabriele, and dialled Paola's number.

'Hello, this is Paola and Alberto ...'

Kennedy left another message, telling them the time they would arrive and reassuring them that Gabriele was fine. Then, her heart pounding in her chest, she dialled Maria's number. The phone rang, and rang, and rang out. Kennedy tried not to let the disappointment show on her face, but she wasn't successful.

Then her phone started ringing.

An unknown number.

'Hello?' she answered cautiously.

'Hi, is that Kennedy?'

Kennedy couldn't believe her ears. 'Maria?'

'Yes. Kennedy?'

'Maria! Yes! It's me!'

Kennedy was so overjoyed, she didn't realise there was no way Maria could have called her unless she'd memorised her number.

(Which, yes, Maria had done, right before her phone battery went flat.

So what.)

'You're okay!' yelled Kennedy. 'Thank God!'

'You're too loud,' Gabriele told her, and Kennedy waved him off.

'Where are you?' they both said at the same time.

'You first,' Kennedy said.

'I'm in Florence. I'm at Rovena's son's house, this is their phone ...'

'Who's Rovena?'

Kennedy heard shuffling and talking in the background. 'Hold on,' Maria told her, and Kennedy heard her talking to someone else. 'Dominic ... Dominic, it's Kennedy, she's my ...'

Kennedy held her breath as Maria paused.

'... she was with me when we first got kidnapped.'

Kennedy felt a brief thud of disappointment, but it wasn't enough to dampen her joy that she had found Maria, that Maria was okay.

'Hello, Kennedy? Where are you?'

Kennedy frowned as she heard a male voice speaking in English. She sat forward in her seat and tried to sound intimidating. 'Who are you?'

'I am a police officer, and I am trying to get Maria to safety.'

'Oh.'

'Are you safe?'

'Kind of. I'm on a train.'

'Kennedy, it is very important that you tell me the truth. Where are you going? What are your plans?'

'Well, uh … I've kind of accidentally got this kid with me and I need to get him back to his parents, so we're on a train to Florence, I guess I'll just keep calling them until they –'

'All right,' Dominic interrupted. 'We will meet you at the station …'

And then the train went through a tunnel, and the call disconnected.

*

'Can I speak to her?' Maria asked Dominic, her heart fluttering way more enthusiastically than she had given it licence to. Rovena, her daughter, her three 'boys' (who were all on the other side of forty), one of their wives and several children were all crammed into the tiny living room and were leaning forward intently.

'I'm sorry, *signorina*, the call disconnected,' Dominic replied, handing her the phone.

Maria tried calling Kennedy again, but the call didn't go through. She was bitterly disappointed, but she didn't want to lose face, so all she said was, 'Oh.'

Dominic turned to the group and explained in Albanian what had transpired. When he got to the part where the phone line had gone dead before Maria could speak to Kennedy, the entire room gave a pitying 'oh!' and looked sadly at Maria. She shrugged and smiled a humorous 'what can you do' smile, but they just kept looking at her sympathetically.

'You poor thing,' said Rovena's daughter, and even though it was in Albanian, Maria knew *exactly* what it meant.

'Maria, do you want to call your family?' Dominic asked.

Maria paused.

Do I want to call my family, she wondered. *Dear God.*

She knew the appropriate answer was 'yes'; objectively, she did want them to know she was safe.

But this conversation was going to be unbearable.

She dialled the only other number she had memorised (as per instructions from Anna, just in case her phone went missing, or was stolen, or overheated due to battery failure and caused a small fire).

The line connected, but no-one spoke.

'Hello …?' Maria asked cautiously.

There was some crackling on the other end, and a delay. And then –

'HELLO? MARIA?'

Maria froze. She could hear them all bustling around the phone, elbowing each other for position, arguing, interspersing each other's sentences with cries of 'she's alive!'

And on the other side of the world, Nonna Lucia burst into tears.

CHAPTER 34

Emotions

'*MADONNA MIA!* WHY HAVE YOU DONE THIS TO ME? MY ONLY GRANDDAUGHTER! WHY?'

'Is that Maria on the phone? Anna, what's going on?'

'I'd be able to *tell* you, Vince, if your mother would *calm down.*'

'LUCIA, *MA STATE ZITTE!* SHUT UP YOUR VOICE!'

'SHUT UP? MY HUSBAND TELL ME TO SHUT UP! OH, *GESU MIO* ...'

'I'm fine, everyone,' Maria cut in. 'Honestly. I'm fine.'

The questioning, once Nonna Lucia managed to calm down, went as expected:

'How did this happen?'

'I got lost.'

'Well, *why* did you get lost?'

'It just happened.'

'So why didn't you call us?'

'I lost my phone.'

'Why did you lose your phone?'

It went on in this vein for a while. The language school had eventually gotten through to Anna, so the Petranellis had known Maria was missing; but, now they'd found her, they couldn't stop asking inane questions. They seemed obsessed with the minute details, which Maria couldn't be bothered explaining because they paled in comparison to getting kidnapped and embroiled in underworld criminal gangs; but because Maria refused to *address* the minute details, they weren't *getting* to the underworld criminal gangs. The circular questioning might have gone on indefinitely, until Vince asked, 'Is this an international call?' and the Petranellis, for whom there was little more sacred than the saving of money on a phone bill, cut to the chase.

'Are you all right?' they asked. 'Are you safe?'

That was the big question, wasn't it.

'I'm with the police,' she said. 'I'm … as safe as possible.'

Dominic gestured for her to hand over the phone, and she did, with relief. He seemed professional enough to pick up that the Petranellis were prone to panic and only needed to know the basics, which were:

1. That she was heading back to Rome;
2. That she was coming home as soon as she could; and
3. That … no, he didn't have any intentions for their daughter, and it was a strange question to ask a police officer.

'*Signorina*,' Dominic said when he was done, passing the phone back to her.

She took a deep breath.

'All right, I'd better go,' she said casually. And then at the last second, on impulse, she added, 'I love you.'

There was a moment of silence, *stunned* silence, and Maria panicked as she realised what she had done.

'What was that?'

'What did she just say?'

'She said "I love you".'

'*Maria* said that? ... Are you sure?'

'OH, MARIA!'

'I have to go!' Maria said, and she hung up the phone.

*

Dominic decided they should get to the station immediately, so they would be there when Kennedy's train pulled in.

Rovena's whole family walked them out the door, hugging and kissing them as if they were farewelling best friends. And Maria didn't understand why, but she was actually feeling *affected*. Emotional, even. First the 'I love you', now the giant lump that had lodged in her throat ... it was ridiculous.

It's probably because I was nearly murdered this morning, she decided, even though, deep down, she knew it was the impending goodbye. She wanted to avoid it, but Rovena grabbed her hand and smiled, which only made Maria more flustered. Then Rovena threw her arms around her; Maria was practically in a headlock, but she was thankful for it, as it distracted her from the strange urge she had to fling her arms around Rovena and sob.

'You're a good girl,' Rovena whispered tearfully. 'Be safe!'

Maria's eyes were welling up, and she was angry at herself. She had known this woman for barely a day and hadn't understood a word she'd said! Why was she being like this?

'Thank you,' Maria finally managed, trying not to let her voice waver. 'Thank you for everything.'

And then they left.

Just in time, because already there were traitorous tears streaming down Maria's face.

*

Dominic didn't say anything as they drove away. But he kept looking over at her meaningfully, and it infuriated her.

'I think you should focus on the road!' she snapped, and Dominic shrugged and looked forwards again.

Hay fever, she decided. *If he asks me if I'm okay, I will say I have hay fever.*

But she was spared from having to justify her rogue emotions when, a few minutes later, one of the tyres blew.

'This shouldn't take long,' Dominic said, getting out of the car.

Maria followed, partly to escape her thoughts and partly out of curiosity, and watched as Dominic opened the boot, removed the spare tyre, and placed the jack under the vehicle.

The weather was glorious that day. Suspiciously glorious. A faint breeze rippled the leaves on the trees that lined the road. In the distance, shopfronts and houses looked like something from a film set. And, strangely, Maria felt like she was entering a test. There was Dominic, effortlessly and gracefully doing manual labour in the sun. The sweat on his brow glistened, and Maria imagined that if he wasn't wearing a button-up shirt, she would probably see his muscles rippling.

As if he had heard her thoughts, Dominic noticed he was getting dirty and removed his shirt, leaving him with just a well-fitted singlet tucked into his unnecessarily tight pants.

Maria decided it was time to get back in the car.

'Have you ever changed a tyre before?' Dominic asked, interrupting her just as she was about to make her move.

'No ...' she admitted.

'Here, I'll show you. It's something everyone needs to know. You don't want to be in a situation where you are alone and don't know how to change one. Would you like to help me with this part?'

'I suppose.'

Dominic smiled and handed her the wheel brace. 'You need to loosen the wheel nuts by turning this to the left,' he explained.

Maria tried to turn the wheel brace to the left, but it didn't budge. 'Nearly got it,' she said, standing up and pushing down hard with both hands.

Nothing.

‘I think it moved that time …’ She put her foot on it and pressed down.

Nothing.

‘Right, just a little more …’ she said, stepping onto the wheel brace with both feet, wishing she was heavier, wishing the stupid thing would move just a little …

‘Would you like some help?’ Dominic asked.

‘I guess,’ she conceded, getting down off the wheel brace.

‘Here,’ he said, placing his arms on either side of her and helping her put pressure on the brace. His breath was sweet and warm on her neck, and Maria knew, after watching variations of this theme in ninety per cent of the romantic comedies she had ever seen, that she should be feeling something – and she was.

She was feeling impatient.

And something that had always been hovering around the edges of Maria’s subconscious finally made itself crystal clear.

As Maria felt the brace move, she leapt up. ‘Wonderful!’ she exclaimed. ‘I did it. Thank you for showing me that, I am sure it will come in handy in the future.’ And she got into the front seat of the car, put her seatbelt on, and locked the door.

Dominic joined her ten minutes later, but all Maria did was sit up properly and clear her throat.

*

‘What do you mean, there’s nothing else you can do?’ Alberto roared.

'I'm sorry, sir,' replied the overworked man behind the ticket counter, 'but we made the announcement three times.'

'He's only eight,' Paola begged. 'Please!'

'Madam, I am not sure what else you expect us to do. You need to go to the police.'

Alberto turned away in frustration and looked desperately through the crowd of transients in Florence station, hoping Gabriele would suddenly stroll out from behind a pillar, announcing 'tricked you!' But there was no sign of him. Alberto was about to turn back when he noticed someone familiar.

'Paola,' he said, grabbing her arm. 'Paola! Look!'

Paola followed his gaze. 'The police officer …' she stammered, and broke into a run.

'Sir! Excuse me! Sir!' she called. 'Please! Wait!'

The police officer stopped and turned. 'Yes, madam?' he said politely.

'I'm sorry, I've forgotten your name,' Paola spoke quickly, 'but you helped us at the station … we had two young people with us, Australian, American …'

'I remember you, madam,' the officer assured her with a smile. 'My name is Officer Spinelli. How can I help you?'

Alberto caught up to the two of them and breathed a sigh of relief. 'Maybe there is a God,' he said.

Roberto Spinelli couldn't help but agree.

CHAPTER 35

Reunion

Maria spotted Kennedy before Kennedy spotted her. She was anxiously looking around the train station, her cap with the Italian flag on it still on her head, an eight-year-old demon trailing behind her …

'There she is!' Maria said to Dominic. 'It's Kennedy!' And try as she might, she couldn't keep the excitement from her voice. Then Kennedy saw her and her whole face lit up with a smile, and Maria's heart skipped a beat, and she realised that this foreign feeling she was experiencing was *joy.* She tried to rein it in, but a new, bold, daring side of Maria decided: if Kennedy chose to hug her, she would allow it. She would bear it heroically. She would not push her off anything or commit any acts of violence at all.

But … Kennedy didn't hug her.

In fact, the closer she got, the more her smile faded.

Maria had no idea what caused the wave of irrationality that swept over Kennedy. But then, from her angle, she couldn't see Dominic – six foot two and the most attractive man Kennedy had ever seen – seeming to appear out of nowhere. And Maria also had no idea about Kennedy's 'you came back for me' fantasy, which – as soon as Dominic put his hand on Maria's shoulder – evaporated like smoke, leaving Kennedy feeling very foolish.

And so, Maria, who had been preparing herself for a display of physical affection and – though she'd rather die than admit it – had nearly been looking *forward* to it, took note of Kennedy's increasingly lukewarm reception, and felt her veins turn to ice.

What was I thinking? she berated herself. *How could I let my guard down like that? She doesn't like me at all. She's angry at me. She's annoyed because I got myself kidnapped at the police station. She's going to judge me for being so weak. Typical. I knew this would happen!*

She tried to shut the voice out, but New Maria had only been liberated for a day and was still very fragile, whereas Maria of Yesterday had had years to develop into the boombox that was ringing around her head. So by the time disappointed, self-conscious Kennedy and internally self-flagellating Maria should have been physically close to each other, they had each schooled their face into casual impassiveness, and stood several feet apart.

'You're here,' Kennedy stated pathetically.

Maria refused to dignify that with a response.

'Ahem,' Dominic broke the silence. 'Maria, this is your friend Kennedy?'

'Yes,' Maria said matter-of-factly. 'Kennedy, this is Dominic. He's an undercover FBI agent.'

Dominic didn't bother to correct her, and Kennedy simply nodded, thinking – like Maria – that the FBI was a global organisation.

'And this young boy?'

'Gabriele,' Gabriele dared.

'He snuck on the train to Rome. I'm trying to take him back to his parents,' Kennedy explained.

Maria raised her eyebrows at Gabriele and shook her head disapprovingly, but he just looked bored.

'Where are you going to meet them?' Dominic asked.

'That's the thing, I can't get onto them. I've got their home number, but it keeps going to voicemail ...'

'What are the parents' names?' Dominic asked, pulling out an old-style flip phone – the kind that looked like it couldn't be tracked.

'Alberto and Paola ... what's your last name?' Kennedy asked Gabriele.

'Sbrana.'

'I will see if I can get a mobile number,' Dominic said.

'How are you going to do that?' Kennedy asked.

But Dominic was already talking to someone on the other end of the line.

Maria rolled her eyes. 'He's FBI, Kennedy.' *If she's going to be annoyed at me for getting kidnapped, at least I have this,* Maria thought.

Maria pretended not to watch Kennedy shuffle around, put her hands in her pockets, take them out, and put them back in again.

Eventually Kennedy attempted to bridge the gap. 'So! How've you been?'

'Fine,' said Maria. 'You?'

Maria didn't understand that this was Kennedy's attempt to make up for her disappointing greeting. But even if she had understood, the narrow window for possible affection had closed, and polite, aloof, unaffected distance was all Maria had left to offer.

'I'm glad you're okay,' Kennedy tried again.

'Well, you too,' Maria replied airily, shutting her down.

Gabriele stood between them, hands on hips, preventing either girl from trying to say anything else.

*

Alberto's mobile rang.

'Answer it, answer it!' Paola hissed urgently, but Alberto wasn't fast enough to stop Officer Spinelli hearing the tune of 'I'm Too Sexy For My Shirt'.

'*Pronto* ...' Alberto answered. His eyes widened.

'Paola! Paola, it's Kennedy!' He passed the phone to her. He admired how easily she broke into English and wished, not for the first time, that he had paid more attention in school.

'Alberto, Gabriele is with Kennedy!' Paola relayed excitedly. 'He accidentally got on the train … they're back here, in Florence …' Paola gasped. 'And Maria is here too!'

'Thank God!' Alberto exclaimed. 'Where can we meet them?'

Paola listened. 'Alberto, do you know where the Hotel Costantini is?'

Alberto shook his head, but Roberto Spinelli spoke up. 'I am familiar with this hotel. I can give you directions.'

'Thank you,' Paola said earnestly, half to Roberto, half to Kennedy. 'Thank you! We will see you as soon as we can!' She hung up and passed the phone back to Alberto. 'Our son is safe,' she said, wrapping her arms around him.

'I'm sorry to interrupt, madam,' said Roberto, 'but if you wish, I can drive ahead of you, show you the way and perhaps help you arrive more quickly. There is still a lot of traffic at this time of night.'

Alberto looked at his watch, shocked at how late it had gotten. 'We can't thank you enough,' he said, his voice full of emotion.

'You are so kind,' Paola agreed, and Roberto Spinelli just nodded.

CHAPTER 36

Split

It was a small hotel with a neon sign in a narrow laneway, but its surroundings were magnificent. The Duomo, which was only a block away, towered behind apartment buildings and hotels, and Maria could see the cathedral's white marble panels laced with emerald green without having to strain her neck too much.

I am going to take in the surroundings this time, she decided. And now that she was being guarded by Dominic the undercover FBI agent, *and* was back together with Kennedy, Maria felt comfortable enough to do so. Not that she and Kennedy were really speaking to each other. Whatever Maria had planned on telling Kennedy when she saw her again – however she might have portrayed those stories in the hopes Kennedy would be impressed, or worried for her, or both – was tightly locked away. *At least now I don't need to worry about her safety*, she told herself, pushing down all those fantasies where she was in Kennedy's arms.

Kennedy's arms were, in fact, quite close to Maria. But only because the lounge area to the left of the lobby desk, which Maria, Kennedy, Dominic and Gabriele were squeezed into, was quite small. They clutched orange juice and sodas from a vending machine; it was way past dinner time, but the group had decided to wait for Gabriele's parents to arrive before eating.

'They're still not here,' announced Gabriele.

The others did not acknowledge this proclamation. It was the fifth time he'd made it.

Gabriele slumped his chin onto his hand and sighed loudly. When no-one responded, he started swinging his legs wildly, making contact with table – and human – legs.

'Gabriele,' Maria said threateningly.

'What?'

'You're kicking me.'

'I'm hungry!'

Maria pursed her lips and tried to bear it, but Gabriele was relentless.

Kick, kick, kick.

Finally, she caved. 'Could we *please* get this kid something to eat?'

'Fine.' Dominic stood up abruptly. 'I will go across the road and get something. You three *stay here*.'

As soon as they were alone, Kennedy took in a large breath.

Here we go, Maria thought, steeling herself for another attempt at conversation.

But Gabriele interrupted them. 'There's Mama,' he observed calmly, pointing out the window. 'And Papa. And a policeman.'

'Thank God,' Maria mumbled, following his gaze. Paola and Alberto were on the opposite side of the street, near the grocery store Dominic had just gone into. Maria stood, getting ready to greet them, but then the policeman came into view and a bolt of fear shot through her. *It can't be*, she thought. But it was. There he was: Roberto Spinelli.

This can't be happening, Maria thought desperately. *This can't be happening!*

But he was unmistakeable. Dread made her vision blurry. Her body felt electric. 'Kennedy!' she whispered urgently. 'Get up! Quickly!'

'What? Why?'

'It's him!' she hissed. 'The policeman, the one who handed me over to Bertoluccio ...'

'Huh?'

'*Kennedy!* Let's go! Now!'

Maria pulled Kennedy and Gabriele out of their chairs. She pushed them both against the wall, where they wouldn't be seen, and peered anxiously out the window to see if Dominic would appear and intervene.

But Spinelli was getting closer to the hotel. And Dominic wasn't appearing. Maria knew she had to act. She waited on edge until Paola, Alberto and Roberto Spinelli had passed the entrance to the lounge area and were at the hotel's front desk, and then, when their backs were towards her, she slipped out the front door. As soon as she was outside, she broke into a run.

'Maria!' Kennedy called after her, but Maria didn't stop.

*

If Maria hadn't been blinded by panic, she would have run into the grocery store and grabbed Dominic. But she wasn't thinking clearly. And this time, the adrenaline made her usual lack of coordination evaporate; she was sprinting like an Olympic athlete.

She could hear Kennedy calling after her, but she couldn't stop. Down barely lit side-streets, past pedestrians taking evening strolls, through squares full of fountains, around flashing mopeds, past the magnificent architecture she had promised to take in, Maria sprinted until her lungs were burning and she had to stop and lean against a wall.

'Do you think we lost them?' Maria gasped as Kennedy finally caught up.

Kennedy might have replied with questions of her own, like 'what the hell is going on' and 'why the hell did you start running', but she was too busy focusing on not passing out.

They were both still doubled over, trying to catch their breath, when Gabriele trotted up to them.

'Gabriele,' Kennedy gulped, the words catching. 'What … what are you doing here?'

'I was following you guys,' Gabriele said innocently.

'Oh my god,' Kennedy groaned. Finally, she summoned the words. 'Maria … what is going on, why …?'

'Kennedy, it was the policeman from the station!'

'Yes, I saw him – but why did you run?'

'He was the one who handed me over to be killed! For being a witness! There was a car waiting outside and he handed me right to the murderers!'

'*What?*'

'Don't you remember, Kennedy?' Maria asked. 'Don't you remember? I went in for questioning, and I never came out! What did you think happened to me?'

Kennedy paused. 'He said you ran away.'

'Why would I do that?'

Kennedy said the next part hesitantly. 'He told us … you were suffering from shock. He said you made up the second body and when you got caught out for lying, you ran …' At Maria's thunderous look, Kennedy repeated hastily, 'He said you were suffering from shock!'

'Kennedy, do I *look* like the type of person who would suffer from shock?'

Kennedy didn't want to reply.

'He said I made up the second body?' Maria's voice nearly broke with the sense of betrayal. 'Is that what you think? Do you think I'm just making everything up?'

'It doesn't matter, Maria! As long as you're safe!'

This statement, intended to be a grand gesture of unconditional love and acceptance, was like a slap to the face. Maria exploded. 'It doesn't *matter*? It doesn't *matter* that I got kidnapped from a police station and held hostage? It doesn't *matter* that I got caught in a mob shoot-out? It doesn't *matter* that I stole a car and crashed it in a field and had to be rescued by an old lady and a man who I thought was a criminal and then got attacked in her farmhouse and ...'

And then the unthinkable happened: Maria burst into tears.

Real tears. Real sobbing. Red, puffy eyes, runny nose, choppy breath, sinking dramatically to the sidewalk and leaning her head against the wall, the whole works.

'I'm fine,' she sobbed. 'I just have hay fever.'

Kennedy shuffled her feet. A few days ago, when they were back in Rome, she would have rushed to Maria's side without hesitation, but now she wasn't sure what the appropriate response was. She felt guilty for doubting her, but she wasn't quite sure Maria was telling the truth.

Gabriele seemed to have no such qualms. He knelt down beside Maria, put his hand on her arm, patted it reassuringly, and handed her a handkerchief.

The fact the two were enemies seemed long forgotten.

'Thanks, Gabriele,' Maria hiccupped.

And it was then that Kennedy realised two things:

1. She had just been shown up by an eight-year-old who apparently carried handkerchiefs; and
2. She had missed her moment. Again.

CHAPTER 37

Exposed

Kennedy's phone rang.

It was Paola, and she sounded anxious. 'We're at the hotel, but you're not here …'

'Well, we were there, but …' Kennedy looked at Maria, who was wiping the last few tears from her eyes and shaking her head urgently. 'Is that policeman still with you?' Kennedy asked Paola.

There was silence on the other end, and then a male voice spoke.

'Kennedy, this is Officer Spinelli. Do you remember me? We spoke at the station.'

'I remember you. What do you want?'

Maria looked at Kennedy, wide-eyed. 'It's okay,' Kennedy mouthed, then turned away so Maria couldn't see her face.

'Kennedy,' Roberto said gently. 'You are with Maria?'

'Yeah?'

'Maria is very sick. She is confused right now. Is that why you ran from the hotel?'

Kennedy paused. Was Maria sick? Was she confused? Had she made the whole thing up?

Kennedy looked at Maria's anxious, tear-stained expression, and her heart clenched.

She made up her mind.

'I know what you did, dirtbag, and you're not coming anywhere near her,' Kennedy said in the most threatening voice she'd ever used in her life, and hung up.

*

Roberto Spinelli dialled the number again, and again, but there was no response.

'What are we going to do?' Paola said, close to tears now. Alberto put his arm around her, frowning and uncharacteristically silent.

Roberto was about to respond when he was punched in the face.

'Roberto Spinelli,' Dominic said. His quest for food had been unsuccessful; he'd realised he must have left his wallet at the hotel, and had returned to get it. That had turned out to be a stroke of luck. With blood oozing out of the knuckles of his right hand, he grabbed Roberto roughly and secured both arms, then lifted him, slamming him against the front desk. The desk clerk just watched, open-mouthed.

'My name is Dominic Cerchi,' he explained to the desk clerk, 'and I am an officer with the ROS. This police officer is corrupt.'

Dominic manoeuvred Roberto's arms so that he could grip both his wrists with one hand, and then dug into his pockets. He would need to call his superior officer. He kept searching.

Where was his phone?

*

'I took these,' said Gabriele, handing Dominic's phone and wallet to Maria.

Kennedy gasped. 'Gabriele, we only steal when we really, really need to!'

Maria raised her eyebrows at Kennedy.

'I took them just in case. And we need them now, don't we?' Gabriele asked. Kennedy was about to concede when Gabriele reached into his pocket and pulled out another wallet. 'Here's yours, too,' he said, handing it to her casually. 'You left it on the train.'

Kennedy gasped again. 'You found it? Why didn't you tell me?'

Gabriele shrugged.

Kennedy's mouth was agape. 'But you made me … we were … we took *so much money from so many people* … why didn't you tell me?'

'You never asked.'

Kennedy gaped, furious, and opened her mouth to give him a piece of her mind.

'Don't yell at him,' Maria interrupted.

And then Gabriele held his hand out to Maria, as if offering to help her to her feet, and *Maria let him.*

Kennedy huffed in disbelief. She was a patient person – *too* patient, some would say – but this was really pushing it. 'We should take Gabriele back to the hotel,' she said to Maria.

'We can't, Kennedy! The policeman!'

'Oh, right,' Kennedy remembered. 'Should we ... go to the police station ...?'

'I don't know how many times I have to explain this to you,' Maria said, clenching her teeth. 'Last time I was at the police station, *I got kidnapped.* We can't trust anyone. We should wait for Dominic. He'll probably try to call his own phone, or he'll call yours, and then we can tell him where we are.'

'I'm still hungry, and I don't know what you two are saying,' Gabriele complained.

Kennedy glared at him for interrupting, but Maria – who was best friends with Gabriele now, apparently – just said in Italian, 'We need to wait for Dominic to call.' Then, seeing the look on his face, she added, 'But we can get something to eat first.'

Gabriele beamed.

Once Gabriele was suitably occupied with pizza, Maria told Kennedy everything that had happened to her. She told her how Roberto Spinelli had herded her out the back of the police station and handed her over to a man named Bertoluccio, who thought she was the daughter of a crime boss and wanted to exchange her for ransom. She told her about the handover, and how she was caught in the gunfire once everyone realised it had all been a mistake. She told her how she stole a car, crashed a car, and woke up at Rovena's.

There was a problem with Maria's re-telling of events, however. Unlike the way she'd rehearsed it in her head – where she was the brave, fearless, sole character, performing feats that would impress Kennedy and make sure she knew she was *just fine, thank you very much* – in this version, she kept adding details about the secondary cast. Such as:

1. How Dominic was unfailingly polite, even though Maria tried multiple times to knock him out;
2. How Dominic had leapt into their getaway car, carried her from the wrecked vehicle, and stopped one of Bertoluccio's henchmen from strangling her with his bare hands; and
3. How Dominic *literally taught her how to change a tyre on the way over.*

There was a reason Maria was doing this. She was mortified that she had cried – her first real display of emotion since she was a pre-teen – and not only had she cried in public, she'd cried in front of Kennedy. Usually, she would try to emphasise to Kennedy – and to herself – that she'd handled all her recent crises without any worries. But Maria's failures were mounting. At this point, *she* was struggling to believe in her own capabilities, so she couldn't expect someone else to believe in them. She also couldn't bear the thought of being challenged or doubted or, god forbid, pitied, so she needed to focus on Dominic's heroism to get her through.

'And now we're here!' Maria finished breezily, making sure not to look directly at Kennedy.

This was unfortunate.

Because if she *hadn't* been so studiously avoiding eye contact, she might have noticed that Kennedy looked like her heart had snapped in two.

'I'm glad you're okay,' Kennedy said, her voice squeaking, which Maria also failed to register.

'Oh yes, I'm fine,' Maria said. 'Once I was with Dominic, I was safe, anyway,' she amended.

Dominic, Dominic, Dominic. Kennedy flinched each time Maria said it, and she was saying it a *lot.*

'So,' Kennedy clarified, 'Lorenzo had nothing to do with it?'

'Nothing. Dominic said his death was a coincidence.'

'So none of this had anything to do with the bracelet.'

Maria didn't reply for a moment, shocked by the change in Kennedy's tone. 'No,' she conceded. 'No, it did not.'

Earlier, Maria had been so wrung out by near-death ordeals that she had actually shed tears. But Kennedy was also being pushed to the limits of her endurance. For the first time in ... ever, Kennedy couldn't help but be a little bit mean. 'Told you,' she said under her breath.

Maria slammed her hand on the table. She was paying attention *now*, that's for sure! 'What is your problem?'

'I haven't got a problem, I was just saying that I knew it had nothing to do with the bracelet.'

Maria glared. She wanted to yell at her, but decided this would be giving her too much ground. 'Fine,' she said, and went back to her pizza.

She knew it would be polite to ask Kennedy what *she* had been up to for the past few days, but Maria found she wasn't interested anymore. Whatever she had imagined, whatever she had – god forbid – *hoped*, she had clearly been wrong about Kennedy. Maria liked to pretend that she didn't have feelings, but if she did, they would be *stinging*.

The three of them finished their meal in silence and walked outside.

'What do we do now?' asked Gabriele.

'We wait for Dominic to call,' Maria answered.

Kennedy scoffed. 'Why don't you just *marry* him then,' she muttered.

Maria did a double take. '*What*?'

'What?'

'You just said something.'

'No I didn't.'

'Did you say something about me marrying Dominic?'

Kennedy rolled her eyes. 'I wasn't being serious.'

Somehow, this was worse. 'Oh, you don't think I could handle marrying Dominic? Is that it? Well, maybe I will marry him, if you keep that up! Maybe I will!'

It was a ridiculous threat, but Kennedy was shaken by it, and turned away so Maria wouldn't see just how upset she was.

Fine, ignore me then, Maria thought childishly, and let her mind wander back to the tyre-changing incident. She thought she had better develop some feelings for the man, just in case. She imagined herself walking down the aisle and passing Kennedy sitting in a pew at the back, looking regretful. *That would show her*, she thought.

CHAPTER 38

Confession

Ten uncomfortable, silent minutes later, Dominic still hadn't called.

And it was getting late.

'Maybe we should find somewhere to wait,' Kennedy said politely, already feeling very sorry for her irrational behaviour earlier.

But Maria showed no sign of opening up again. 'Yes,' she agreed stiffly. 'Dominic would want us to find somewhere safe.'

'Let's go then,' Kennedy said, doing a very good job at hiding the fact that Dominic's name was stabbing her in the heart. 'You ready, Gabriele?'

Gabriele nodded, and they wandered – with Maria keeping an eye out for assailants – until they found a cheap hotel. Their room wasn't fancy; a double bed, a small ensuite, a TV.

There were no chairs to sit on, so they took off their shoes, sat on the bed, and tried to understand what was on the TV. Gabriele was content, but the other two kept checking the digital alarm clock.

8.00pm.

8.05pm.

8.07pm.

Before, when they were out on the streets, Maria had wanted nothing more than to sleep for a week; now, she was full of energy. Sleep didn't seem to be on the cards while there was so much uncertainty.

And, apparently, animosity.

Maria kept glancing over at Kennedy, who was pretending to be interested in the television, but looked noticeably forlorn. Maria still felt a bit cross, but she knew it was going to be a long night unless she tried to break the standoff.

Plus – she had missed Kennedy. She still missed Kennedy.

Would it kill her to admit it? Maria wrestled with herself. It would be painful, yes, but she'd been through worse. And maybe she could bear it if it meant things could go back to normal.

'All right! Enough is enough!' she finally snapped, making Kennedy jump. She waited until Kennedy was looking at her, then said firmly, 'Thanks.'

Kennedy's eyebrows scrunched in confusion. 'Sorry?'

Maria huffed, annoyed that Kennedy was making this so difficult. 'I *said,* thanks!' And then she said, softly and truthfully, 'I'm glad you're here. With me.'

Kennedy blinked several times in quick succession, and stayed silent. Maria knew Gabriele was listening, but it couldn't be helped. She had to say it, even with a witness there. At least he didn't understand English. She took a deep breath and continued.

'Okay, you've been a bit of a jerk about the bracelet,' she said, 'but you believed me about the policeman. And you stayed with me. I'm just really ...' Stuck for words, she repeated herself. 'I'm glad you're here. I ... I missed you.'

There!

She'd said it!

Maria was proud of herself. It felt good to say, as if she were getting something off her chest.

Kennedy didn't say anything for a long time. *Too long,* Maria thought, getting annoyed with her again.

'I missed you too,' Kennedy said, and when Maria didn't snap her head off, she continued, 'and I know I was being a jerk. Sorry about that. It isn't normal for me. I was, uh, you know. A bit jealous.'

Maria stared at her, unable (or unwilling) to process this information. 'Of what?'

'Oh, you know.' Kennedy laughed self-consciously.

Maria didn't know. Not really. But the atmosphere in the room had become so much lighter, it was practically sunny. And hearing Kennedy's laugh made Maria's heart start doing little flips – much to her chagrin. Somehow, they had stumbled onto very shaky ground, and she needed to reel things back in. 'Well,' she said, ever the poet.

'There's no need to be jealous about something that doesn't exist.'

'Right, sorry.' Kennedy laughed self-consciously, shaking her head, her smile growing wider and wider. Her whole body relaxed, and the bed – which had a *very* unsupportive mattress – made her lopsided, and dangerously close to rubbing her shoulders against Maria's.

Maria got up and opened the window.

She looked at the street below her. It was so different from her neighbourhood back home, with its streets that looked deserted and suspicious as soon as the sun went down. Her family, and all the old Italians in her part of town, would be well and truly in bed by now, locked safely inside houses with windows reinforced by impenetrable roller shutters. But this neighbourhood was still so full of *life*. Maria watched as groups of people ambled slowly by, bathed in the yellow tinge of streetlights, while others dined in restaurants over the road. She could hear music. It looked so happy outside.

'It's beautiful here,' she said, sticking her head and arms out the window and feeling the warm breeze on her skin. 'I wish we could go for a walk.' She sighed.

'Why can't we?' Kennedy asked, opportunistic as ever.

'Well … the murderers …'

'It's well-lit outside, and there are lots of people out,' said Kennedy, whose only experience with the criminal element had been the short journey in the boot, and who had a very short memory anyway.

Maria looked unsure.

'We'll have Dominic's phone with us, for when he calls,' Kennedy said.

'What if he doesn't call?'

'I don't think we should worry about what ifs – we'll deal with what happens, when it happens.'

Maria bit her lip, trying to decide if she should agree. She did not care for Kennedy's laissez-faire approach, but she was right – there were lots of people around. Surely there was safety in numbers. Plus, if they didn't go for a walk, what else were they going to do? They couldn't understand the shows on the TV. They had already had a heart-to-heart. And Kennedy was looking at her with hopeful eyes, and smiling … it made the events of the past few hours, even the past week, seem foreign. The idea that there were murderers out to get her suddenly seemed ridiculous. Maybe it *was* ridiculous! Maybe it would be nice to just go for a walk, completely carefree. Maybe they could just be two normal people with two normal lives, enjoying the evening air. Two people …

And Gabriele, she remembered as she watched the eight-year-old flick through the TV channels. She envisioned what he would do in the hours to come, when he got bored, or hungry …

That clinched it. 'Put your shoes back on,' she told him.

CHAPTER 39

Musician

It was a spectacular night. Everywhere they walked they heard music playing, whether it was from a restaurant or a busker or a car with its windows down. The city alternated between modern and ancient, and once they reached the river, Kennedy leaned over the edge in wonder.

'This is the most beautiful city.'

'Yes, it's quite nice,' Maria agreed, looking around – partly to take in the scenery, and partly to check for any suspicious activity.

Kennedy pointed to two men walking past, each wearing a Robin Hood style cap. 'Those are interesting hats, I wonder why they're wearing them? Is it a traditional folk dress thing?'

Maria saw them too. 'I don't know. Gabriele?' she asked. 'What type of hats are those?'

'They're soldier hats,' Gabriele replied.

Maria and Kennedy both nodded with respect.

Safe in the knowledge there were soldiers nearby, Maria started to relax. 'Just look at this,' she said, waving her arm along the riverside, lit by circles of lamplight and crossed with arched stone bridges. 'Have you ever seen anything like it?'

'No, I haven't,' Kennedy agreed, looking into her eyes and smiling softly.

Maria felt her knees go unstable and her stomach feel weak. Her brain went into overdrive.

It's the music in the background. It's the soft lighting. It's the near-death experiences, her rational voice lectured, trying to snap her out of it.

But it wasn't working. Maria's heart raced, she felt warm all over, and in an uncharacteristic surge of daring, she committed the most wanton act she'd ever committed: she smiled back, with *full eye contact.*

If Alberto had been there, cheering Kennedy on, he would have been beside himself. This was *it!* This was the moment to be seized!

But Kennedy wasn't able to seize anything, because suddenly, a few metres away, a car mounted the kerb.

Maria grabbed Kennedy's arm. 'It's them!' she yelled. 'We have to go!'

They both grabbed at Gabriele, who didn't seem particularly concerned, and they were about to start running to safety when the car *un*-mounted the kerb, paused, and did a very painful thirteen-point turn.

It turned out it was not Luca, or one of Bertoluccio's other men, or someone working for Angelo Petranelli, or someone connected to a corrupt cop.

It was just a terrible driver.

Maria frowned.

'Are you okay?' Kennedy asked, worried.

'Yes. I may have overreacted. I apologise,' Maria said, feeling very stupid. 'But we should probably get back to the hotel.'

'Good idea. Which way is it?' Kennedy asked.

They looked at each other.

'Well, what's it called?' Maria asked.

Kennedy looked at Gabriele. Gabriele looked at Maria. Maria looked at Kennedy.

'I can't remember,' Kennedy admitted finally.

'The room key card!' Maria said. 'It would be on the room key card, wouldn't it?'

Kennedy didn't say anything.

'You forgot it, didn't you?'

'Why was the room key card my responsibility?' Kennedy asked.

Maria rolled her eyes.

Perfect night ruined.

'Well, let's start walking, and hopefully we'll see it,' said Kennedy, somewhat sheepishly.

'We'll go that way,' said Maria, gesturing. 'It's north.'

They walked (south) to a well-lit square. It was surrounded by shop windows, and filled with people laughing and strolling and stopping at various vendors.

But Maria couldn't relax. She looked around the crowd. The car on the kerb had shattered whatever illusion she had of safety, and her nerves were on edge.

Kennedy wasn't faring much better. 'What's that guy doing?' she muttered, frowning. Across the square, a man was walking towards them.

'Where?' Maria asked, shooting her head around wildly.

Kennedy tried to play it cool, and nodded towards the man.

Maria cursed her five-foot genetics. 'I can't see anyone!'

'He's walking towards us.' Kennedy switched languages. 'Gabriele, can you see that guy?'

'The angry one?' Gabriele said.

'Yes,' Kennedy said.

Maria felt a jolt of fear. She strained her neck, trying to see who they were talking about. She didn't know how Gabriele had managed to spot him. There were so many people. There was so much noise. *Everyone* seemed to be walking towards them.

'Kennedy, what do we do?' she asked, fear in her voice.

'It's okay,' said Kennedy calmly. 'There are those soldiers again.'

'The same ones?' Maria asked. 'Oh wait … there's another one!'

'There are more over there.' Kennedy pointed. 'We're safe!'

'What's going on?' Maria asked. 'Gabriele, is today some kind of special day, like a celebration for soldiers?' If it was, she couldn't believe their luck. Even if it wasn't, she couldn't believe their luck. They were saved! Nobody was going to try anything in a square full of military!

'Maybe,' said Gabriele. 'Maybe that's why they're selling those.'

And only then did Maria and Kennedy see the stand of Alpini mountain troop hats, going for ten euro apiece.

Maria gulped.

Suddenly a trumpet exploded behind them. They turned to see a score of men and women – all wearing the Alpini mountain troop hats and holding brass instruments and snare drums – marching their way.

'It's a marching band!' yelled Kennedy unnecessarily. 'We have to get out of here!'

'Typical Americans,' sniffed an old Italian couple that Kennedy accidentally elbowed in her haste to get away.

'Wait! Kennedy!' Maria tried to call over the trumpets. 'I've got a plan!'

Maria still couldn't see her pursuer, but she was *not* going to let him catch up.

And so, Maria decided to implement yet another plotline from another bad film: the old 'Escape by Pretending to be Part of the Marching Band' trick. She yanked both Kennedy and Gabriele by the arm, pulled them into the thick of the trumpet section, and fell in step. Both she and Gabriele were quite short and felt very protected. But Kennedy's head was protruding, and in among the authentic Alpini costumes, her cap with the Italian flag on it stood out like a sore thumb.

'Maria ...' she complained.

'Trust me!' she yelled.

'*I'm trying my be-e-est,*' Kennedy sang through gritted teeth, trying to smile and blend in.

'It's working,' yelled Maria. 'We're marching right through the square to safety!'

But she spoke too soon. The trumpets ceased, the drums rolled, and somebody blew a whistle. A trombone handle swung around and narrowly missed Kennedy's head.

'They're spinning!' yelled Maria. Everyone was turning on their heels, changing direction and walking two steps forward, one step back, and the three runaways were exposed.

'We have to get out of here!' Kennedy yelled, panicking and pushing a saxophone player out of the way. The saxophone player recovered quickly and pretended nothing had happened, to his credit, while Maria and Gabriele ducked a little more considerately out of the marching band's throes.

'Is he still chasing us?' Maria asked once they were out of the musicians' way.

Kennedy looked around worriedly. There he was – the same determined look on his face, the same clenched fists – yelling at another man who had parked his car *very* badly, and was blocking the vehicles around him.

Kennedy swallowed hard. Maria was vibrating with ferocity and looked as if she was prepared to lead them straight back into the marching band. And Gabriele, who could see the car exchange very clearly, looked Kennedy right in the face.

And she knew that he knew.

Oh god.

Kennedy steeled herself as he opened his mouth to embarrass her once again.

'We lost him,' Gabriele said, and Maria deflated with relief.

And despite everything the kid had put her through, in that moment, Kennedy felt so much solidarity with Gabriele, she could have cried.

'This way,' he said confidently, and led them back towards the river.

'This looks familiar …' Kennedy murmured.

'There's the hotel,' Maria announced. 'Look!'

And there it was.

The distant music of the marching band wasn't quite the same as the angelic choirs that should have been proclaiming their find, but it did the job.

CHAPTER 40

Found

As soon as they got back to their hotel room, Gabriele ran to the bathroom. Maria and Kennedy had just collapsed on the bed (Kennedy, flopping her whole body; Maria, sitting formally, hands on knees) when they both heard a noise.

Buzzing. Vibrating.

'Dominic's phone …' Kennedy said.

Maria jumped up. 'I can't find it!' she said, frantically searching around the room.

'Where did you leave it?'

'I can't remember!'

Kennedy leapt up and joined in the search. She found it underneath her zip-up jumper. But it wasn't ringing.

'It's yours! It's *yours!*' Maria cried, pointing to Kennedy's phone, which was plugged into the opposite wall.

Kennedy grabbed it. 'Hello?'

'Who am I speaking to?' came the voice from the other end.

'Who am *I* speaking to?' Kennedy demanded.

'Just give it to me,' Maria huffed, grabbing the phone from Kennedy's hand. 'Dominic? Is that you?'

'Maria, yes, it is Dominic here. Where are you?'

'We're in a hotel!'

'You are safe? You have Gabriele with you?'

'Yes, we're all fine.'

'Good. Tell me where you are. I will bring Gabriele's parents and then we will get you somewhere safe.'

Maria picked up the hotel brochure from the nightstand and read out the name, address and room number.

'Thank you – it is close. We will be there soon. Maria?'

'Yes?'

'It is nearly over now.'

Dominic hung up.

'Why did he take so long to call?' Kennedy asked.

'I don't know …' Maria replied honestly, before noticing the mobile screen.

Seventeen missed calls.

'Seventeen missed calls!' she exclaimed. 'How did we miss that?'

Neither said anything. Kennedy didn't admit she'd accidentally left her phone in the hotel when they had gone for The Walk. Maria didn't admit she had forgotten that Kennedy's phone existed.

But both let it go. They were safe, and their ordeal – and their time looking after Gabriele – was nearly over. Maria sighed with relief. She turned to Gabriele as he emerged from the bathroom. 'Your parents will be here soon,' she said.

'Okay,' said Gabriele, as if the idea didn't bother him, but he'd be fine either way.

*

Paola, Alberto and Dominic arrived shortly afterwards. They raced past the receptionist and took the elevator straight up to level four.

'It's all right, Alberto, we're nearly there,' said Paola, trying to calm her agitated husband.

'I know, I know,' Alberto said, urging the elevator to move faster. When the door opened, Alberto rushed out and was at Room 403 before the others had even stepped into the hallway.

'Gabriele!' he yelled, pounding on the door.

The door creaked open slowly, revealing … no-one.

The room was empty.

'Gabriele!' Alberto yelled again, panic in his voice, as Paola and Dominic caught up with him.

Maria emerged from behind the door with a lamp in her hand. 'He's in the bathroom,' she said, as Kennedy crawled out from behind the nightstand.

'Maria put him in there in case it was one of the bad guys at the door,' Kennedy explained. Her weapon was a pair of shoes – there hadn't been a lot of time to prepare, so Kennedy could only work with what she had.

Alberto laughed with relief and Paola let out a cry as Gabriele opened the bathroom door and walked calmly over to them. They knelt down and wrapped their arms around him, kissing him, crying, and reciting the usual parental pattern of concern: are you all right, we were so worried, don't ever do that to us again, we are so glad you're okay, where have you been all this time …

'We were waiting for you to call your phone,' Maria told Dominic, putting the lamp down. 'We didn't think you'd call Kennedy …'

'That phone makes calls, it doesn't receive them,' Dominic said. 'But it doesn't matter now. We have found you.'

'What happened to the policeman?'

'He is in custody.'

'So we're safe from him now?'

'Yes. However, Roberto Spinelli is a corrupt police officer, and if there are others, they will be anxious to make sure he is not convicted …'

'I'm a witness for that too, aren't I?' Maria sighed. 'And Bertoluccio, and Luca, and Petranelli, have they …'

'They haven't been arrested yet, no. That is why it is important we get you to your embassies.'

Across the room, Alberto and Paola finally released Gabriele from their group hug and made their way over. 'Kennedy …' they chorused. 'Maria …'

And then Kennedy and Maria were being smothered.

'Thank you so much for saving our son!'

'What would we have done without you?'

'Was he any trouble?'

'We can never repay you for what you have done.'

'You really are the most amazing young people.'

It was hard to breathe, but Maria and Kennedy bore it stoically.

'Be honest,' Paola said finally. 'Was he well-behaved?'

Maria and Kennedy didn't dare look at each other. 'Very well-behaved,' they replied.

Paola wiped the tears from her eyes and took both of Maria's hands into hers. 'And you,' her voice wavered. 'I am so glad you are safe. We thought you had run away! I am so sorry.'

'Oh, don't worry, I was completely fine,' said Maria.

'I am still so glad you are safe,' Paola repeated, seeing through Maria entirely.

Maria pretended she didn't notice.

Alberto had also stopped crying and was back to his usual cheerful self. He pulled Kennedy to the side. 'So?' he asked, grinning.

'Oh, that,' Kennedy said sheepishly.

Alberto read her easily. 'Don't worry,' he said. 'The moment will come.' He clapped a hand on Kennedy's shoulder and winked. Kennedy laughed nervously and turned to make sure Dominic and Maria weren't watching. Dominic was.

*

'Maria, Kennedy, we need to take our son home,' Alberto said. 'This has been too much adventure for us!'

'But we will see each other again,' added Paola. 'Our fates are intertwined!'

The farewell didn't seem real to any of them. They'd been through this before, and found saying goodbye was much more cheerful this time around.

Maria and Kennedy looked at each other, then knelt down so they were at Gabriele's height. Kennedy took a deep breath, as if getting ready to say something profound and moving.

'Bye,' said Gabriele, beating them to it.

'... bye,' they both replied, startled. Even Maria had expected it to be more emotional than that. But apparently not.

'Goodbye and good luck!' shouted Alberto.

Kennedy kept her eyes keenly on Gabriele, to make sure he actually went with his parents and didn't casually stroll out of the bathroom or appear from behind the curtains or crawl out from under the bed ten minutes after they left. But Alberto and Paola had similar ideas. They each had a hold of one of his hands and were holding on for dear life. Kennedy was glad; Gabriele looked calculating.

CHAPTER 41

Water

By the time Paola, Alberto and Gabriele left, it was late.

'Let's stay put for the night,' Dominic suggested. 'I'll take you to your embassies first thing in the morning.'

Kennedy agreed readily, already yawning over in the corner, and of course Maria wasn't going to argue, but she felt very frustrated.

This would be the *third time* she was spending the night with Kennedy – first in the barn, then in the hotel Alberto paid for, and now this. Maria's feelings about this were all over the place. She'd made peace with the fact that Kennedy had an effect on her. She'd given up trying to pretend otherwise. But sometimes she was so infuriating! Hot one minute, cold the next, losing room keys, bringing the bracelet into everything. And yet Maria *still* wanted her around – and those thoughts of having Kennedy's arms around her hadn't stopped.

Now they'd be forced to share a bed together, again, and Maria frowned in consternation.

God forbid she be given space to process her feelings in her own time!

Not that there's much time left, said the irritating inner voice that had been getting louder and louder the longer she'd been in Italy. And Maria quickly pushed down the realisation that 'going home' meant 'leaving Kennedy', because that's the last distraction she needed while she was focusing on staying alive …

Maria had no idea that her warring emotions were making her facial expressions positively fierce.

'Do you, uh, want me to sleep on the floor …?' Kennedy asked, rubbing the back of her neck.

'Oh! No, of course not, ha ha. Not like we haven't done this before!'

'Ha ha! Phew! Ha ha.'

'Ha ha ha!'

Why they felt the need to turn into comedians when they were nervous, Maria did not know.

Dominic, who was fluffing a pillow and gallantly preparing a place to sleep on the limited carpet space, looked at them curiously. Maria turned her laughter into a cough.

'I'm going to, uh, take a shower, if that's okay?' Kennedy asked, sobering.

'Of course!' Maria waved her off. She fussed around for a while, straightening the nightstand Kennedy had hidden behind, straightening her shoes, straightening Kennedy's shoes, sitting on the bed, standing up from the bed, straightening the covers …

Kennedy was taking a long time. Maria listened as she heard the water stop running, and felt her breath catch … and then she heard the sound of the hotel's cheap hair dryer.

Maria huffed. Why did Kennedy need to make such a production out of everything!

She decided to stop waiting and get it over with.

As soon as she lay down, the cheap mattress dipped dramatically and she rolled right into the centre.

Of course.

'Sorry I took so long,' Kennedy announced, emerging from the bathroom. She looked … *soft*, Maria thought, her heart suddenly in her throat – and her usually absent powers of observation became so acute then, so honed, that she registered that *Kennedy wasn't wearing a bra.*

She felt like she had sinned, just for thinking it. This changed *everything*.

Kennedy seemed to have no idea what she had done to Maria; she just walked over to her side of the bed and slipped under the covers as if nothing was amiss.

And then the mattress collapsed.

And Kennedy rolled right into Maria.

She was only there for a few seconds, max, but it was enough for Maria to feel Kennedy's whole body pressed against her, and register that she was soft, and warm, and smelled like soap, and that her own body was reacting, in a *positive* way, and *this*, this was *far* too much to handle.

For goodness' sake! she thought, throwing out her arms and clawing at the edge of the bed to pull herself away.

'Oops! Sorry! Didn't mean for that to happen!' Kennedy said.

'Ha ha ha!' Maria replied.

'Ha ha ha ha!'

And then it was painfully awkward.

And frustratingly quiet.

The earlier nightlife – the pedestrians and mopeds and yet more versions of Frank Sinatra's 'My Way' being played on piano accordions – had died down, and the silence was thick.

And of course, Kennedy had to break it.

'Goodnight, Maria,' she whispered. And then, 'I'm really glad you're safe.'

And even though her body was so far away from Kennedy that Dominic probably could have fitted between them, the words felt so intimate that Maria burned right up.

She knew she should say something back. But what should she say? That she was glad Kennedy was safe too? That she didn't feel right when they were apart? That, believe it or not, she was *attracted* to her, physically? That none of this made sense to her and she was furious with herself for feeling this way, but it seemed completely beyond her control?

But Maria didn't say anything. Maybe Kennedy would think she was asleep, instead of wide-eyed and clinging to the edge of the mattress. She stayed that way, frozen, until she heard Kennedy sigh, and reshuffle, and eventually snore softly.

She felt guilty for the rest of the night.

*

Maria woke up uncomfortably. She had managed to wedge herself into the narrow gap between the mattress and the nightstand, which was the only thing preventing her from falling off the bed altogether.

'Morning,' Kennedy said neutrally, from the other side of the mattress.

'Morning,' Maria replied, wondering if she should say something to make up for the night before.

'Morning,' Dominic joined in from the floor, before she had the chance.

That's all anyone said until he led them to his car.

'What's going to happen once we get to the embassies?' Maria asked.

'We'll get your travel documents in order.'

'Will I need to testify ...?'

Dominic nodded. 'You are a very brave girl, Maria.' (Maria didn't respond to this comment, but she was secretly glad someone had finally noticed.) 'But,' he continued, 'it is not safe for you in Italy. Bertoluccio is a dangerous man. Petranelli is worse. That's why you must return to your home country right away.'

This is it, then, she realised. Maria was going home. *Really* going home, unlike all the other times when she was supposed to be going home but had ended up in shootouts and strangers' homes and various hotels.

Which meant she would be safe, soon. And with her family.

And away from Kennedy.

She peered up at the rear-view mirror and caught a glimpse of Kennedy; she was staring out the window, deep in thought. And Maria allowed herself a brief, indulgent moment where she wondered if, maybe, Kennedy was thinking about her.

*

The car ride to the embassies was taking a very long time. Dominic was driving unbelievably slowly. The traffic was impenetrable. When they got onto a road by the riverside, they stopped completely.

'Come on,' cursed Dominic.

'Is it usually like this?' Kennedy asked from the back.

'Sometimes, not often,' Dominic said, sighing impatiently.

Maria leaned over the dashboard so she could get a better look. 'I think there's been an accident.'

'What? How do you know?' asked Dominic.

'There are police.'

They crawled closer and closer, but there was no accident. The police were mostly waving people by, and occasionally pulling a vehicle to the side and asking to speak to the driver. As soon as Dominic's car approached, they gestured for him to stop.

A policeman knocked on the window, and Maria's heart started to thud.

'What now …' Dominic muttered. 'It will be okay,' he said to Maria and Kennedy before opening the window. He looked up at the policeman. 'Yes?'

'I'll need you to step out of the car, sir. All three of you,' the policeman said in Italian.

'What for?'

'Step out of the car, sir. Now.'

Maria gulped.

Dominic was arguing with the policeman now, and they were both speaking louder and faster, too fast for her to understand. She considered doing what she had done before, and slamming her foot on the accelerator, but Dominic was in the way. The road ahead had cleared a little. Why wasn't Dominic slamming his foot on the accelerator?

'Miss,' the police officer spoke to Maria over Dominic's head. 'You must trust me. He is a dangerous man. Get out of the car. We will help you.'

'You lying son of a bitch!' Dominic yelled. 'Maria …'

Maria frowned. Dominic wasn't dangerous! This had to be a mistake …

'Get out of the car, miss,' the police officer repeated, and then another police officer made his way to Maria's side, and immediately Dominic reached over her and pushed the lock down on her door. She was either saved, or she was trapped. Which was it? Should she trust Dominic? What if he *wasn't* an undercover agent? What if Dominic was playing both sides, and this was all some complicated plot to betray Bertoluccio and return her to Petranelli for the two million euro?

Now the policeman was opening Kennedy's door.

'Get off me!' Kennedy yelled as the police officer tried to drag her out.

Maria desperately tried to decide what to do. Should she try to get Kennedy back in the car? Or should she try to get out too? What was going on?

The car hiccupped forward.

'Damn gears,' Dominic cursed, adjusted the gear stick, and slammed his foot on the accelerator. Kennedy kicked the man off her and managed to slam her door shut. They sped forward, leaving the police officers behind.

'It's a trap. You know it is a trap,' Dominic said, trying not to yell, even though the tension was evident.

Maria faltered, her head still screaming in doubt, but Kennedy immediately said, 'We know.' And when Maria heard Kennedy say it, she realised it was true.

'We know,' she echoed. 'We trust you.'

Dominic nodded, and gave Kennedy a brief but grateful look. He turned his attention back to the road. They were moving again, thankfully, but the traffic was thick.

Dominic reached into his pocket, then cursed. 'My phone,' he snapped. 'Who's got my phone?'

Kennedy nervously handed it over from the back, and Dominic dialled a number while manoeuvring the vehicle with one hand. Someone on the other end picked up, and Dominic started yelling. Kennedy and Maria looked at each other helplessly. They had no idea what he was saying, but they assumed … hoped, rather … it was something about backup.

After only a few hundred metres, they had to stop near a bridge. There was a wall of cars in front of them, and nowhere left to go. Maria looked behind them. Two police officers were fast approaching on foot.

'Get out,' Dominic shouted. 'Get across the bridge!' and all three of them exited the car and ran. Pedestrians who saw them coming tried to duck out of the way, but others weren't so lucky and were shouldered to the side, Kennedy apologising every step of the way.

It wasn't until they were midway across the bridge that they saw people coming at them from ahead, too. They were trapped.

'Bertoluccio's men,' hissed Dominic, recognising them. 'Stay behind me.'

Two men lunged at Dominic, and Maria gasped and grabbed Kennedy's arm.

'Stay behind me,' Kennedy copied, but that made Maria realise she was *holding onto Kennedy.*

She released her immediately.

But there was no need for fear. Dominic blocked the first man's punch and grabbed hold of his wrist while the other man attacked. He ducked the second assailant's blow too, responded with a kick to the stomach, and elbowed the first man in the head.

'Run!' he yelled, and the three of them were back to tearing across the bridge.

As soon as they got to the other end, Dominic yelled, 'Down here!' He led the way down some stone stairs to the embankment. Maria saw why: more of Bertoluccio's men were rushing towards them, quickly approaching the other side of the bridge.

Step after step after step; Maria's legs were tired. Who knew bridges were so high? Something flew past her and collided with the stone wall on her right. She noticed the bullet hole it left.

'They're *shooting* now?' Kennedy yelled, shocked.

They shot again.

'Jump!' instructed Dominic. 'We will have to jump.'

'Jump where?' Maria asked.

Dominic didn't answer. He just pushed.

As Maria fell into the river below, she decided that – no matter what happened with Kennedy – she would not be marrying Dominic after all.

*

When she reached the water, she just kept falling. And falling. Only now she couldn't breathe. She thrashed her arms and legs, trying to stop herself. She couldn't breathe, or see, and she didn't know which way was up.

Was this it?

Was she dying?

She didn't want to die.

She kept thrashing.

Thankfully, the river was flowing gently and Maria wasn't being swept away.

But that didn't change the simple fact that Maria couldn't swim.

CHAPTER 42

Slaughterhouse

Kennedy watched Maria fall and was filled with horror.

'What did you do that for?' she yelled as another bullet collided with the wall next to her.

Dominic didn't reply, just pushed again.

Kennedy was slightly better equipped and landed somewhat more gracefully than Maria, quickly rising to the surface and treading water. 'Maria!' she cried, swirling around desperately.

'Kennedy!' Maria spluttered.

Kennedy grabbed one of Maria's flailing arms. Maria wasn't trying to be obstructive, but in her panic she clung to Kennedy like a limpet, pinning her arms to her body.

Kennedy started sinking.

Thankfully, Dominic dove in shortly after, barely making a splash. He streamlined over, grabbed a hold of Kennedy's shirt, and pulled them to the riverbank. They coughed and spluttered their way out of the water.

'Thank you,' Maria gasped, having not yet relinquished Kennedy.

'No problem,' Kennedy said, her voice higher than usual.

Dominic sighed. 'This way,' he said, leading them along the embankment, under the bridge, and ducking behind a pile of crates.

The people chasing them were still a long way away, but Maria could see them moving quickly, silently, murderously down the stairs. So far, Maria, Kennedy and Dominic were hidden. But if they tried to run, they would be out in the open; exposed.

'Here,' said Dominic.

'Where …' Maria started, but then realised. In among the crates was a door in the stone wall. There was no handle, only a heavy lock bolting it shut. Effortlessly, Dominic pulled out his gun – which, fortunately, had a silencer – shot the lock, and opened the door. And before Maria could tell him that she didn't like small spaces, Dominic pushed them inside and closed the door behind them.

It was pitch black. And musty. And Maria imagined she could hear rats, crabs, and giant cockroaches scurrying and plotting a full-scale attack. She frowned.

'Kennedy?' she whispered, unable to keep the urgency from her voice.

'Here,' Kennedy said.

The two girls fumbled around until they found each other's arms, and, once again, Maria clung to her. And it seemed all Maria's usual hesitancy for physical contact had gone right out the window.

There was silence now, except for the sound of their breathing – and Dominic, who was cursing because his waterlogged phone was now useless. He tried to get his lighter to work.

It didn't.

'What do we do?' whispered Maria.

Dominic replied from somewhere behind her, keeping his voice low. 'There's a staircase here. It leads into a small room that's attached to an underground storehouse. We just need to wait until our eyes adjust to the dark, and we will see which way to go.'

'Are you sure?' Kennedy asked. 'What if it's a dead end?'

'It's not a dead end,' Dominic replied. 'Keep your voice down! We can't let them know we are here.'

Neither of them asked any more questions, but Maria was not happy about where they were headed. She had seen the films. Bad things happened in storehouses. Like shady meetings. And drug deals. And serial killers who hung people from the roof by hooks …

'Move forward, slowly,' Dominic instructed. 'Shuffle your feet so you can feel the edge of each step, and walk down carefully.'

The darkness was terrifying. All Maria could think about was bumping into a gutted corpse that was hanging from the ceiling. She heard dripping. Was it blood? Her mind overwhelmed her.

Now was not the time for Maria to acknowledge this, but the truth was, all her years of 'prepared for anything' bravado were made completely void by being in a dark, enclosed space. Maria's imagined threats – and even her real ones – had always been *above* ground. This was something she had never conjured a plan for.

'Kennedy!' she whispered again, holding onto her arm.

'It's okay, Maria,' Kennedy said comfortingly as they reached the bottom of the stairs.

Drip, drip, drip, Maria heard. Drip, drip, drip.

It's blood, she thought. *I know it is.*

And then the unthinkable happened.

And it was worse than running into a gutted corpse with its intestines pouring onto the floor. Much, much worse.

She ran into a spiderweb.

Maria shrieked in terror as her arms and head were coated in thin, sticky mesh. 'Get me out of here!' she hollered, the revulsion rising in her throat. Suddenly her whole body seemed sensitive; she imagined black widows and redbacks and funnel web spiders that had transcended continents, was sure she could feel them crawling inside her clothes, into her shoes, down her back, in her hair … she lashed out wildly with her arms and legs, and when Kennedy and Dominic tried to hold her, she hit them both, multiple times.

'It's okay!' they tried to tell her. 'Maria! Hold still! Calm down!'

But Maria would not hold still, and she refused to calm down. She needed air! She needed light! She needed to be rid of the army of insects that was surely swarming all over her! She couldn't see a thing, but she was moving fast, pushing over containers and kicking unknown obstacles out of the way in her quest to get back outside.

Suddenly, far on the other side of whatever space they were in, a door flew open. There was light.

It flooded the room, revealing nothing but piles of sacks, crates and barrels. There were no corpses (gutted or otherwise) hanging from the ceiling, and no insects crawling on her; she could even see the room's exit, which, as Dominic had predicted, led down into a wider storage area (which was also well lit).

Maria slowly – and guiltily – turned to face Kennedy and Dominic. She had screamed so loudly she had probably led their enemies directly to them. Now, if she was going to be hung from the ceiling by a hook, it would be her own fault.

Already, she could see several men and women searching the warehouse, but – miraculously – she and her companions had not been seen. And they were not yet ready to concede defeat. Dominic motioned for them to take cover, and was quietly sneaking towards another entrance, gun in hand. And, unbeknownst to Maria, Kennedy had also come up with a plan.

In the past half hour alone, she had watched Dominic successfully fend off multiple foes, rescue them both from drowning, shoot locks off hidden doorways and lead them to safety. Now it was her turn to repay the favour.

She gestured for Maria to hide with her behind a large

barrel. She waited, and waited, until their enemies were lined up in the barrel's path.

And then she pushed.

But the barrel was quite heavy, and not easily overturned. Kennedy strained, but the barrel wouldn't budge.

'Come on!' she whispered, using her full body weight.

Nothing happened.

And then the group started walking towards them.

'Kennedy, what are you doing?' Maria whispered.

Kennedy threw her hip and shoulder into the barrel … and bruised both.

Their attackers were getting closer.

'Kennedy?' Maria asked.

Finally, Kennedy gave up. 'Never mind,' she sighed, grabbing Maria's hand. 'Let's go.' She led Maria towards the back corner, where there was plenty of cover.

'Were you trying to push the barrel into those people?' Maria whispered.

Kennedy looked behind them, embarrassed. 'Yes,' she admitted.

'That was a good plan,' Maria whispered. She had also seen that film plotline before. 'I'm not sure why it didn't work.'

And even though her barrel move had been a complete failure, Maria's praise made Kennedy feel buoyant.

But it didn't last long.

Kennedy felt Maria grip her arm, and then squeeze painfully tight.

Because there, in the centre of the room, was Bertoluccio.

CHAPTER 43

Confrontation

And it wasn't just Bertoluccio. His people were all over the place.

'What do we do now?' Kennedy asked.

Maria took stock of the room they were in. It had cement floors and walls. There were no hooks, but there were ceiling-high shelves stacked with large, wooden containers, and at least six machines designed to move heavy loads (Maria couldn't remember what they were called).

'I know,' Maria said. 'Do you think you could drive one of those things?'

'What, a forklift?' Kennedy asked.

'Yes.'

'Maria, I don't think that's a good idea ...'

'How else are we going to get out? We can take a run up and it will burst through the wall, and then we'll be outside ...'

Kennedy was concerned. Maria had clearly not thought this through. She was also missing the obvious escape route, which was the staircase against the opposite wall, leading back up to ground level.

Luckily, Dominic appeared. 'Follow me,' he commanded.

They obeyed. They didn't head up the stairs, just wove their way among the shelves, where they were less exposed to gunfire.

'Where's your gun?' Maria gasped, realising he was empty-handed.

'I don't have any bullets left,' Dominic admitted, trying to hurry her out of sight as the sound of footsteps came closer.

'Dominic!' someone yelled, throwing out a string of swear words (which Maria understood, thanks to Vince). She knew they were probably trying to be intimidating, but the swearing had a strangely calming effect on her. Silent bad guys were terrifying; she preferred the ones who shouted and cursed. At least then she knew where they were.

Dominic motioned for Kennedy and Maria to stop. They listened carefully, and heard the sound of a door opening.

Maria looked at Kennedy, her sense of direction once again confounding her. What door? She didn't remember a door.

'At the top of the staircase,' Kennedy whispered, which of course Maria didn't remember either.

Dominic snuck across the room and peered up the stairs to see who it was, then quickly moved back to safety.

'Is it backup?' Kennedy mouthed.

Dominic shook his head, worry written all over his face. He didn't need to explain that the people who were now heading towards them were reinforcements for the wrong team.

'How many?' Kennedy mouthed again.

Dominic held up eight fingers.

Maria's eyes widened.

Eight?

Eight ...

No gun, and eight more armed enemies.

'We'll have to use the forklift,' she whispered to Kennedy.

Suddenly they heard shouting. And guns cocking.

Dominic stuck his head out from the shelf he was hiding behind.

'Is *that* backup?' Kennedy mouthed.

Dominic shook his head again. He looked grim.

'Bertoluccio!' Angelo Petranelli called angrily.

'Not now,' Bertoluccio replied.

'What do you mean, *not now?*'

More guns cocking.

'You took three million.'

'It was two million!'

'I want my daughter back.'

'We don't have your daughter!'

This is getting ridiculous, Maria thought, but she was starting to feel bold. All the hostiles were focussed on each other. Maybe that's all this was – a long-time feud and a missing daughter. Maybe now that they were facing each other, they wouldn't care about her anymore!

'This will end badly for you,' said Angelo Petranelli, who didn't have a weapon out, but was well covered by his own bodyguards. 'You need to tell me where my daughter is. I will count to three. One … two … three.' Petranelli pulled out his gun, and randomly shot one of the men who was right next to Bertoluccio.

Maria gasped. The man crumpled to the floor. Had he just been killed? Murdered, point blank? Maria's heart raced. The people who weren't on Petranelli's side looked visibly shaken. She crept into another position, still hidden.

'Let me ask you again,' said Petranelli, slowly and menacingly. He aimed at another man. 'Where is my daughter? I will count to three …'

'Wait!' yelled Bertoluccio. He held his gun high in a symbol of surrender, made his way over, and whispered in Petranelli's ear.

Petranelli seemed to be listening patiently while Bertoluccio explained whatever he was explaining.

'Here?' Petranelli asked, finally.

Bertoluccio nodded, and Petranelli looked dangerous. 'Search the room,' he ordered.

*

Dominic, still hidden among the shelves, put a finger to his lips and motioned for them to move forward, slowly. Kennedy nodded and reached for Maria.

But Maria was gone.

'Dominic!' she whispered desperately.

He looked around, realised Maria was missing, and mouthed, 'Where is she?'

'I don't know!' Kennedy mouthed back.

Only a moment ago, both Petranelli's and Bertoluccio's people had been standing in a clearing in the middle of the room with their guns pointed at each other. Now, they were silently moving up and down the rows of shelves. There was nowhere to hide.

'Here!' someone shouted, and a second later, there were guns pointed at Kennedy's face. And at Dominic's too.

Kennedy wondered if Dominic would fight back, but he held up his hands, resigned.

They were out of chances now.

It was over.

Kennedy couldn't believe this was happening. The only hope she had left was that Maria had gotten out.

One of Bertoluccio's men pushed Kennedy and Dominic along until they were in the clearing, then forced them to kneel in front of Luca.

'This one's a cop,' Luca announced, looking far too happy about outing his former partner. He struck Dominic twice before bending down so he could look him in the eye and gloat.

Without missing a beat, Dominic snapped his head back and landed it with brutal force on Luca's nose, which immediately spouted blood.

'You bastard!' Luca screamed, clutching his nose as two other men leapt in for him and pounded Dominic with their guns, splitting his forehead open.

'Enough!' shouted Angelo Petranelli. He made his way over to Kennedy, who was wide eyed and breathing fast, and Dominic, who was struggling to lift his now-bleeding head up to look Petranelli in the face. 'Who are you?' he barked at Kennedy.

'Uh, no-one ...?'

'Where is the other one?'

Kennedy cringed, but kept silent.

'You will tell us what you know,' Petranelli said. It was an order, but it was calmly spoken, with the confident air of a man who expects to be obeyed without question. 'You will tell us where the girl is.'

Dominic spat blood at his feet.

It was a stupid thing to do, Kennedy thought; Petranelli hit him, then swung his gun on her, close to her face.

Kennedy was not as cool as Dominic, and she did not do any spitting. Her teeth were gritted and her eyes were clenched shut. But if these people expected pleading, begging, and an immediate pointing out of Maria's whereabouts, they would get none.

She would never give Maria up. Ever.

'I will count to three!' Petranelli cocked the gun and pressed it firmly underneath Kennedy's jaw, but all Kennedy did was hold her breath and steel herself ...

And then an engine roared to life.

Kennedy's eyes shot open as everyone turned their heads towards the noise, then aimed their guns at the forklift ambling slowly towards the centre of the room.

'*You will not harm her!*' yelled Maria from the seat of the forklift as she tried – and failed – to gain some speed.

The seventeen armed attackers, including Petranelli and Bertoluccio, released fire, bullets pinging off the forklift's metal exterior, but the shooting stopped when they realised it was headed right for them. Everyone dove out of the way as the forklift split the crowd in two. It kept ambling until it slammed into a reinforced wall with a loud crash.

It took a moment for the smoke to clear. When it did, everyone looked at the wreckage.

The wall was intact, but the forklift was not.

'Maria!' Kennedy screamed, berating herself for not explaining earlier that Maria's forklift plan would end in death.

'Put your hands in the air!' someone else screamed, bursting in through the door at the top of the stairs. And if, for the third time, Kennedy *had* turned to Dominic and mouthed 'is it backup?', thankfully, *finally*, Dominic would have been able to say 'yes'.

But Kennedy wasn't paying attention to the members of the ROS who were streaming inside and placing everyone under arrest. She wasn't relishing the moment of victory, or scoffing at the curses and threats the criminals made as they were handcuffed and led out of the building. She wasn't narrowing her eyes at the jeering Bertoluccio or the glowering Petranelli, both of whom were loudly confident that no court could convict them. She wasn't doing any of those things because she was too busy running to the forklift, which was now on fire.

Kennedy coughed as she tried to see through the flames, desperate to find Maria.

She would pull her out. She would save her. It wasn't too late. 'Maria!' she called.

'Kennedy,' she heard, and turned to see Maria sprawled on the ground a few metres behind her.

'Maria!' she cried, surprised and overjoyed, as both she and Dominic made their way over and knelt beside her. 'You're okay! I thought you were still in the forklift … I thought you were … did you jump? You must have jumped! Of course you would have jumped. Maria, that was the smartest, bravest, *stupidest* …'

'I've been shot,' Maria said.

It was only then that Kennedy saw the blood.

CHAPTER 44

Quiet

Death was a funny thing, Maria mused.

All her life she'd been planning, preparing, doing what she could to avoid it.

Now it was here, and she wasn't afraid.

She was in a great deal of pain, but she was also calm. Peaceful. Accepting.

Though she did have regrets.

'How …' Kennedy was rambling. 'It's not possible. This can't be happening. I thought you were in the forklift. How can you be shot …?' Her voice grew quieter and quieter as her face started to crumple.

Maria knew she had no more time to waste. No more running. No more pretending, or trying to protect herself. If there was ever a time to be honest with herself, it was now. She gathered all the strength she had left. 'I'm really sorry, Kennedy,' she said.

Kennedy lifted Maria's head and shoulders gently off the ground. 'For what?' she asked, tears pricking her eyes.

'When we were at Rocco and Nicolina's farm, remember? And they accused us of kissing? And I said I didn't even like you like that?' Maria winced. 'I was lying.'

There.

She'd said it.

Her greatest shame, spoken aloud.

For the first time in her life, she felt free.

And then she closed her eyes and surrendered.

'Maria,' Kennedy said softly, and then, when Maria didn't open her eyes, she repeated it, more urgently. 'Maria. Maria!' She was crying now, holding her close, sobbing. 'This can't be happening. No, this can't be happening. Maria! Oh God, no! Maria!' She threw her head back. 'Why, God?' she cried, ignoring the startled looks of the criminal element and the hardened undercover agents alike. 'Why?'

Dominic cleared his throat. He, too, was kneeling by Maria, but he was much more aware of the people around them, some of whom were starting to laugh.

'Maria,' he said, his voice as kind and understanding as could be. 'You are not dying. You have only been shot in the leg.'

Maria's eyes snapped open. Dominic had both hands pressed against her wound, stemming the bleeding. Kennedy had tears streaming down her face and was looking at her with a mix of confusion and joy.

'Thank God!' Kennedy cried. 'You're alive!'

Maria felt everything it was possible to feel, then. But her emotions were complex. She felt a bit cross: how could people be laughing at a time like this? She'd been shot! She couldn't be blamed for thinking she was on the brink of death! She also felt a bit foolish, obviously, and annoyed, like she'd been tricked into pouring her heart out. But then she looked at Kennedy again, who was laughing, and weeping, and – yes, she could admit it, beautiful – and Maria realised that, all things considered, she didn't regret saying what she'd said.

But it did feel like someone was driving a hot poker into her leg.

'Kennedy,' she said.

'Yes?' Kennedy looked so hopeful it made Maria's heart clench.

'Don't be alarmed, but I think I might go unconscious for a minute.'

Kennedy hiccupped a relieved laugh and said, 'All right, I'll be here.'

And Maria smiled and closed her eyes.

CHAPTER 45

Recovery

Maria regained consciousness long before she opened her eyes. She tried to assess her surroundings with her eyes shut. She was lying in a bed, that much she knew. And she was being watched. She could feel it. Her body tensed.

Her eyes snapped open, ready and furious, and there, standing much too close to her bed, was Gabriele.

What was he doing here?

And where was she?

'She's awake!' Vince Petranelli roared. 'Maria's awake!'

Startled, Maria sat up quickly, then sank back into her pillow as the room burst into life with a lot of weeping, wailing and gnashing of teeth. Nonna Lucia threw herself across Maria's chest. Nonno Franco grabbed one of Maria's hands with both of his; he seemed intent on crushing it. Her father was criticising the service in the hospital … where was the doctor? Where were the nurses? His daughter was awake!

Her mother was shaking her head and saying, 'I told you. I knew something like this would happen.'

Her family ... Gabriele ... hospital ...

That's right, she remembered. *I'm in Italy.*

She tried to ignore her family's outpourings as she looked around urgently.

There she was, in the corner, smiling sheepishly.

'Kennedy,' Maria said, and her family gasped audibly, then faded to silence, all eyes on the girl in the corner.

'Hi,' Kennedy said and gave an awkward wave, her voice cracking.

She was there. Kennedy was there. Without even thinking about it, Maria smiled.

'Maria!' boomed a loud, joyful voice from the doorway. It was Alberto.

Immediately Nonno released her hand, Nonna got up off her chest, and the Petranellis all moved in an orderly fashion to one side of the room. They'd all been introduced while Maria was unconscious – Paola and Alberto wisely said they'd met Maria while she'd been on an excursion, and Kennedy, just as wisely, explained she was a friend from the language school. But the Petranellis didn't care for strangers, especially ones with a Florentine accent, so they just looked on with suspicion as the family entered cheerfully.

'Feeling better? It's about time you joined us!' Alberto said with a pointed look from Maria to Kennedy.

Paola elbowed her husband in the ribs. 'How are you feeling, Maria?'

'Fine, thank you,' Maria replied. 'How long has everyone been here?'

'A while,' said Alberto. 'You've been in and out of it for a day.'

This disturbed Maria somewhat. She hoped she hadn't said anything embarrassing in her sleep. But she hadn't lost too much time – just enough time, apparently, for the Petranellis to arrive. Anna had immediately enacted her 'a family member has gone missing overseas' plan with the frightening efficiency of someone who had been preparing for such an event for years. The whole clan had been camped out at Maria's school in Rome in less than forty-eight hours.

'Maria, we were so worried!' said Nonna Lucia. 'I cried for days. I cried for the whole plane trip. I just cried, "what has happened to my Maria?" And I prayed, "God, if you take my Maria from me …"' Her voice cracked with the pain of it all and she started wringing her hands.

Nonno Franco snorted. 'She's fine, Lucia. She was always fine. She only got shot in the leg.'

'Only got shot in the leg!' shouted Nonna. 'Only got shot in the leg! What if the infection got her? What if …' Her voice lowered, and she crossed herself. 'What if they had to amputate? Oh, *Gesu mio, Madonna mia* …'

'I'm fine, Nonna,' Maria interrupted. 'They didn't have to amputate.' (Though she subtly checked, to make sure.)

'Well, don't say we didn't warn you,' said Anna, shaking her head. 'At least now you know how dangerous travelling is, you might listen to us next time.'

‘What about your exchange, Maria?’ Vince asked. ‘Did you have a good time? Did you get a boyfriend?’

Alberto didn’t understand the last portion of the conversation, which had turned into English. But he could see that Maria was getting tense. ‘Maria, you look tired!’ he exclaimed. ‘You probably need to rest.’ He turned to the Petranellis. ‘Why don’t we wait outside until the doctor has seen her?’ He moved so that he was behind Maria’s family, and started herding them out the door. ‘We’ll just wait in the hall,’ he said in his booming voice. ‘You will be fine, I’m sure.’

Maria’s family grumbled every step of the way – in English, of course – muttering ‘who does he think he is, telling me what is best for my own daughter?’ and ‘we’ve come all this way, he doesn’t understand what we’ve been through’, but they kept moving. They were united, at least. Nothing unites like a common enemy.

*

Kennedy followed them as they shuffled out the door, but just as she too was about to exit, Alberto turned back and held his hand in her face. ‘Not you,’ he said, glancing not at all subtly from Kennedy to Maria and back again. Then, in case Kennedy hadn’t got the message, he winked at her.

Maria pushed her elbows back against her pillow and sat up nervously as Kennedy settled into a chair beside her bed.

‘So,’ Kennedy said. ‘How’s your leg?’

'Fine,' Maria said, and then added, on reflex, 'how's yours?'

'Fine,' Kennedy replied, confused.

The two girls sat quietly for a moment.

'Where's Dominic?' Maria asked eventually.

'He's been in a few times, to check how you're going.'

'Oh. So ... are we safe?' Maria asked, starting to feel anxious.

'Yeah. Dominic said we are,' Kennedy replied, smiling, and Maria relaxed. 'He said that Angelo Petranelli guy will probably go to jail, and so will that policeman who sold you out at the station. And now they've got a warrant out for the boss of those guys who kidnapped us. We still have to give our testimonies, but we're going to do it through our embassies when we're ... back home,' Kennedy said, and she held Maria's gaze for a moment too long.

Maria's heart pounded as she looked at Kennedy. Kennedy, who had rescued her in so many ways, ever since she arrived. Kennedy, who was shy, hopeless, and incredibly kind. Kennedy, who, just by being close to her, made Maria feel goosebumps and the bizarre desire to cling to her.

Kennedy, who Maria would probably never see again.

Maria swallowed hard, trying to suppress the overwhelming desire to reach out and hold Kennedy while she still had the chance. She blinked a few times and tried to think of something to say. 'So ... I guess it's all over?'

'Yeah,' said Kennedy, and her voice was a little sad.

They sat quietly once more, and then Kennedy opened her mouth to say something just as a young nurse opened the door to check on Maria. As soon as the Petranellis saw him enter the room, they poured in, too – Alberto couldn't hold them back any longer.

Vince led the way. He took one step inside, saw the nurse holding Maria's hand while checking the IV, and stopped. 'What's this?' he shouted, realising he had the perfect opportunity. 'Who is this? Maria! Is this your boyfriend?'

The other Petranellis, confused at first, gathered around him to join the hilarity.

'What's going on?' said Nonno Franco.

'What are we laughing at?' asked Anna.

'Maria's got a boyfriend, everybody!' Vince shouted, pointing at the nurse, then turning to her with a ridiculous grin. 'Maria? Have you got a boyfriend?'

And Maria was *furious.* Not because, after everything she'd been through, her family were still making boyfriend jokes – that was to be expected – but because, before they'd interrupted, it looked like Kennedy had been about to say something important. Maria did not have time for this anymore!

'No,' she snapped. 'And I won't be getting a boyfriend, thank you.' She took a deep breath, then said, 'Because I am a lesbian.'

Vince paused.

Kennedy looked at her, shocked.

And Maria grabbed her hand and said, 'Yes, it's true. Also, I'm in love with Kennedy.'

Kennedy's breath hitched. 'Really?'

'Yes,' Maria informed her curtly.

Saying it out loud felt like the most natural thing in the world.

Something had unlocked in Maria – and, rather than worrying that her words would make her look weak or vulnerable or unprepared, Maria found she just didn't care.

Kennedy seemed unsure until Maria finally made eye contact, and smiled *(again!)*, and Kennedy – face burning and grinning so much her cheeks hurt – looked like she might combust on the spot.

Vince stood, mouth agape, looking like he didn't know whether to shout or cry. 'Why didn't anyone tell *me* about this?'

Alberto seemed overjoyed by the news. 'About time!' he shouted, knowing at least enough English to recognise the words 'lesbian' and 'in love' and to understand the significance of Maria holding Kennedy's hand.

But nobody commented further. Maria had that fierce look on her face, the one her family knew meant she had taken a position and was prepared to defend it to the death, so everyone just settled into their respective areas of the room. Alberto and Paola alternated between smiling politely at Maria's family and grinning joyfully at Maria and Kennedy, who did not release each other's hands, even though they were both embarrassed and were now avoiding eye contact.

The Petranellis – whose narrowed eyes kept moving from Maria to Kennedy, from Kennedy to Maria, and then to their entwined hands – rumbled their unhappiness for the rest of the day. Not wanting to have an open confrontation in front of the strangers (Maria thanked God fervently that Paola, Alberto and Gabriele were quite happy to hang around in her hospital room), they had to content themselves with criticising everything they could find to criticise, including:

1. The hospital food;
2. The size of the room;
3. The air-conditioning;
4. The Italian health care system, in general; and
5. Anna's choice of perfume, which was giving Nonna Lucia a headache.

Alberto and Paola stayed as long as they could, but eventually, after Gabriele had disappeared from Maria's room three times and been returned by dishevelled nurses with stories of thievery and disturbing other patients, they had to take him home.

'Make sure you keep in touch,' Paola said, hugging them both.

Alberto didn't say anything. He just grinned cheekily at Maria and gently punched Kennedy's arm.

Finally, the Petranellis stood, one united mass of discontent, ready to confront the apparent lesbians in their midst. Kennedy felt Maria stiffen, and saw a blank look settle over her face. It was a look Kennedy was beginning to recognise – the one that Maria always conjured when she was afraid, the one that said *you're about to leave me, aren't you,* and meant she was preparing herself to pretend she didn't care. So Kennedy picked up Maria's hand, kissed it, and held on for all she was worth.

And suddenly, Maria couldn't see anyone else in the room but her.

The Petranellis didn't notice this, of course.

'Maria says she's gay, Anna,' Vince yelled. 'And you didn't tell me?'

'Oh, she's not *gay,* Vince!' Anna argued. 'She's just saying it to get attention!'

'A homosexual in the family!' Nonna Lucia cried. 'We won't live through the shame!'

'Nobody ever said anything to me about this! Not once! And that ... *American* ... hasn't asked my permission to date my daughter. Hasn't even asked my *permission*!' Vince carried on.

'The devil has entered our house,' said Nonna Lucia. 'And it must have come from the mother. It is the mother's job to raise the child right ...'

'What's that supposed to mean?' Anna shrieked.

Only Nonno Franco was quiet. Watching, silently, his granddaughter and the girl she apparently loved. Watching the way the more the family yelled, the more Maria leant into Kennedy, until eventually Kennedy had her arm around her, and Nonno Franco realised he had never in his life seen Maria look like she didn't have her guard up.

He stood up quietly and made his way over to them. He looked at Kennedy. 'American?'

'Yes,' Kennedy replied.

Nonno Franco shook his head.

Maria wondered if this was it; the confirmation of her family's rejection. Anna, Vince and Nonna Lucia were reacting as usual, and Maria was used to that. But the thought of her nonno disapproving had a weight to it she hadn't expected, and Maria realised she was dreading it.

She steeled herself as Nonno Franco turned to Kennedy once again. 'America is too far away. You'll have to come live in Australia,' he said.

Maria's mouth dropped open.

Kennedy choked a little. 'Okay,' she stammered.

And once Maria realised what had been said, her heart soared.

Nonno Franco patted Kennedy's shoulder and walked to the door. 'We're leaving,' he announced.

'What?' Nonna Lucia cried. 'We're not done here!'

'Yes,' Nonno Franco said. 'It's time to go home.'

It was not up for argument. Despite the protests, the passive-aggressive tears, and the brief moment when Nonna Lucia claimed she couldn't walk so she'd have to stay (until Anna handily supplied a wheelchair), the Petranellis were soon gone. And Nonno Franco, who made sure he was the last one out, turned back and smiled at his granddaughter – and at the tall, lanky girl who made her so happy.

*

Finally, Kennedy and Maria were alone. Kennedy shifted her chair to a better position, and Maria adjusted her blankets.

'I'm so sorry,' Maria said.

'About your family?' Kennedy laughed. 'Oh, I've seen worse!'

Maria smiled, but only a little. 'I'm sorry I didn't say anything before. I've been very ... afraid.' She took a deep breath and forced herself to look Kennedy in the eye. 'But truthfully, I *am* very attracted to you. I think I always have been. I want you around when you're not with me. And I shouldn't have pushed you off the bed when you tried to kiss me.'

'I wasn't trying to kiss ...' Kennedy started, but Maria looked at her sharply. 'Okay, I *was* trying to kiss you.'

Mollified, Maria continued. 'It was a knee-jerk reaction and I'm sorry. I got caught off-guard. But I probably would have liked it.'

Kennedy was stunned. 'Yeah?'

'Yes,' Maria agreed. 'In fact, I wouldn't mind if you kissed me now,' she said in an offhand tone.

'You wouldn't mind if I kissed you now?' Kennedy repeated, still sounding very unsure.

'No, I wouldn't mind,' Maria said, sitting up, putting her hands in her lap, and looking very proper, though she was thinking to herself, *what is taking her so long?*

Kennedy couldn't suppress a smile. 'So, is it okay if I ...' She reached out slowly, and Maria shifted, still trying to pretend she could take it or leave it.

This is it, this is happening, her brain declared loudly. Kennedy reached out far too slowly, and tucked Maria's hair behind her ear, and usually Maria would have been appalled at how clichéd the move was, but it was happening to *her*, and – though it still pained her to admit it – she liked it. And then Kennedy was holding her face gently, and leaning forward, and pressing her lips sweetly against hers, and –

Oh – *this* is what kissing is supposed to be like, Maria realised, her heart hammering and something warm rushing through her body as their lips moved together.

Yes, Maria thought, the voice in her head still speaking in a proper accent. *I'll allow it.*

Epilogue

In the end, the Petranellis came around.

Nonna Lucia continued to claim that the devil had come into their house for about as long as it took her to realise that Anna felt the same way. That was when Nonna Lucia had the loud, public epiphany that a mother should never reject her daughter – or her daughter's choice of partner. And so, Nonna Lucia set about being the model of acceptance to show Anna *exactly* how it should be done.

This, of course, infuriated Anna, who started a local Supportive Parents group in retaliation.

Vince took the longest to adjust. He spent months and months sulking: as usual, nobody asked him; nobody respected his views; nobody cared about his opinion at all. But then, one Sunday lunch, when the Petranellis had gathered to celebrate Kennedy's first (and definitely not last) visit to Australia, Vince found himself sitting at the table with her. Nonno Franco was asleep on the couch. Nonna Lucia and Anna were trying to out-clean each other, and Maria was trying to stop them from wearing holes in the kitchen counter. Vince and Kennedy were alone, and Vince realised he had nothing to say to her. So he grabbed a serviette and half-heartedly twisted the four corners so it looked like a roast chicken.

'Look,' he said sadly, holding it up to Kennedy.

And Kennedy burst out laughing. 'That's hilarious!' she said. 'Show me more!'

It was hard to stop Vince's enthusiasm for Kennedy after that.

Maria decided not to go through with an exchange program; after all, her first attempt at that particular adventure had not gone as planned. But she felt open to travelling again. She felt like an expert now, having already learned the most important lessons:

1. Make sure you check which airport bus you get on;
2. Make sure you drive on the correct side of the road; and
3. Make sure you know the phrase 'remove your hands immediately, I'm not paying a cent' so you can use it if someone grabs your arm and tries to put a bracelet on it.

Even though Maria had no idea what she would do with the rest of her life, she was certain about one thing. She was no longer alone, and she was *happy*. As soon as Kennedy had gotten over her jetlag, Maria took her on a much-less-dramatic tour of the streets of Adelaide, and they took photos together (yes, selfies, which Maria of the Past would never have abided). They sent some to Rovena, who reciprocated with photos of her sons and their families, and some to Rocco and Nicolina, who reciprocated with photos of Pope Francis and various saints. They didn't need to send photos to Alberto, Paola and Gabriele, because they had already booked a holiday to Australia, so they could see them in person.

Maria and Kennedy didn't hear from Dominic again. They had both given their testimonies through their embassies, but Dominic wasn't involved – he was probably off undercover somewhere, saving some other innocent civilians, speaking a thousand languages, and rippling his muscles all over the place. But Maria wished him well, regardless. There was even a small part of her that hoped he could find someone he loved, too.

That's right. Maria was a romantic now.

Because now she didn't need to pretend that she had no emotions and no attachments. She didn't need to build walls, and constantly push people away, and rush from one place to another with no idea where she was going just to prove she could navigate the world on her own. Now she had new things to keep her strong and fierce:

1. A girlfriend she loved, who loved her back;
2. A family that, for better or worse, was definitely not going anywhere; and finally, and most importantly,
3. A new-found willingness to use to Google maps.

THE END

Acknowledgements

Thank you so much to the many people who've supported me to get *Maria* to the point where she can be shared with the world.

To my little brother, the first one I shared *Maria* with, who's been the most enthusiastic supporter – right back from when we were young adults living in a transportable, where I'd read sections out loud by the light of the bar heater, in between episodes of *Xena*.

To the very early readers, Liz, Laura, Lauren, and Johnny, who read drafts back when Maria (and the author) were dabbling with heterosexuality and had to be gently encouraged to review whether or not the romance was ringing true. It took us a while, but we got there eventually.

To Steff, who has read my drafts, my pitches, my submissions, this acknowledgement, and has taken each one as seriously as a PhD. You have no idea how grateful I am for your friendship and support.

To my PIC crew, past and present, who make work worth going to, and are very good at reminding me that publishing a book is something to be excited about, not terrified of!

To the wonderful people at Hardie Grant, particularly Marisa Pintado and Luna Soo, from whom I've learned so much. You are genius editors, and have been so encouraging and kind – I am incredibly grateful for this experience.

To my family, who've provided me with so many stories to draw on ... particularly my cousins Dana and Isaac, who took me on my first 'unsupervised' adventure to Italy and whose experience at the Spanish Steps sparked the whole idea for this novel.

To my mum, Meredith, who has shared her own passion for writing and kept encouraging me to go for it, even when 'Tom' was rewritten to become 'Kennedy' (and all the other things that went along with that). I always feel better after talking to you.

To Darryl and Dianne, the best parents-in-law a girl could ask for, whose unwavering love and fierce support is something I still can't get my head around, but appreciate so much.

And of course, to my beautiful wife, Kylie. You are my best friend, and the person I'm most excited to share queer content with. I love you!

About the author

Photo by Kierra Resce

Elisa Chenoweth is a high school teacher who lives in the Adelaide Hills. She has a terrible sense of direction, and a bad habit of bringing up politics and religion at the dinner table, but she can type *very* fast. She enjoys writing stories drawn from her Italian/Australian/religious upbringing and is passionate about queer content and representation. Her first novel, *Maria Petranelli is Prepared for Anything (Except This)*, won Hardie Grant's Ampersand Prize.

To learn more about the Ampersand Prize and discover other great novels, visit: go.hardiegrant.com/ampersandprize